EXILE OF THE CHOSEN

GOD'S HEROES

FROM SOLOMON TO MALACHI

D1481508

SALLY PIERSON DILLON

REVIEW AND HERALD® PUBLISHING ASSOCIATION

Since 1861 | www.reviewandherald.com

The author assumes full responsibility for the accuracy of all facts and
quotations as cited in this book.

This book was
Edited by Gerald Wheeler
Cover designed by Trent Truman
Cover art by Greg and Tim Hildebrandt
Typeset: Berkeley Book 12/16

PRINTED IN U.S.A.

13 12 11 10 09   6 5 4 3 2

R&H Cataloging Service
Dillon, Sally Pierson, 1959-
    Exile of the chosen.

    1. Bible. O.T.—History—Juvenile works. I. Title.

        221.09

ISBN 978-0-8280-1703-9

DEDICATION

To Jacob and Lucas Beebe
who also understand how it feels
to start a new life in a new place.
To my personal reading committee
Cassie and Sasha Brauer
for their input and enthusiasm.
To the Galbraith Girlies
Katie and Kristie
for all the joy you bring to our house
(and all of us who live here).

Other books by Sally Pierson Dillon:
    Hugs From Jesus
    Little Hearts for Jesus
    Michael Asks Why
    Survivors of the Dark Rebellion
    Victory of the Warrior King
    War of the Invisibles

To order, call **1-800-765-6955.**

Visit us at www.reviewandherald.com for information on other Review and Herald products.

Contents

Πατηαπ

athan felt as if all the blood was draining out of his head and rushing down to his big toe in his left foot.

"But, but why?" he stammered. "Why do you want me to leave home?"

"It's not that we want you to leave," his father explained gently. "Now you are 12 and you've become a son of the law. You are a Levite. Part of your job is serving the Lord."

"Yes, I know that. You've explained that to me before," Nathan said slowly. "But I thought that when I became a man, I would work with you in teaching others."

Father nodded. "Yes, I hope that is what you will do. But this is a wonderful opportunity, Nathan. Your grandfather Ethan was a close friend of King David and has been an advisor to King Solomon on the building of the Temple. He's invited you and your cousin Zachary to come stay with him in Jerusalem and help him. This is the most exciting time ever in the history of Israel to be in Jerusalem. You'll be able to watch the construction of the great Temple. Since you'll be with your grandfather you may even get to meet the king. And you will learn more in a day there than I could teach you in a year here."

Nathan stared at the floor. He loved his grandfather Ethan and had heard stories about him all his life. But he'd never been away from home before. Just the idea of it made his stomach hurt.

"Your grandfather has gotten a place for you and Zachary in one of the choirs that will sing in the Temple. You will be learning all the psalms being especially written for when the Temple is dedicated and open for worshiping God. This could be the greatest adventure of your entire life."

Although Nathan nodded he said nothing.

I looked with compassion at the boy standing on one foot then the other. While it was legally true that he was a son of the law now that he was 12 years old, there was still a lot of him that was still a child and not yet a man. I wished I could put my angel arms around him and comfort him, but he was totally unaware of my presence. Still I quivered with excitement clear to my wingtips.

The Temple in Jerusalem had been in planning for many years and the actual building had continued for more than 10. I was delighted to have an assignment that would take me to Jerusalem where I could observe the wonderful building these humans were erecting for worshiping the Almighty. Surely in a place like that the glory of it would overwhelm Nathan and he would forget to be afraid and homesick.

Then I shook my head. Perhaps not. Sometimes humans can be in the presence of all kinds of things and still miss them because they have been blinded by their own internal feelings.

Still, this would be exciting. I was thankful that his cousin Zachary would be accompanying him. Perhaps that would comfort the young lad.

Nathan's father had finished talking to him and left. The boy wandered out into the courtyard. Peleb, his pet goat, bumped his leg playfully. Absentmindedly Nathan scratched her ears. "Peleb, what are you going to do without me?" he asked.

The animal blinked at him with her black goat eyes.

"I know," Nathan laughed. "You'll still do what you do every day—chew on things you're not supposed to. Drop little presents in the way where Mom will have to complain and sweep them out. And like as not you'll try to kick over the bucket every morning when they milk you."

Peleb bleated in agreement, her little tail flapping joyfully.

Nathan rubbed her head. "Sometimes I wish I were a goat," he said. "I'd be fed well. I wouldn't have to worry about anything. And I could stay home. Nobody would make me leave."

"Baa-aa," Peleb answered.

The boy laughed. "At least somebody agrees with me," he muttered.

* * * *

"Come in! Come in!" Grandfather Ethan bellowed. He scooped Nathan and his cousin Zachary into a huge bear hug. "Look at you men," he said. "It seems only days ago that you were little boys running around and now you're men ready to enter the service of the Lord."

Nathan glanced at Zachary. He still felt like a little boy. Any part of him that had seemed grown-up had shrunk and disappeared as they entered the big city. He felt like a very tiny fish in a very large pond.

Grandfather Ethan seemed totally oblivious to any of his fears. "Did you have a good trip? Are you hungry? Come this way. Let me show you where you will sleep."

Nathan's father smiled and followed along as Grandfather Ethan led the boys to the sleeping space they would share.

"There's a chest in the corner you may put your other clothes in," he said. "We'll fit you for some appropriate choir robes tomorrow. For now you can just relax and learn your way about. My chambers are over there." He pointed. "Everything in the courtyard and every building opening into it is part of our family dwelling. The gate at the front goes out into the street. Perhaps it would be best if you did not go out there without someone until you learn your way around the city."

"That building over there"—he indicated a small door on one side of the courtyard—"with the oven out in front of it, is the kitchen. I imagine that will be your favorite spot here if I remember what life was like when I was 12."

Father and Grandfather both laughed. Nathan and Zachary just looked at each other. They had never lived in such a big compound before and they both felt a little lost. It seemed too soon when Father hugged them both and left.

Nathan lay for a long time staring at the ceiling unable to go to sleep. What would life be like here? And why did he even have to be here? Could God's plan want him in Jerusalem? Or was it just Father's idea? Didn't his parents want him at home anymore, or did they just feel he would be able to get a more important job if he lived near the Temple with Grandfather, making connections with powerful people? Whatever it was, he had never felt so alone. He even missed his annoying little sister.

Whenever Father or Grandfather talked about God they spoke in reverent tones. They would never even say His name out loud. Nathan frowned. How could they love a God that they couldn't even see, and who hadn't done anything that he knew of for years and years? How did they know that He was still interested in them? What if he was just the God of the olden days? Nathan's thoughts were becoming a confused jumble as he finally drifted off into a restless sleep.

Morning came way too early, although Zachary was already up and humming a psalm.

"Come on sleepyhead," he said. "We're going to the Temple today."

"The Temple?" Nathan asked foggily. "I thought they were still building it."

"Well, we're gonna go watch them do that," Zachary said, "if we can ever get you moving."

Suddenly Nathan remembered where he was and the heavy feeling of homesickness washed back over him.

"What's the matter?" Zachary asked, noticing his expression.

Nathan shook his head. "Give me a minute. I'll be right with you."

"Fine," Zachary replied, "but you better hurry. They've made fresh bread out here and it is so good while it's warm. If you like, I'll eat yours for you."

"Oh, thanks," Nathan responded to his cousin's good-natured teasing. "Just what everyone needs," he mumbled to himself. "An early bird for a roommate."

On the way to the Temple Zachary seemed filled with endless questions though Grandfather didn't seem to mind.

"When King Solomon started working on the planning," Grandfather explained, "he planned on three basic sets of workers—officers, stonecutters, and carriers. The officers are priests and those that have administrative skills or who have studied the plans God gave us for building the tabernacle."

"Are you an officer?" Nathan interrupted.

"Yes. That's what I've been working on for many years. In fact, King David, when he was still alive, had wanted to build the Temple and he and I had even worked on some of the plans. But the Lord said that David couldn't do it and so it became Solomon's project."

Both boys had heard the story before.

"How close is it to being finished?" Zachary asked.

"We're getting there," said Grandfather. "It's becoming very exciting, especially for those of us who have been involved in it for so many years. Part of my job is to visit the various manufacturing sites and see how things are going, so you'll be able to see, too."

"Who are the other workers?" Nathan wanted to know.

"The stonecutters and the carriers," Grandfather explained. "We need highly skilled people to work the stone since it is to be put together so precisely. It has no mortar or anything holding the blocks together."

"Oh, like the pyramids in Egypt," Zachary suggested brightly.

"Nothing like the Pyramids," Grandfather snapped. "This is the holy house of our God, the God of Abraham, Isaac, and Jacob. It will be nothing like the pyramids. But the precision needed for the stone cutting could be similar," he finished lamely, embarrassed at his outburst. "The carriers help bring the stone from where it is cut to where the stonemasons work on it and then to here, but they also bring the other things used for building, such as the cedarwood and the brass. They are probably the biggest group of workers. We will check with Korah and find out when your practice times are for the choir. Then I will try to schedule some of my trips to avoid those times so that you boys can go with me. This is an opportunity that few others will have, and you will know so much more about the Temple of the Holy One by the time it is finished. Both of you will serve in the Temple, and you will be able to teach younger people what you have learned as they come to worship here. This is the most exciting time in which a worshiper of our God could live."

Zachary nodded but Nathan frowned. The most exciting time? Hardly! He had heard so many stories of King Saul and King David and of the hero Gideon who had stopped the Midianites. The elders had told of miracles and other wonderful things that God had done for Abraham, Isaac, and Jacob. But he had not heard of anything like that happening in his lifetime, and no one had fought a Philistine for years. There was nothing going on in Israel except a lot of building projects and politics. It didn't strike him as an exciting time.

Nathan was so absorbed in his own thoughts as they rounded the corner and walked onto the building site that when he saw it, it took his breath away. The unfinished Temple reached abruptly into the sky in front of him. The sun glinted on the white limestone, and its brightness took his breath away.

Grandfather chuckled. "See what I mean? It's wonderful. Just imagine what it will be like when it's finished."

The boys stared at everything around them.

"This area here," Grandfather flung his arm, gesturing toward the Temple courtyard, "is part of the threshing floor of Araunah."

Nathan's brow wrinkled again. "Araunah?" He knew threshing floors were important places. They served not only for actually threshing grain, but also where the families divided up the grain, and where people often negotiated legal contracts. He remembered the story of Gideon and how an angel had met him at the threshing floor.

"Who is Araunah?" he asked. "Is that someone important?"

Grandfather smiled. "I guess Araunah himself was not all that famous, but something very important happened here. King David was not always perfect, and he committed a great sin during his reign. A plague fell upon the people and many died. David confessed his sin and begged God to stop the plague and not punish the people anymore. The angel of the Lord came here to the threshing floor of Araunah. The plague spread until it stopped here. It is the place God chose to forgive His people and to save them from death."

"Oh," was all Zachary could say.

Nathan remembered now. King David had conducted a census of the people—a symbol of his trusting human resources more than God's power. The boy looked around. It was a holy place where God would continue to forgive His people again and again and save them from eternal death.

"That's not the only story here," Grandfather said, as if reading his thoughts.

Nathan glanced up.

"Do you know the story of Isaac and Abraham?"

Both boys nodded. Every Jewish boy knew the stories of Abraham and Isaac.

"Well," Grandfather continued, "this area is Mount Moriah."

"Mount Moriah!" both boys echoed, catching their breath.

"Yes," Grandfather said. "In fact, see that flat rock over there?"

They looked.

"It was on that flat area that Abraham built the altar that he was going to use to sacrifice Isaac."

Nathan shuddered. He thought of how alone and rejected he felt with his father bringing him to Jerusalem to be left with Grandfather. It must have been nothing compared to how Isaac had felt with his father bringing him up the mountain to be sacrificed. *How could he bear it?* he wondered. Perhaps he would understand someday. Still, it seemed as if Isaac and Abraham had been much stronger and more committed to God. At least they weren't like people today.

My wings twitched. I desperately wanted to swoop down and try to explain things to Nathan, yet I must not. Explaining wasn't my job.

Nathan turned to stare at a group of sweating men hauling huge planks of cedar into the courtyard. "Those carriers are working really hard," he observed. "Look at them. Are they slaves, Grandfather?"

Grandfather Ethan shook his head. "No. Some of our carriers are slaves, but those men are Hebrews, just like you. They have come from the villages as unskilled laborers and work a period of time for the king, then return to their village."

"But what about their families?" Nathan asked. "Don't they need them at home to help with the animals or their farms?"

"Yes. In some families it can cause a real hardship for the men to leave and do their terms of service for the king. I suppose that's what Samuel was warning us about when he tried to convince the people of Israel not to insist on a king. He promised them that the king would take their sons and daughters for labor. But nobody cared. They wanted a king really bad."

Nathan thought for a moment. "But everyone else has a king. How did Israel survive without one? It seems as if that would be something every country would need."

Grandfather Ethan smiled. "That's what most people thought," he said, ruffling Nathan's hair. "The prophet Samuel handled most of our governing before we had a king, and God told him what to do. It was God through Samuel who settled disputes and advised us on foreign policy, things such as when to go into battle and when to negotiate."

The boy shook his head. "I just can't imagine life without a king."

"Of course you can't. Neither can I. There have been kings in Israel during my whole lifetime and yours. But living here at the Temple you will learn stories of life before we had a king."

"Was God mad at us for getting a king then?" Zachary asked.

Grandfather shook his head. "The God of Israel is patient and loving. I believe it hurt Him deeply when His own people wanted a human king rather than His leadership. However, He still promised to bless us as long as we were faithful to him. We just need to have kings who remember who put them there and who gave them their authority."

His grandsons agreed that was a good idea.

"We've only had three kings," Grandfather continued. "The first one was King Saul. He was the king when I was a young lad."

"Was he a good king, Grandfather?" the boys asked.

Grandfather paused. "Please tell us," Nathan begged. "Whenever I ask Father about things like this, he says it's something I need to talk to you about when I'm older."

Grandfather Ethan sighed. "That's probably wise," he said. "But now that you are both over 12 you are men, and I think you should know."

Nathan grinned at his cousin. He couldn't help it. After all, he didn't get referred to as a man very often.

"When Saul first became king," Grandfather began, "he was so surprised that the whole thing scared him a bit."

Nathan could understand that. The thought of being part of the Temple choir still frightened him. He felt some sympathy for King Saul.

"When the prophet Samuel went to introduce the new king they couldn't find him anywhere," Grandfather explained.

The boys' eyes widened in surprise. "Didn't God know where he was? Couldn't He tell the prophet?"

"Well, yes. And that's exactly what happened. It turned out the new king was hiding behind the baggage. He was having a panic attack."

Zachary burst out laughing. "The king?"

Nathan didn't laugh. He had an idea how King Saul must have felt.

"Yes, the king was hiding behind the baggage," Grandfather said. "The prophet pulled him out and introduced him to people. They were delighted with Saul. He was very handsome and taller than any of them. And he looked like someone whom they could respect as long as he would stand tall and didn't hide."

Nathan chuckled again, then became serious. "Then why won't my father talk about him?"

"Saul had some problems," Grandfather sighed, "and he really didn't want anyone to tell him how to deal with them. He didn't want God to tell him what to do now that he was king either."

"But—but God made him king," Nathan protested, "so God had every right to tell him what to do. And besides, the whole country would have been better off with God helping him."

"You are very wise. Unfortunately, Saul wasn't always as wise. As time went on several disagreements arose between him and the prophet, Samuel. Samuel felt terrible and rejected because of it, for he had loved and nurtured the new king and been like a father to him. But really the king was rejecting God even more than he was Samuel. The Lord was patient with Saul again and again, but eventually the king totally rejected the God of Israel and tried to run the country on his own. That is why before Samuel died God had him anoint another king to replace Saul."

"King David," Zachary piped up.

"Yes, it was."

"I bet the people were really happy to have another king who would follow what God wanted."

Grandfather smiled wearily. "It didn't really work that way," he said. "God told Samuel to anoint King David, who was much younger then, but it wasn't quite time for him to be king. David waited until God let him know it was time. He was very loyal to King Saul and was best friends with Saul's son, Jonathan. But Saul was afraid of David and his growing popularity. It would have been even worse if he had known about the anointing. David had to run for his life and hide. Saul tried to find him and even killed people who wouldn't tell him where David was. Many times he executed even those who had no idea where David had gone."

"That's terrible!" Zachary exclaimed. "Father didn't tell me that part of the story."

"No," Grandfather said. "It's not a particularly noble thing to remember about our first king, but it's true. That was how I lost my family. Doeg the Edomite had betrayed the high priest and told Saul that David had been there seeking advice from the Lord. Even though none of them knew where David had gone after that, Saul had all the families of the priests killed. The high priest was my father. Abiathar and I ran away to join David and his men. We were barely older than you two boys now. That was how I became a friend of King David."

His grandsons nodded solemnly. They knew that Grandfather had been a friend of King David and that he had been one of his men in exile, but they had never known the whole story. Nathan felt a huge lump in his throat. He had been so homesick and miserable just being far away from his family. Now he couldn't imagine what it would be like to know that he would never see them again.

Grandfather Ethan shook his head as if it was all a bad dream. "Come," he said, "let's talk about the Temple instead."

Nathan followed along thoughtfully behind them. Although he wanted to know many things about the Temple, he also wanted to learn everything about his family and Grandfather's father and grandfather. "I guess I'm in the right place for learning those things," he mumbled to himself and smiled. "God probably had several reasons for bringing me here. I'm glad Father made me come after all."

That night as they sat around the fire in the courtyard after dinner Grandfather asked, "Do you boys have questions about things that you saw today or anything else that might have come to you since we talked earlier today?"

Nathan's mind had been churning with hundreds of questions. "Yes, when you spoke of your parents being killed and you going to live with King David in hiding, who was your friend Abiathar? Was that Abiathar, the high priest?"

"No, silly, it couldn't be him," Zachary interrupted. "He's a filthy traitor."

Grandfather's eyes flashed with fire for a moment, but his voice remained gentle. "No one may call the high priest Abiathar a filthy traitor in my home," he said firmly.

Zachary looked as if he had shrunk two inches in height, but Nathan frowned. "Was it the same person?" he asked. "Is that who your friend was?"

"Yes," Grandfather replied. "Abiathar was my best friend, and he and I joined King David together."

"But then why do our fathers . . ."

"It's OK to ask questions," Grandfather said. "All of us have many choices to make in life. For the big ones we ask the Lord's guidance. But the many little ones we often feel that we can take care of ourselves. There was a time," he said with that faraway look in his eyes that usually meant a long story, "when King David was very old. He was ill during the last years of his life. And naturally everyone was concerned about who would be his successor. David's oldest son, who many had viewed as the rightful heir, had rebelled against him years before that and was dead."

The boys had heard the story of Absalom and how he had rebelled against his own father and led an army against him. And how King David even had to leave the city of Jerusalem.

"Since Absalom was dead," Grandfather continued, "many felt that the obvious successor to David should be Prince Adonijah. And Prince Adonijah especially believed that," he said with a twinkle.

Nathan frowned and rubbed his head. He didn't remember any King Adonijah from his history lessons.

"Adonijah was afraid that one of his other brothers would feel that he should be the king, so he went to Hebron and arranged to have himself proclaimed king before David died. That way there wouldn't be any questions or any fighting over it. My friend Abiathar was the high priest at the time. The plan made perfect sense to him, for Adonijah was not leading people in rebellion against David. He just wanted to secure the succession for himself. So he supported him. The problem was that God had promised David, and David had promised Solomon and his mother, that Solomon would be the next king. Adonijah knew about this, but he didn't feel that it was a promise his father needed to keep, especially considering that David's great sin had been with Solomon's mother."

"But if God had promised it," Nathan said, "then Abiathar should have known that. He was the high priest."

Grandfather nodded. "Yes, if Abiathar had consulted God and asked Him, God would not have kept that as a secret from him. But it just seemed logical to Abiathar and he supported Adonijah."

"But Adonijah isn't king now. What happened?" Zachary asked.

"King David called everyone to Jerusalem and had Solomon crowned king," Grandfather explained. "Then he and David shared the throne until my old friend the king finally died. Everyone knew who David had chosen as his successor. And Adonijah, to his credit, did not lead a great army against his father or try to fight it. However, my friend Abiathar, because of his mistake, has not been able to be here, even though building a Temple was one of the greatest dreams of his heart too."

"What happened to him?" Nathan wanted to know.

"Solomon was kind to him. Our king is very wise and merciful, and he had great respect for Abiathar, not only because he was a priest of God, but also because he had been such a good friend to his father, David. So he sent Abiathar out to live in a country house in retirement. And even though that doesn't sound too bad to you boys, he is missing being a part of building the Temple, and it just breaks his heart."

"I never knew that even high priests could make mistakes and do wrong things," Zachary exclaimed.

Grandfather laughed. "It's part of the human condition. Sometimes we don't like to admit it, but all of us make mistakes and bad choices sometimes. That's why we are so thankful for a forgiving God. No matter what we do, we can take our lamb and go to the sanctuary and confess it to Him. He knows our hearts and forgives us— just like Moses said. The Lord is patient and long-suffering. His kindness and mercy endures forever," Grandfather said, his eyes filling with tears.

Nathan watched him. Grandfather got so emotional sometimes talking about the God of Israel. The boy hoped that someday he would have such a love for God too. But right now the Lord just seemed so big and important and far away.

Grandfather's voice rose and fell with his storytelling, and while Nathan intended to listen and was fascinated with what he heard, he soon dozed off with his head on Grandfather's shoulder. Even though he was a grown man 12 years old, he was not too big for Grandfather to scoop up in his arms and carry gently to his sleeping quarters.

It had been a long day and he was still a very young human. I smiled. This one did not know much about the Mighty One, but he had a tender heart and an inquisitive mind, and he would learn. Oh, how soon he would learn.

* * * *

"Today," Grandfather announced, "you will want to take a few extra pieces of bread and dried food and bring them with you."

"Are we going on a trip?" Zachary asked eagerly.

"We are—we're going to head out to the stone quarries and see how the stonemasons are coming along."

Nathan's forehead wrinkled into a frown.

"What are you frowning about now?" his cousin demanded. "You always frown like that when you have questions."

"Well," Nathan replied, "it's just that it looks as if the Temple is already built. What do we need stonemasons for? I thought they were just working on the inside now. Remember, we saw them bring all of that cedarwood for the interior?"

"Yeah," Zachary agreed. "What are the stonemasons working on, Grandfather?"

"You are very observant," Grandfather said with a smile. "Yes, the main part of the Temple building is complete, and the workmen are working on the interior now. They will cover the wood with gold leaf. However, the plans do not just involve the building with the holy and Most Holy places. The stonemasons are still working on the surrounding buildings and area. So they're still quarrying stone, although it isn't for the Temple itself. There will be a large wall surrounding the courtyard and a lower wall within it. We will need paving stones and chambers around the edge for storage and other things. All of these will require stone. We will be going down to talk to the officer in charge of the stonemasons, and you can see how they do everything."

The boys broke into huge smiles. They loved going on trips with Grandfather. Although they enjoyed singing in the choir and their practice time, and though Korah, the Levite in charge, was a very nice man, nothing compared to trips with their grandfather. He always told stories as they went.

The activity in the rock quarry fascinated the boys. Men scurried everywhere.

"Watch carefully," Grandfather said. "These are some of the less experienced rock cutters, although they will be more skilled someday as they learn. They're quarrying large blocks of stone."

"How do they do it?" Zachary asked.

"Look over there." Their grandfather pointed. "See those wooden wedges. They have to choose the spots where the stone is perfect. They don't want a limestone block with big ugly flaws in it, especially for the Temple. Then they drive the wedges into the cracks that they make. Finally they soak the wood with water."

"Why?" Zachary demanded.

Grandfather smiled. "What happens when wood becomes wet?"

"Oh," the boy remembered. "It swells and expands."

"That's right. Limestone, when we first find it in the quarry, is fairly soft. The stonemasons are able to use their picks to make a crack. Then after the men force the wooden wedges in and soak them, the wood expands and widens the crack. The quarry workers can then break out a block of limestone."

Nathan picked up a piece of stone from the ground and rubbed it. "I guess fairly soft is a relative term," he mumbled.

Grandfather laughed. "Yes, it would still feel hard if you bumped your head on it. It all depends on what you're planning to use it for.

"Once the stonecutters have broken the rock out of the cliff and gotten it into a rough shape, they bring it to this other area." He gestured over to one side. "Here the more skilled stonemasons do the fine shaping. They make the pieces so smooth that they fit together perfectly and hold together even without mortar."

This time neither boy mentioned anything about the pyramids. They knew better.

"Now," Grandfather said, "you two walk around. Watch closely but don't get in anybody's way. I have to talk to the foreman here, then I'll be ready to go in a couple hours. Shoo."

The boys wandered off to explore the quarry.

Too soon it was time to leave. As they sat around their campfire that night, Nathan asked, "Are we going back home now?"

"No," Grandfather answered. "I need to stop by the clay pits and talk to the metalworkers also."

Nathan's forehead wrinkled again. Another question was brewing. "Why are the metalworkers in the clay pits?" he asked. He was familiar with the clay pits along the edge of the river between the Dead Sea and the Galilee, because his father had come there before, though not to see a metalworker.

Grandfather smiled. "Think about it," he said. "The metalworkers are making things for the interior of the Temple. To work metal you need to heat it up and then pour it into a mold to shape it unless you are making gold leaf."

"Oh," Zachary said, his face lighting up. "I get it."

"Well, good. Tell me," Nathan demanded. "It doesn't make any sense to me why a metalworker would be in a clay pit. There's less trees and wood for stoking your fire."

His cousin laughed. "That's true. But they need something to make the molds out of. They make the molds in the clay pits."

"That's right," Grandfather said with a smile.

"But I've seen metalworkers work before," Nathan protested, "and they brought the clay and the molds to where they were working."

"Yes," Grandfather replied, "that would usually be easier. But it depends what they're working on. For the smaller things (some of the basins and spoons and incense burners) that could be practical. But they have some *huge* pieces to prepare for the Temple that could not be made anywhere else. They dig the actual molds for them in large pits in the ground. This week we will check on the pillars for the front of the Temple. It will have two huge bronze pillars that will be nearly as tall as the Temple itself. Something that size takes a huge mold, and it was easier to construct the molds here in the clay pits than up in Jerusalem."

As Grandfather finished explaining, the boys rounded the curve and saw exactly what he meant.

"Ooo, they're huge!" his grandsons exclaimed. "Is the Temple really that tall?"

"I'm sure they've measured it," Grandfather said, "but these pillars do look enormous."

The pillars had already been cast and loaded onto long wooden carts.

"Take a look," Grandfather suggested. "Here are the pits they were molded in."

The boys peered down into one of them, then Zachary playfully shoved Nathan. Slipping on the smooth clay, Nathan tumbled into the pit. Grandfather laughed and gave Zachary a shove. He slid in next to his cousin.

"Look at this," Zachary shouted. "I can stand all the way up in the mold. Those pillars are as wide as I am tall."

His cousin laughed. "Yeah, well, those pillars are a couple inches short of being as wide as I am tall. I'm glad I don't have to live inside of one."

The boys giggled.

"Hey, let's lie head to toe and see how long these things are," Zachary suggested. "We'll find out how many of us could fit inside one of these pillars."

Zach and Nathan took turns as they measured out the length of the clay mold.

"Seven," Nathan shouted. "It could fit seven of us standing on each other's shoulders."

Grandfather laughed. "Those aren't quite the measurements that the workmen were going by, but I guess that works." He turned to the metalworker. "How much do these two pillars weigh? Do we have any idea?"

The man shook his head. "I have no idea. These things are so huge, they're unweighable now. And they took such huge quantities of brass to cast them, none of us know."

Grandfather nodded. "I'm sure that's true. It's a good thing that King Solomon has the wealth to provide for all these things. This will be the most magnificent building ever constructed."

The boys continued to play in the clay molds as Grandfather and the men talked about basins and lavers and other Temple needs.

Then he shouted, "Come on, boys. Look at this one over here. You will like this too."

"What is it?" they asked. The object was huge.

"Well," said Grandfather, "by you boys' way of measuring things, I guess it would take about nine of you standing on each other's shoulders to span this."

"It's true," said Nathan, who was a little better at math than Zach. "What is it for? It looks like a huge basin."

"It is," the workman said. "Although you'd be quite a giant to need one of these for a bath."

"I'll say," Nathan agreed. "Who's going to be bathing in this?"

"Only the priests," Grandfather explained. "They have 10 other lavers for washing sacrifices. But this huge one is just for them."

"But why so big?" the boys chorused.

"Everything has been planned to be as magnificent as possible to remind people of our glorious God," Grandfather Ethan told them.

"It's going to look even bigger," the metalworker told the two boys. "We are casting cattle right now. There are going to be three bronze cattle facing east, three west, three south, and three north, all supporting the basin. So the priest will need steps to get up to it."

"This would be a wonderful thing to play in," Zachary whispered wistfully.

Nathan frowned at him. "Zachary, it's sacrilegious to even think such a thing. It's for the Temple, remember?"

His cousin looked apologetic. "It is truly magnificent. And I try really hard to think reverent thoughts, but every once in a while these things just pop into my head."

Grandfather had overheard him and started to laugh. "I imagine," he said with a chuckle, "that the Mighty One does not forget that you were little boys not so long ago. Apparently He likes little boys anyway or He wouldn't have made so many of them."

Nathan smiled, but Zachary squirmed uncomfortably. He hadn't realized Grandfather was listening.

Grandfather resumed his discussion with the metalworkers.

"Yes," the metalworker commented, "right now we're at about 6,000 talents of gold just for the interior of the Most Holy Place. And we have no idea how much we have put into the rest of it."

"By the way you boys measure things," Grandfather commented, "the gold in the Holy Place would weigh about the same amount as 40 of you."

Both boys shook their heads. Neither had come from wealthy homes. They couldn't imagine that much gold. However, for a Temple for their God only the best was good enough. And as much gold as King Solomon wanted to put into it was fine with them.

"You must feel greatly honored to be working on these things for the Temple," Zachary exclaimed to one of the metalworkers.

The man laughed hoarsely. "Oh, yeah, real honored. I'm real honored to work in gold for any god that will pay me well."

Nathan and Zachary were astonished. Grandfather Ethan's mouth pressed into a firm line and the muscles in his jaw tightened.

"Speaking of which," the man said to Grandfather, "did your God happen to send the monthly payment along with you on this trip?"

"Yes," Grandfather Ethan said as calmly as he could. "I left it with the supervisor as always." He gestured toward the tent where another officer worked.

"Well, one thing I have to say," the workman continued, oblivious to Grandfather's anger. "The God of Israel at least is a little more prompt with paying His bills than some we've worked for."

Several of the metalworkers around him laughed.

Grandfather turned on his heel and strode away. The boys hurried to keep up with him. It was half an hour before he slowed his pace.

"That metalworker was terribly disrespectful," Nathan blurted, still thinking about the incident.

"Yes," Grandfather agreed, "he was. And he is fortunate that the God of Israel is merciful and slow to anger and didn't strike him dead with a lightning bolt like I might have enjoyed doing right then."

Surely, the boys thought, their God was patient and merciful to put up with such disrespect.

"Wouldn't it have been better to get—well, you know—Israelites to do the fine metalwork for the sanctuary?" Nathan asked. "I have heard that King Hiram sent these men from Tyre."

"Yes, but do you want to hear something even more amazing? They *are* descendants of Israelites. That craftsperson you were talking to who was so disrespectful is a direct descendant of Aholiub."

"Really?" both boys asked at once. They knew Aholiub from the stories their father had told them when they were little. The man had been a slave in Egypt and had learned metalworking there. When Moses led the Israelites out of Egypt, Aholiub received the honor of making the ark of the covenant and all the sacred metalwork funishings within the first sanctuary that Moses had erected in the wilderness.

"How could that be?" Zachary exclaimed. "He was so, well—rude."

"Yes. Through the years our people apparently didn't pay enough, and the descendants of Aholiub found that they could make much better money casting metal objects for the kings of the other nations around us. Business was pretty good. That fellow we spoke to—Huram—was actually from the tribe of Dan, or at least his mother was. His father was from Tyre. He is more interested in getting wealthy than serving the God of his mother."

The boys solemnly nodded.

I had to agree with them on this one. It seemed to those of us observing that Solomon might have been better off using local metal smiths who, while perhaps less experienced than the skilled workers from Tyre, would have had more respect for the God they were working for. After all, because they would be committed to Him, He would have endowed them with the skills they needed to make the holy things for His home. It was the Mighty One who gave the skills to Ahoilab and his sons in the first place, and there was no reason why He could not do it again. Still these were the choices Solomon had made and, in spite of the greed of the metalworkers, God was blessing the building project.

* * * *

It was hard to believe that almost two years had passed since the boys had come to live with their grandfather. The air almost buzzed around them with excitement. The Temple was at last finished. It seemed as if they had been practicing their songs for the dedication forever, singing each one again and again to make sure it was absolutely perfect.

"It finally makes sense to me," Nathan said.

"What finally makes sense?" his cousin asked.

"Well, it never made sense to me," he said, "that the ark was in the palace with the king, but the high priest was banished out to his country home and the tent of meeting with the bronze altar was in Gibeon. Where was God's real residence?"

"Well, I don't think it was that big a deal to God," Zachary commented. "After all, He's the King of the universe. The earth is just His footstool."

"I know. But the whole reason for having the tent of meeting and the entire wilderness tabernacle was so that He would have a place where He could be near us. And then it was all split up and I always wondered which one He was actually at."

Zachary laughed. "Probably He can be more places than one at a time. He may not be made the same as we are."

Nathan nodded. "I'm sure it wasn't a problem to Him, but it always bothered me. I'm glad that He has a beautiful Temple now. I just hope He will always want to be with us."

"Why wouldn't He?" Zachary asked.

"Perhaps I phrased that wrong," Nathan said slowly. "Perhaps I should have said I hope that we always make Him welcome."

"Yes, I guess you're right. Well, tomorrow's the big day. We still have things to do to get ready."

"I finally figured something else out today," Nathan continued, totally ignoring Zachary's comment about preparing for the ceremony.

"My, you've been busy thinking today," Zachary laughed. "What else did you figure out?"

"Why God wanted them to use cedar on the inside of the house."

"Oh, that's easy. It's because it smells nice. The Lord wants things that are sweet smelling."

"Well, if that's true," Nathan smirked, "you're in real trouble."

Zachary burst out laughing. "Well, I don't think God minds people who got sweaty practicing to sing for Him. Better than somebody who smells good and just sits around and doesn't praise Him."

"Perhaps God is like your mom."

"What does that mean?" his cousin demanded.

"Well, you know, she just adores you no matter how you smell because you're her son."

As Zachary reluctantly nodded, Nathan continued, "Unlike the rest of us who would really appreciate you bathing before the ceremonies tomorrow."

After Zachary gave him a playful punch, the two were soon wrestling in the courtyard.

"Hey, break it up you two," Grandfather's voice ordered. "Look, I have new robes for you two to wear tomorrow."

The boys caught their breath. They were white ephods like the other Levites wore. But they had beautiful blue tassels on the corners.

"They look expensive," Zachary blurted.

"That's because they were," Grandfather commented. "But you're worth it. And it's to celebrate the dedication of the Temple, and the Lord is worth it. Besides, in Moses law God said that all the sons of Israel should wear at least one thread of blue in their garment."

The deep blue dye was very expensive, because the snails that the dye was made from came from the ocean and were very tiny. It took many of them to produce just a small amount of pure dye.

"Thank you, Grandfather," the boys said together.

ELISHEBA

lisheba crouched near the doorway, straining to hear what was being said. Grandfather Nathan had called a secret family meeting. Both of her uncles were there and three of their eldest sons. The girl had had a prickling at the back of her neck that someone was watching her or talking about her. And while it seemed pretty far-fetched, she just had to know what they were saying.

So many things had happened that week that had left her confused and worried. The king was dead. Now Prince Rehoboam would be the king. The whole land grieved for King Solomon. He had been a wise and good king. Elisheba had seen him several times when he addressed the country or worshiped at the Temple. This was the first time anyone important that she knew of had died since she had been too young to remember the death of her father.

"Elisheba!"

Hearing her name, she jumped and looked up guiltily.

"What are you doing here?" her mother demanded. "Come back out and help me with the cooking. We must prepare something for these men." She smiled and winked.

The girl grinned to herself. Mother wanted to know as badly as she did what was going on.

"What do you think they're talking about?" Elisheba asked.

"I don't know," her mother whispered. "There's a lot going on. But I have a hunch it's not about the weather or they wouldn't be hiding in the back room whispering among themselves."

"Our uncles and cousins are here," Elisheba said. "Everyone who is of age." She wrinkled her nose. If she were a boy, she would be almost old enough to be a man now. Instead, she was just a girl and would never be included in this kind of meetings.

"Well, if they were just chatting about King Rehoboam's coronation," Mother said, "they could do that out in the courtyard. Here, you carry this platter, and I'll bring something for them to drink."

The two quietly pulled back the curtain that covered the doorway to the room in the back.

"Won't that be considered treason?" Uncle Seth asked.

"I guess that depends where you are at the time," his brother, Reuben, retorted. "If you're in Rehoboam's court, then, yes, it would be treason. But if you are in Jereboam's court, then it would be considered loyal behavior."

The conversation stopped abruptly as the men realized the curtain had moved.

"We brought you something to eat," Elisheba's mother said as she set the platter in the center of the room and the jug of grape juice beside it.

"Thank you," Grandfather Nathan said.

Elisheba's uncles just looked at the floor, but her cousins stared at her curiously.

"What?" she asked as she saw the questioning look in their faces.

"Never mind," her cousin Joab said. "This conversation is not for women."

Mother made a small coughing noise but said nothing.

Grandfather Nathan smiled. "Eventually it will affect everyone in this family," he said.

Elisheba and her mother left the room.

"See," Mother said, "they're talking about the coronation and Jereboam."

"Who's Jereboam?" Elisheba asked.

"Jereboam was around a while back. When King Solomon married so many women from other countries, he started building them temples to their gods so they would have a place to worship and not be so homesick."

"Wasn't that wrong?" Elisheba interrupted. "Isn't that disloyal to our God?"

Mother nodded. "Yes, and the Lord thought so too. Your father told me that the prophet Ahijah went to Jereboam one day and tore his robe in half."

"Why? Clothing is too expensive."

"Apparently the prophet told Jereboam that God was going to tear the kingdom in half—not even really in half. He was going to give the smaller piece to Solomon's sons and the larger piece to Jereboam. But God told Jereboam He didn't want him to do anything about this until Solomon died.

"None of us really knew whether it was a true story or not, although it was a rumor that many people believed. But the next thing we knew Jereboam had fled to Egypt and was staying in the court of King Shishack. Now within a week of Solomon's death, here he is back in Israel again. Makes you wonder."

Elisheba looked thoughtful. "Do you think that Grandfather and our men are trying to decide which king to be loyal to?"

"Well, there's only one king right now. It's Rehoboam. But if the rumor is true and if God really does divide the kingdom, then I guess everyone will have to decide who should receive their allegiance."

Elisheba didn't say anything for a moment, then asked, "Who are you going to be loyal to?"

Mother laughed. "We don't get to choose, Elisheba. Remember, we will be a part of Grandfather Nathan's household. And whoever he gives his allegiance to we will be loyal to also."

Elisheba's shoulders sagged for a minute, then she perked up. "But you've always said that Grandfather Nathan was very wise and a godly man, so he'll choose the right king, won't he?"

"Of course," Mother said as she hugged Elisheba. "And no matter how things turn out, it will be fine. We will live here with your grandfather and your uncles and they will take care of us. And we'll all get to stay together because—because of your little brother."

"Why because of him?"

"Because he's your father's heir. So we'll be fine. Life would be very different if I had been childless when your father died."

Elisheba had heard of other widows and the terrible times they had had. Life was good here on Grandfather Nathan's family compound. And even though the family had not been as prosperous as most Levites had been during the time when the Temple was first built, life was still good.

"As King Solomon became distracted by his foreign wives and their gods," Mother continued, "many in Israel began worshiping the foreign gods also. They stopped attending the Temple. Since the

Levites depended on the gifts and offerings brought to the Temple, this meant there was less to go around."

"Will King Rehoboam worship God like King Solomon did?"

"I don't know about him. Sometimes he seems committed and sincere in his worship. Then other times, well—" She shrugged. "Perhaps he can't help it. His mother was an Ammonite. I think Prince Rehoboam has always felt pulled two ways. But now that he is the king, he'll have to make up his mind. Perhaps that's what the men are talking of too."

"If the story about Prophet Ahijah and Jereoboam is true," Elisheba said pensively, "then perhaps God felt that Jereboam would worship Him and lead the country in a more godly way than Prince Rehoboam."

"Perhaps, but we don't know about any of this, and it would be very dangerous to speak of it where anyone else could hear you. You're old enough to know some of these important secrets, but you must be very careful."

Elisheba nodded. "I certainly will."

It was long after Elisheba had laid down on her sleeping mat in the room she shared with her mother before the men completed their secret meeting. The girl had not fallen asleep yet. She strained her ears to pick up the whispered conversations as they headed for their respective sleeping spaces in the family enclosure.

"I still think we should offer Elisheba as a wife to him."

Her ears perked up. She recognized Uncle Seth's voice.

"You know Father would never let us do that," another voice replied.

"But why?" Seth protested. "True she's not royalty, but she could be a concubine and that would give us a basis of power and access to Jereoboam's court. If things didn't work out well and we decided to stick with Rehoboam, it wouldn't be a problem either. She's only a girl and a niece. It's not as if we're giving one of our daughters."

"I agree," her other uncle answered. "The plan has merit, but our father is determined that she should marry some respectable Levite and raise a whole family of little Levites. And have the same financial problems that all the rest of us do."

"Humph," Uncle Seth growled. "Maybe we can talk him into a compromise. He certainly is a stubborn old man."

Elisheba leaned against the wall as she sat in the darkness. She felt as if her heart was pounding so loudly it would give her away. Had she heard correctly? Surely she was misunderstanding them. Were they really thinking of giving her as a wife to Jereboam? He was older, and besides he had a wife. She stared out the window at the twinkling stars for what seemed like hours. The lump in her throat wouldn't go away.

Finally she gathered her courage about her and crept out the door and across the courtyard. Carefully she slipped in through the curtain covering Grandfather's door.

"Grandfather, Grandfather," she whispered.

"Elisheba, what are you doing up so late?" he said from the darkness.

"I couldn't sleep and—and I'm scared."

"Why are you afraid, Elisheba? Did you hear something? You know we have a sturdy gate with a heavy beam barring it. No one can break in here and hurt you."

"That's not what I heard," she whispered guiltily.

"Hmm. Come sit here by me. And here, put this around you. It's chilly in the middle of the night this time of year."

Grandfather handed her his daytime cloak. She wrapped up in it and then leaned against him.

"You heard some of your uncles' discussion," he said flatly.

She nodded and even though it was dark, Grandfather Nathan understood.

"They said they wouldn't give their daughters, but because I was only a niece, I didn't matter," she blurted.

Grandfather put his arm around her. "You matter," he said firmly. "They were wrong to say that."

"Are you really going to send me away from here to marry him?"

"No, we are not. As long as I'm head of this household, I am the one to make those decisions."

The girl took a deep breath and let it out with a sigh of relief.

"Elisheba," he said gently, "you understand that when girls reach marriageable age they do leave home?"

"But Grandfather, I'm not quite that age yet."

He smiled in the darkness and hugged her closer. "I know. And I'm glad you're not. It's hard to imagine you all grown up and living somewhere else as someone's wife. But you do know that that will happen someday?"

"Yes."

"Meanwhile there are many things happening in our country that make circumstances different than they were a week ago. Your uncles and I are trying to decide what to do—what would be best for our whole family."

Elisheba squeezed his arm in agreement.

"And even more important than being loyal to the family," he continued, "is your loyalty to God."

"I am loyal to God," she protested.

"Yes, I know. Your love for the God of Israel is one of the things that has bound you and I so closely, more so than my other grandchildren."

Elisheba smiled to herself. It was true. Grandfather Nathan loved the God of Israel. He worked at the Temple as one of the assistant instructors to the new members of the choir. They said that he knew every psalm King David had ever written and most of the rest of them. He had taught many of them to Elisheba, and she loved to sing them with him.

"It is my plan," Grandfather explained, "that you will marry a good

Levite man when you are old enough. However, our family has had some financial problems, and we do need to think of other things."

"Like which king?"

"Where'd you hear that?" he demanded.

"Just talk," she said guiltily.

"Be very careful and don't say anything until we see what happens with our country," he cautioned. "Such talk can be very dangerous if it's heard by the wrong person."

"I'll be careful," she whispered. "Tell me about Jereboam."

"You have heard the discussions, haven't you? There are lots of rumors about. I will tell you what is truth, if you promise not to ask anyone else questions."

"I promise," she said solemnly.

Grandfather Nathan drew a deep breath. "Jereboam is a good man. He was one of King Solomon's mighty men of valor and a highly skilled soldier. In addition, he supervised the men doing temporary service for the king in the district of the house of Joseph. Organizing the local labor, he directed them on several construction projects for the king."

"He sounds like an important man," Elisheba said.

"Yes, and a man gifted with strong leadership skills."

"Is the story about the prophet Ahijah true?"

"Yes, and because of that Jereboam has been living in Egypt for his own safety. But he's back. Prince Rehoboam is heading for Shechem. We think he's planning the coronation there and have been wondering if Jereboam is going to make his move then."

"Will it be dangerous? Will there be fighting?"

"I don't know," Grandfather answered slowly. "None of the men in this family will lift a sword against the Lord's anointed king. It's just that both of these men seem to be anointed. One is the son of Solomon. The other was called to be king by the prophet Ahijah. We are very confused. But Jereboam has always been loyal to the God of

Israel. Rehoboam—well, sometimes it seems it depends on the weather."

Suddenly Grandfather changed the subject. "The wife of Jereboam is very young."

"How young?"

"A few years older than you. This is a difficult time for her, too. And she needs a companion and a maidservant. I'm making arrangements for you to go to the house of Jereboam and be a maidservant and companion to his young wife."

"Is that different than what my uncles were saying?"

"Absolutely. They wanted to give you to Jereboam himself. Being a companion and a maidservant to his wife is not the same. You will belong to her and you will care for her, but you will return to our family when we have found a husband for you and when I have a suitable dowry."

Elisheba caught her breath. She didn't know whether to be relieved or to burst into tears. While she was leaving home, at least she wasn't being married off to someone she didn't know. Not yet, anyway.

Grandfather hugged her. "These will be difficult days," he said. "I know you will be lonely and I will miss you terribly, but it may be a safer place for you right now. And you will be in a wealthier home until we get back on our feet financially here. Just remember that wherever you are, the God of Israel will be with you and you can always talk to Him. You'll never be alone."

"I will always remember that, Grandfather."

"Now," said Grandfather gruffly, "get back to your bed before morning. You don't want to be still sitting up when the sun rises. Otherwise you'll be exhausted tomorrow."

Elisheba bit her lip. "I love you, Grandpa." After giving him a hug, she scampered back across the courtyard.

I watched my young charge toss and turn the remainder of the night. By the time she had awakened in the morning, decisions had been made, provisions had been packed, and she had only time for a brief and careful goodbye to her mother before she, her grandfather, and her uncles set out for the gathering of the men of Israel. First, though, they went to the home of Jereboam in Shechem.

"Your granddaughter, Elisheba, is welcome here," he told Grandfather. "I received your message and, in honor of the respect that my father, Nebat, had for you, and your friendship with him, I will care for her respectfully in my home as long as she is a guest here."

Elisheba was surprised. She didn't know that Grandfather Nathan had been friends with Nebat, the father of Jereboam. I smiled. There were lots of things she didn't know.

"This is my wife, Sarah. She will be pleased to have a young companion. The only other women in our family compound are some older servants."

Jereboam's wife smiled shyly at the girl.

Before long the men had left and the two girls were alone together. I was thankful that the Mighty One had planned to put these girls together for both were young and lonely and needed the friendship of each other. I was even more glad that He had posted extra guardians around her, for the entire country was restless and impending conflict seemed to lurk everywhere. Today the men in Israel were going to meet with young Prince Rehoboam and make plans for the coronation.

The girls spent very little time worrying about that as Sarah showed Elisheba around the compound and they got to know each other.

"Your home is almost the same size as Grandfather Nathan's home near Jerusalem," Elisheba observed. "But there were a lot more of us living in it."

"Yes, my husband's family used to be bigger. I think many of them died while he was in Egypt."

Elisheba smiled bashfully. "Also it appears that Jereboam is more—well, you know, prosperous."

Sarah laughed. "Yes, we're very blessed. This is a good place to live and he is prosperous, but"—she swallowed hard—"I miss my mother."

Suddenly Elisheba's eyes also filled with tears and she was unable to speak.

When Jereboam and the other men returned that evening, the girls were eager to hear the news.

"What happened today? Did you see Prince Rehoboam? Is there going to be a coronation?" Sarah asked.

"Stop, stop. One at a time," Jereboam laughed. "The men of Israel gathered altogether and, yes, Rehoboam was there. The elders presented some of our concerns to him. The economy has been terrible for the common people here in Israel. And even though wealth has poured into the country during Solomon's reign and he was very prosperous, not much of it has filtered down to ordinary people. Toward the end of his reign taxes just went up and up and people are hardly able to bear it. The elders petitioned Rehoboam to lower our taxes and relieve the burden on us."

Grandfather Nathan shook his head. "In the old days," he said, "there were no rich and poor in Israel. Some were more prosperous than others, but there was not such a division. That was before we had kings. Under the kings the royal family and their favorites became very wealthy and the poor became more destitute and the gap between them became so large. It is not that anyone wishes to take anything from those who are wealthy, but just to relieve the burden of taxation on those who are barely making it as it is."

"Well, what did he say?" Sarah asked. "Is he going to do it?"

Jereboam shrugged. "He says he wants to talk with his advisers and he'll get back to us. So everyone is waiting to see what he decides."

"And you?" Sarah looked pointedly at her husband.

"I'm waiting, too," he said. "The Lord will tell me what to do and when to do it, and until then I wait."

Grandfather Nathan nodded and smiled. "That's all we can do."

I was pleased, although I knew not everyone in their group was as willing to wait for the Almighty to fulfill His plans.

The next day, several hours after Jeroboam left, the girls could hear shouting outside the walls of the compound.

"Summon the servants to help," Sarah exclaimed as the noise increased. "We must bar the entrance."

Unfortunately, the only ones home at the moment were only two elderly men, an older woman who was the cook, and two small children. Everyone else had gone to the public gathering for Rehoboam's coronation. They pushed the gates to the compound shut and, after struggling to put the heavy beam across it, they dragged over a few pieces of furniture and piled them against the gate.

It was difficult for the girls to tell who was shouting in the streets and what they were saying. Sara, Elisheba, and the servants clung to each other in a large central room at the back of the courtyard. They found themselves torn between trying to listen and trying not to hear what was going on so close to them.

"I thought I heard shouts of 'Long live King Rehoboam,'" Sarah said. "Then I thought I heard them say 'Jereboam,' but now I don't know which."

"Whatever it is, they're certainly angry," Elisheba said, swallowing hard.

It seemed like hours before their men returned. And when they did there were many others with them. They poured into the courtyard and stood gathered around the front gate.

Jereboam raised his hands and some of the noise died down. "You have called on me to be your king," he said, "and I humbly accept."

The crowd roared its approval.

"Many years ago," he said, "the prophet Ahijah told me this would happen." He shared the story of Ahijah tearing his garment and telling him not to do anything before Solomon's death.

"Now," he said, "Rehoboam has gone back to Jerusalem to gather an army and we may have to fight. We need to pray and dedicate ourselves to the God of Israel for we are Israel, whether we are 10 tribes or the previous 12. He is our God and perhaps He can save us from war right now. And if not, then He will give us victory."

The crowd roared its approval again. "Long live Jereboam! Long live Jereboam!" they yelled.

Elisheba turned to Sarah. "Sarah, if Jereboam is the new king of Israel, you're the queen."

The older girl's chin dropped.

"Your highness," Elisheba said, dropping on her knees before Sarah.

"Don't be silly. Get up," Sarah insisted. "You're my best friend. I'll have other people for servants and slaves. You're my companion."

"As you wish, your highness," Elisheba said with a smile.

* * * *

Elisheba stood in her chamber, her elbows on the windowsill, staring out at the night sky. Tears welled up in her eyes. "God of Israel, are You paying attention? It wasn't supposed to be like this. When Rehoboam refused to listen to any of the people's requests and Jereboam became king, it all seemed so perfect. You appeared to have had planned everything that way, but now I'm so confused. I was so happy being brought together with Sarah, and I assumed it was Your plan for me to be here. But now, I don't know what to think. I thought that Jereboam was truly committed to you, but I don't understand what he's doing now. He has had those two golden calves made—one to be put in Dan and one to be put in Bethel. He says we're not really worshiping the calves, that we're worshiping You and that the calves are substitutes for the ark of the covenant. But it doesn't feel right to me.

"Grandfather Nathan taught me that one of Your commandments was about not making any graven images. And I remember the stories about Moses and the children of Israel when they built the golden calf. God of Israel, I don't understand what's happening, but I want You to know that no matter what, You are the One I worship and You are the One I love."

She put her head in her hands. I hovered close, wishing that I could wrap my wings around her and comfort her. It was confusing. Both kings claimed to worship the God of Israel. Rehoboam's allegiance seemed to shift back and forth though he did continue to worship God in the Temple his father, Solomon, had built. Jereboam, to whom God had given the 10 tribes of Israel because of the behavior of Solomon and Rehoboam, was now erecting rival places of worship.

Elisheba's mind drifted back to a conversation she had heard earlier that evening.

"I can't have all the men of Israel trotting off to Jerusalem," Jereboam exploded. "It's enemy territory now."

"Not necessarily," his wife protested. "God told us that we all needed to go to the Temple four times a year, so He would protect us. He kept Rehoboam from going to war with us when the people crowned you king of Israel. He could do it again."

"It's just not practical," the Israelite king insisted. "I've talked it over with my counselors, and it makes much more sense to establish two more convenient places central to most people in Israel. That way they can make it easily to one or the other. I'll build temples. I can put the golden calves there, since there is only one ark of the covenant. It will be fine."

Sarah just shook her head and Elisheba said nothing.

In human terms choices of loyalty can be difficult. Sometimes you have to deal with whatever situation you are in and be as honest and straightforward as you can and give your true loyalty to the Mighty One and trust Him to work everything else out. At times that's all humans can do, and this was one of those times.

The months flew by. Jereboam had the planned temples built with beautiful altars and the golden calves just as he had wanted. He appointed friends and political allies instead of Levites to be priests at them. When it came time for the great feast when all the men of Israel used to go to Jereusalem, Jereboam sent out a message.

"It is too much for you to go up to Jerusalem," he urged, "so there will be feasts in Dan and Bethel for your convenience."

The morning of the great feast arrived. Sarah looked pale with dark circles under her eyes. She and Jereboam had been arguing the night before. Elisheba could hear them from her bed chamber. Now Jereboam was standing in the courtyard with his hands on his hips.

"All of my household will accompany me to the sacrifice," he said sternly.

Sarah's chin quivered. "I can't," she said in a tiny voice.

"You will," he bellowed.

Suddenly she bent over and threw up on the ground.

"Don't even think that a little bit of phony hysterics is going to change my mind," he shouted.

Everyone stood around, aghast.

Sarah crumpled to the ground. Elisheba ran over and wiped her face, cradling her head in her lap. For the first time she met the steady gaze of Jereboam and said as calmly as she could, "She's going to have a baby."

Silence fell on the courtyard. Jereboam looked at the ground. Then with swift strides he walked over and picked his wife up. "An heir," he said, "an heir to the throne. This is wonderful." And he carried her back into their chambers.

Elisheba and the two other servants hurried after him. Since Jereboam had become king they had a lot more servants.

In a few minutes Elisheba and the servants had Sarah cleaned up and reclining on pillows. The young queen's chin quivered and the tears poured down her cheeks in spite of how hard she tried to hold them back. "This isn't how I wanted it to be," she said. "I wanted you to be happy. I wanted to tell you at just the right time."

"I am happy," Jereboam said. "The timing was—well, don't worry about the timing. I am happy. It's an heir for Israel. You may rest." He planted a kiss on her forehead and turned to Elisheba. "And I expect you with the rest of the household to attend the sacrifices." He turned on his heel and walked out.

Elisheba squeezed Sarah's hand and followed the king out to the courtyard.

Two of the older women servants remained to care for Sarah and everyone else made the trip to Bethel. Elisheba was hot and tired and worried about Sarah. As she walked with the royal procession she kept praying, "God of Israel, what do I do? This isn't the way You asked us to worship. What do You expect of me? I've never stood up to Jereboam before until today. I'm not sure I can again. I need Your help."

I noticed several guardians in the group and warriors with their swords of light shielded for the time being. Obviously the Almighty had some major action planned. I wanted to comfort Elisheba and tell her, "He hears you. He's got it under control. He has everything all planned." But I wasn't permitted to do that. So I followed the girl in silence.

At Bethel Jereboam stood with the priests. Most of the men were not Levite priests, for all the loyal Levites had returned to Judah, much to his great bitterness. They had refused to officiate at shrines that were not built according to the Mighty One's guidelines. Arrogantly Jereboam stood before the priests at Bethel and raised his hands.

"Behold the shrine of our God who brought our ancestors out of the land of Egypt," he proclaimed, waiting for everyone to bow in worship.

Suddenly a shout came from the watching crowd. Elisheba opened her eyes and saw that many had not yet bowed. A man strode toward the front of the crowd. Ignoring the king, he spoke directly to the altar. "Oh, altar, listen to what the Lord says. A child is going to be born into the house of David. A prince named Josiah. And on you he shall offer the priests of these places and the men that burn incense on you. And you will be desecrated totally by having old dead bones burned on you instead of incense."

A murmur rippled through the crowd. Burning bones on an altar would be the ultimate insult. It could never be made holy again after that.

"And here's a sign to prove to you that this is from the Lord," the man continued. "This altar will split in half and the ashes that are on it will be dumped out all over the ground."

"Arrest him!" King Jereboam ordered. Suddenly they heard a loud roar. The ground shook and the altar split in half and in front of the king and everyone the ashes poured out all over the ground, just as the prophet had said. Many in the crowd fell on their knees and prayed to the God of Israel. Who could stand against a sign like that? Obviously the Lord was not pleased with worship in this place.

The voice of Jereboam interrupted their prayers. "Stop," he shouted. "Grab that man." He reached across the altar, pointing at the prophet.

Suddenly a strangled cry came from his throat. Everybody watched in horror as his hand curled up into a gnarled position and shriveled. Hoarsely he whispered, "Help me, somebody. Help me. I can't move my arm."

Quickly one of his advisers grabbed his shoulder. "Can you put it down, your majesty?"

"No," he choked out.

Now the crowd buzzed with excitement. If the broken altar and the spilled ashes hadn't been enough, that certainly was.

"Please," the king croaked, "bring the man of God to me. Please ask God," he begged the prophet, "please ask him to restore my arm and my hand to me."

The prophet stared at him for several moments and then prayed. In amazement Elsheba watched as the king's hand filled back out again and then unclenched. Gingerly Jereboam pulled his arm down and rubbed the recently shriveled hand with his good one.

* * * *

Scooping up young Abijah in her arms, Elisheba groaned, "Oh, child, I must be getting old."

He giggled and wrapped his tiny arms around her neck.

"Let's go see how your mother is," she said.

Sarah had given birth to Abijah, Jereboam's heir, and later Prince Nadab. It seemed such a short time since Jereboam had become king, and yet so much had happened. Even though she had been in Jereboam's court for almost five years, Elisheba was still homesick. She had not seen Grandfather Nathan or her mother in a long time. Although the Lord had been merciful and had prevented conflict at the time of the split, Israel and Judah had been attacking each other ever since.

Jereboam seemed repentant only briefly after the incident with the destroyed altar and his withered hand. Soon he resumed his practice of mingling pagan rituals with the worship of the true God. Not only did he appoint anyone he wanted to reward as priests in the northern shrines, he even made himself one.

Elisheba felt queasy at the pit of her stomach every time she thought about it. She continued to whisper her private prayers to the God of Abraham and Jacob every day. Yet she wondered how long He would put up with Jereboam's behavior, especially since God had chosen him as ruler because the last king had become disloyal to him. Jereboam was even worse than Solomon had been.

The squirming child in her arms kept her from dwelling on Israel's idolatry for long.

"Oh, good, you two are awake," Elisheba said as she entered the royal nursery.

Sarah cradled Nadab in her arms. "He's always cranky when he first wakes up."

"Like his mother," Elisheba replied with a grin as she sat on the floor in front of her.

Both girls laughed.

"So what have you two been doing?" Sarah asked.

"Playing," Abijah announced. "Playing outside."

"Good," his mother declared.

Prince Abijah flopped over and laid his head on Elisheba's lap. "I don't think he feels well today," she observed. "The whole time we were playing he just acted tired. He didn't really want to eat at lunchtime either."

Sarah nodded absently. "He's just like that some days."

"No, not like this. I think there's something wrong."

"Yoshebel," Sarah called.

"Yes, my queen," the servant answered.

"Was Abijah OK earlier? Elisheba thinks he's not feeling well."

"He seemed all right this morning," the older servant replied. "Sometimes children just do this. He'll eat when he's hungry. When my children were little they would go through periods where they ate as though they were expecting a famine and at other times seemed barely interested in their food. But whenever they started eating like a wild beast it usually meant they were about to become much taller."

The girls laughed. "Well, Abijah," Elisheba said, "you had better perk up and eat a little more. You've got some growing to do yet, my child."

Abijah stood up to his full height. "I'm this big," he said defensively.

"Yes," his mother said, "you are a big boy."

The little prince laid his head back in Elisheba's lap. "Should we lay down for a little while?" Elisheba asked.

"No, no naps!" the child shouted and started to cry.

"There, there, nobody said anything about a nap," Elisheba said soothingly. "How about if you curl up in my lap here and I tell you a story?"

Abijah stopped sobbing and curled up in Elisheba's lap. "Stories are good," he said and stuck his thumb in his mouth.

Elisheba's eyes met Sarah's. "He feels really hot," she said.

The boy's mother reached over and felt his face. "Yoshebel," she called, "bring some cool water to bath Abijah's face with and bring him a drink."

"Don't want a drink. Want a story!" the child insisted.

"Yes," Elisheba said, "you shall have a story. Once upon a time . . ."

"Not a 'Once upon a time' story," said the young prince. "Want 'When I was a little girl' story."

"OK. When I was a little girl I lived in Jerusalem with my mother and my Grandfather Nathan." Her gentle voice had lulled him to sleep before she had gone far in her story. Elisheba laid him on the couch where his mother and little brother had been resting earlier.

"I hope he feels better when he wakes up," she said. "His face is so hot, and I think he has a fever. Perhaps we should have the court physician take a look at him."

"Let's wait," Sarah suggested. "This happens sometimes. He used to run fevers when he was cutting teeth."

They both slipped out of the room to let the little prince sleep.

Abijah dozed fitfully through the afternoon. Sarah and Elisheba grew more concerned as the hours wore on. His fussiness and crying was so unusual for him. And the longer it went on the more frantic they became.

The next morning they were even more worried. The child no longer tossed and turned or fussed. He just lay there with his little eyes half open, staring into space. The court physician had made an herbal potion for him that the boy refused to drink. The little they were able to get into him came back up immediately.

Jereboam stood with his arms folded across his chest, staring down at his little son. "Is there nothing else you can do?" he asked.

"Your Majesty, we're doing everything—" began the court doctor.

"You're all useless," the king snapped. "Get out."

"Yes, your majesty." He and several other officials bowed and retreated hastily from the room.

Sarah turned to her husband.

"We could pray," she said.

"We've already had sacrifices offered for him," Jereboam growled.

"I mean to God," Sarah stated coldly. "The God of Israel, or the God who was the God of Israel, the God who was the God of Jereboam."

"Leave us," the king ordered the servants in the room. Only Sarah, Elisheba, and the child on the couch remained. "Don't ever speak to me like that in front of the servants again," Jereboam exploded.

Sarah turned to him with tear-filled eyes. "Our son is sick. Surely God would have mercy on him. He's an innocent little boy."

Jereboam's face softened. "The prophet Ahijah is still alive," he said after a moment.

"Really?" Sarah and Elisheba responded in unison.

The king nodded. "He's been ill and I understand his eyesight is poor. But he's still around and lives in Shiloh."

"Just like the prophet Samuel did," Elisheba exclaimed.

"The very place," Jereboam replied. The king turned to his wife. "Look, if you want to go to the prophet Ahijah, it's fine with me. But I can hardly show up there. He's not that happy with me. Things haven't gone the way he hoped."

Sarah nodded and shot a glance at Elisheba. Things hadn't gone the way she had hoped either.

"But if you go," he continued, "at least wear a disguise so no one will know that you are my wife. Take him gifts, but nothing special that he would recognize as from the palace. You know, a few loaves of bread, maybe some cakes and a jar of honey. Ask him to inquire of the Lord and find out what's going to happen with our son. Perhaps he will ask the Lord to heal him. I'm obviously not in a position to request it myself."

"I'll get ready right away," Sarah said. "Come, Elisheba. Let's go to the servant's quarters. We'll get some clothes from there."

I shook my head. How could this man whom the Lord had chosen to be king over Israel do this? He had seen God's power both in putting him in his position of power and in healing his withered arm after his flagrant disobedience. How could Jeroboam think that by having his wife wear a disguise he could somehow fool the Lord into doing favors for his son? Did he assume that just because the old prophet had bad eyesight that the Mighty One was blind also? Sometimes these humans were so—well, dense. I frowned as I remembered how they had been in the beginning when the Mighty One had first created the world. He had made them to be highly intelligent. How could they be so smart about some things and so stupid about the important ones?

Turning, I swept out of the room to follow the young queen and her confidant. I did not believe for a moment that their disguises would fool the old prophet. And I was right.

Ahijah heard the women as they approached. As Sarah raised her hands to knock he called, "Come in. I already know who you are. You are the wife of King Jereboam. Why are you pretending to be someone else? I have very bad news for you."

Sarah dropped to her knees before the prophet.

"Go home," he said. "Tell Jereboam that the Lord has a message for him. The Lord is the God of Israel. He says, 'I chose you from among the people. I made you the leader of my people Israel. I tore the kingdom away from the royal house of David, and I gave it to you. But you have not been obedient like My servant David. He followed Me with his heart and David was right in My eyes. You have done more evil things than all the kings who lived before you. You have made Me very angry, because you have made other gods for yourself. Statues out of metal. Because of that I am going to bring horrible trouble on your royal house. I will cut off from you every male in Israel, whether they be slave or free. I will burn up your royal house just as someone burns up trash. I will consume it until it is all gone. Some of the people who belong to you will die in the city and the dogs will devour them. Others will die in the country and the birds of the air will eat them.'"

Sarah gasped. Ahijah's voice softened. He put his hand on the young queen's head. "'Now go home,'" he continued. "'When you enter the city your son will die. All the people of Israel will sob over him and then his body will be buried. He is the only one who belongs to Jereboam who will be buried. That is because he is the only one in Jereboam's royal house in whom I have found anything good. I am the Lord, the God of Israel, and I will choose for myself a king over Israel.' He will cut off the family of Jereboam. This day your son will die."

Sarah's sobs drowned out the final words of the prophet. Numbly she walked toward the door. Elisheba put her arm around her and helped her as they started up the dusty road toward home.

"Do you think it's true?" Sarah finally gasped out, raising her tear-filled eyes to Elisheba's.

Her friend nodded. "You know it is."

The trip home seemed to last forever. As they entered the courtyard a wail rose from the queen's bedchambers. Sarah and Elisheba broke into a run. The servants and physicians stood clustered around the bed.

Jereboam burst out the door as the women approached, scowling.

"It's over," he said. "Your little trip didn't do any good at all."

Elisheba flung her arms around Sarah and they burst into tears again.

As Jereboam left the women's quarters he paused and called over his shoulder to a servant. "Bring Nadab to me. He is my heir now."

The whole city went into mourning for the little prince. Condolences came in from the other cities in Israel. Emissaries constantly arrived at the palace. Elisheba sat with Sarah dull-eyed, hearing little of what went on.

An older man approached the young queen. Sarah didn't even lift her gaze from the floor, but a bolt of recognition shot through Elisheba. Something familiar about the man caught her attention. As he rose from his deep bow she recognized him. It was Grandfather. She drew a deep breath, but he motioned her to keep silent.

"We cannot talk here," he whispered. "It is dangerous, what with the war and everything. I've come to take you home. I had thought Israel would be a safe place for you. I had thought—well, it doesn't matter what I thought. I was wrong. I've come to take you home."

Suddenly Sarah seemed to realize what was happening. "Oh, Elisheba," she whispered. "So many losses in such a short time. How can I bear it?"

Grandfather Nathan looked at her gently. "The God of Israel and the God of Judah knows your needs, your highness. And He cares very deeply about you. He will bring you comfort. When you were young and lonely He brought you Elisheba. And He will bring you more children and another friend and comforter. But He has sent me to bring Elisheba back to Judah. I will take her to our home in Jerusalem. Things are better there now for our family. She will marry and have children. Her time with you was God's gift to you. But God has other gifts. Now it's time to go."

Sarah clung to Elisheba for a long time.

My heart ached for the young queen; yet we all knew the court of

Jereboam was not the place for Elisheba, worshiper of the true God, to live any longer.

"I have a traveling cloak waiting for you and a disguise," Grandfather said. "It will be best if you just leave with me now. There's no time to get your things."

With a last embrace to Sarah, Elisheba turned and walked with her grandfather out of the royal court. She was going home. Home to Jerusalem. She took a deep breath, grabbed Grandfather Nathan's hand with a firm grip, and began the journey.

JEDEDIAH

ou may now take a break," the boys' teacher said. Jedediah stretched and took a deep breath. "I don't know why we have to learn all this boring historical stuff," Ahaziah complained.

"Well," Jedediah laughed, "I understand why *you* have to learn it. You're the son of a king—the crown prince. Someday you'll be king."

"When I'm king, I'm going to be like my father, Ahab, and will have a really good man in charge of all of my business and the palace. I'll have a steward of the royal houses, lands, and possessions so that I can spend my time enjoying being king. That's why *you* should study this stuff. When we grow up and I am king, I'll make you prime minister and you can do all the work and I will do the playing. We'll be a perfect team."

"It doesn't work exactly that way," Jedediah said carefully.

"Of course it does," Prince Ahaziah insisted. "I see it every day."

Jedediah was quiet. As the prince's best friend, he had learned there were times when it didn't pay to argue with Ahaziah. The boy's father had also taught him that there were times when it was best to be silent around royalty.

Even though they lived in the land of Israel, a country that God had separated from Judah, it wasn't safe to be too enthusiastic about worshiping the God in the ways of Judah. It hadn't been for some time, but especially now.

King Ahab had married Princess Jezebel, the daughter of King Ethbaal. Ethbaal was king of Tyre, a center of Baal worship. Jezebel came to Israel with the primary goal of converting the country to Baal worship, and she had been fairly successful.

Jedediah's father, Obadiah, top minister in Ahab's administration, had taught him that they should keep silent outside their home and only worship the God of Israel in secret. The boy knew that his father did several things for the God of Israel that Ahab would find upsetting and Jezebel would be furious over. Thus now he did not say anything to Ahaziah.

"So what shall we do this afternoon?" the king's son asked. "We've done everything interesting that I can think of."

"I don't know. Do you want to go riding?"

"No. We've been on all the good trails around here. Everything's boring.'"

Their teacher strode back into the room. "Boys, don't make too many plans for this afternoon. We've been discussing the laws of Israel, and I would like you to come and sit in the king's court this afternoon and watch how he settles disputes."

"Oh, no," Ahaziah groaned.

Jedediah chuckled. "Oh, you didn't want to go horseback riding anyway."

"But to just sit there and listen to Father all afternoon. He's not exactly Solomon, you know."

Jedediah decided this was another good time to stay quiet.

"Someday, Ahaziah," the teacher interrupted, "you are going to have to settle disputes in this court, and it would behoove you to learn a little bit about the laws and how they apply. You don't want to be known as one who had no wisdom or justice."

Ahaziah shrugged. Jedediah wondered whether the prince really cared about anything. But it didn't matter anyway—they were going to spend the afternoon in Ahab's court.

"Now go get some lunch, because I want you in the courtroom when the king is ready to start."

"Yes, sir," the boys said and headed for the dining area.

In the courtroom King Ahab of the nation of Israel sat on his carved ivory throne. Prince Ahaziah sat on a smaller throne at his side. Obadiah stood on the right side of Ahab's throne and Jedediah next to his father. It was an honor to be allowed to stand so close to the throne. Most people had to remain much further away or could not enter the courtroom at all. Being the son of the second most important man in Israel and best friend of the crown prince did have its advantages.

People came and went. Some of the cases were interesting, but many of them seemed to Jedediah to be petty complaints about injustices that could have been settled a different way if people weren't so selfish. Ahaziah slouched in his chair and tried not to yawn.

Suddenly a commotion erupted near the entrance of the courtroom. An odd-looking man burst in without invitation or announcement and before the soldiers could stop him took a position directly before the king.

Jedediah stared. No one just entered the courtroom without invitation or announcement, and no one approached the throne without kneeling totally prostrate with their faces clear to the floor for the king's blessing before they stood. The boy glanced at his father. Obadiah stood motionless, but the muscles in his jaw were tight and a little spot on his cheek twitched like it did when he was worried about something.

Ahab glowered like a thundercloud and roared, "What are you doing in my courtroom? And how dare you enter this way."

The strange man lowered his gaze to make eye contact with Ahab. He didn't flinch or blink, but answered the king coolly and directly. "I am Elijah, the Tishbite. I serve the Lord. He is the God of Israel. You can be sure that He lives. And you can be just as sure that there will not be any dew or rain on this entire land. None will fall during the next two years nor will it start again until I say so."

A hush fell over the courtroom. For a moment no one knew what to say. Elijah turned on his heel and strode out as unexpectedly as he had appeared.

As he disappeared, Ahab exploded: "How dare he come into my courtroom like this! How dare he threaten me! How dare he think he can decide who the God of Israel is! I'm the king! Doesn't he know that?"

The courtroom broke into a buzz of discussion.

"Well, what are you doing just standing there?" the king shouted. "Get him! Kill him!"

The soldiers rushed out of the courtroom. Ahab sat for a moment waiting for them to return with the prophet. When nothing happened, it became embarrassing. He threw the scroll he'd been holding on the floor and stomped out of the chamber.

Ahaziah and Jedediah left by a different exit. They hurried to their favorite place on the rooftop of the palace where they could sit and dangle their legs and talk privately without anyone hearing them.

"What was that all about?" Ahaziah demanded. "I couldn't believe that guy just marched in there. And what was he wearing?"

"I think that was camel's hair," Jedediah replied. "It certainly doesn't look comfortable."

"Well," Ahaziah commented, "if he wasn't so rude to rich people, perhaps he would be able to afford something better than that."

Jedediah smiled. Probably so. Those who kept their mouth shut did fairly well in Israel. But he couldn't help feeling a secret admiration for the oddly dressed man.

"So what's the deal with no rain?" Ahaziah continued. "Baal is the god of rain." And he broke into a chuckle. "I get it. The God of Israel wants to take Baal on at his own game in his own territory."

"That's what it sounded like to me," Jedediah said cautiously. "Although the God of Israel probably considers Israel His own territory."

"Well, it used to be," Ahaziah muttered. "He's just a sore loser."

Again Jedediah remained silent.

"This should be interesting," Ahaziah mused. "Do you think the God of Israel really can shut up the heavens? He might be able to for a month or two, but the rainy season is coming. Maybe He will announce that it is OK to rain before that happens." And he laughed at his own joke.

"I wonder if your father's soldiers will find him," Jedediah said.

"Of course. Then they'll kill him. And it will never ever rain again because he said it couldn't happen until he said so."

Jedediah smiled. "Maybe they should keep him alive at least until he gives permission for it to rain again."

"Nah. The guy's crazy."

"You really think so?" Jedediah asked.

"Sure. Who else would come into the royal court force like that? He's a goner."

"We have a good view from up here," Jedediah commented. "That way we can watch the soldiers searching for him. I haven't seen 'em dragging anybody back yet."

"No, not yet," Ahaziah agreed.

Although Jedediah nodded, secretly he hoped that they wouldn't find the prophet Elijah, or if they did, that God would keep them from hurting him too much. He couldn't help admiring the man.

Later the two boys resumed their lessons.

"Any questions?" their teacher asked when he had finished.

"Yes," Jedediah said.

Ahaziah rolled his eyes.

"In Sidon do they worship Baal, too?"

The teacher nodded.

"Yet they tolerate people of other religions and those who worship other gods. Why do we kill the prophets of the previous God of Israel?"

"That's a very good question. As you know, the worshipers of Baal are kind and benevolent people and historically they have been very tolerant of others and any god they choose to worship. Although it is foolish to worship anyone other than Baal if one hopes for fertility in the land and prosperity in the cities. The decision to kill the prophets of the God of Israel is more one of politics."

"Why?" Jedediah persisted.

"Well, as you know, Israel has been a theocracy, or it was supposed to be, before it became a monarchy with kings, and its people only worshiped the God of Israel. He was always so exclusive about it, forbidding the people to worship anyone else. Hardly a tolerant religion," their teacher commented, rolling his eyes. "Therefore, though the worshipers of Baal are tolerant and benevolent, the previous God of Israel insists on being the only one. For Baal worship to become the official worship in the country, rather than the worship of that God, one would have to wipe out those who would preach against it. And certainly over the years there have been some who have been very vocal against Baal. But that is treasonous since both our king and queen are avid worshipers of Baal. And our queen is the highest priestess in the land."

Jedediah knew that was true. Ahaziah sat up straighter and stuck his chest out. He looked very proud.

"Therefore, the only way to silence the opposition and get them to behave in a more tolerant manner was to kill them," their teacher concluded.

Ahaziah burst out laughing. "Yup, dead prophets of God are much more tolerant than live ones."

It was true, Jedediah had to agree silently to himself. Take Elijah for example. The boy could never imagine the prophet being tolerant and allowing Baal worship. It made his stomach twist a little, though, as he thought about his father. Best not to even think such things when around other people, and he steeled his mind away from the topic.

Both guardians assigned to Jedediah stood between him and his teacher so that the teacher could not read the look on the boy's face. It had only been a few nights before that he had made a disturbing discovery. His father Obadiah was governor of the palace and country and so frequently had to leave on business. However, he usually traveled with a retinue of servants, scribes, and assistants.

Two nights ago he had pulled on a dark-colored servant's cloak that veiled his face and slipped out through the kitchen courtyard. Jedediah was curious. What could Father be doing? The boy followed at a distance so that Obadiah would not discover him and send him back to bed.

As his father hiked on and on, Jedediah wondered whether they would ever get to wherever he was going, and several times the boy considered turning back. It was bad enough on the main roads and then the trails leading up to the rocky hills, but when his father left the paths completely Jedediah began to worry that he might not keep up with him and would get lost. His father climbed up the rocky wadi, then he disappeared. Panic-stricken, Jedediah called his name, but it bounced off the rocks in the darkness and echoed again and again. He scrambled up to the point where his father had been standing when he had seen him last.

"Father," he shouted. "Father, it's Jedediah. Where are you?"

Suddenly strong arms grabbed him and clamped a hand over his mouth. Kicking and trying to scream, the boy felt himself dragged into a cave. Then someone lit a torch and held it over his head.

"It is my son. Let him go," he heard his father say.

Whoever was holding him now let go, and Jedediah crumpled to the floor.

"Father," he said as he looked up.

Obediah knelt beside him. "Jedediah, are you all right? What are you doing out here? Do you know how far from home you are?"

His son broke into sobs. He considered himself almost a man, but even men get pushed to a breaking point sometimes.

Finally his sobbing hiccuped to a stop as he became aware of all the men standing around him. "I followed you," he said. "I was curious as to where you were going."

Some of the men glanced down nervously. "Did anyone else follow him? Has he given away our hiding place?"

"No," Jedediah said. "Just me."

His father ruffled his hair. "You have the makings of a great spy, Jedediah. Why did you follow me out here?"

"I just wanted to see where you were going."

"I guess it's time I told you. But this is a secret you must keep. We'll all lose our lives if you don't."

Jedediah nodded solemnly.

"These are some of the prophets of the God of Israel."

The boy glanced around. "I thought all the prophets of the true God were dead. Didn't Queen Jezebel order their execution? That's why everyone was so surprised to see Elijah."

Father smiled grimly. "She especially was surprised to see him. And Jezebel did make a law that all the prophets should be killed. However, some of them are hiding here."

"But there are so many," the boy exclaimed, glancing around.

"Yes. About 50 of them. There are 50 here and 50 in another cave further down the wadi."

"One hundred! Father, how could 100 men survive hiding in caves? Who has been feeding them? Someone would have to be organizing all of that."

Suddenly a look of understanding crossed Jedediah's face. "You're taking care of them."

"Yes. I rarely come out here. I make arrangements, though, and God's people will survive and be fed until such a time as things are safer. I don't know what the God of Israel plans to do, but whatever it is, I'm sure He will need some prophets to straighten out the mess this country is in when it is ready to worship Him again."

Many of the men surrounding him nodded. "I should never have followed you," Jedediah confessed. "But I promise I will never let your secret out."

"It will mean the end of our lives if you do," his father said.

The boy knew that it was common when someone was executed for treason that his entire family was killed along with him. "I will not tell," he repeated, standing and drawing himself up to his full height. "I, too, am a worshiper of the God of Israel."

* * * *

It had been almost three years since the last rains.

"This dry spell is miserable," Ahaziah complained. "Nothing's any fun anymore. And when we leave the palace people look at us as if it's our fault or something."

"My father says that people get angry and always blame their leaders whether it's their fault or not," Jedediah replied.

"That makes it even less fun to be the crown prince," Ahaziah pouted. "It's bad enough in good times."

"What do you mean? Being the prince can't be that bad. You're given everything you ever want. Your life is probably the best of anyone in the country."

"Yeah, in the daytime. At night I lay there and think about things we learned in our history class."

"You mean you were listening?" Jedediah teased.

Ahaziah frowned at him but continued. "Yeah, how often does the crown prince actually become the king in this country? In some countries families rule for a long way. But not in Israel. Look at our recent history. Grandfather Omri was king for 12 years and he did OK. But before him Zimri was king for only seven days or so, and before that Elah was the king. Zimri didn't die of old age and neither did Elah. Baasha ruled 24 years, but only because he killed the people who tried to assassinate him. Nadab was only king for two years. Nobody in their right mind would want to be the crown prince in this country if they thought about it or studied our history."

Jedediah thought a moment, then nodded with a serious expression on his face. "Yes, it is a little scary. Why do you think it is that kings of Israel rarely die of old age? I mean King David and King Solomon all had long lives. It appears as if history is telling us that worshiping the God of Abraham, Isaac, and Jacob made kings a little safer and helped them live a lot longer than those who worship Baal."

Ahaziah raised an eyebrow. "You're sounding a little treasonous."

"No, just being observant," Jedediah said with a shrug. "It seems that studying history has no other use than to help us figure out what previous kings did right or wrong so that we can know how to make the best choices and decisions."

"Humph," snorted Ahaziah, then sat down thoughtfully.

"Anyway, it's just a idea," Jedediah said. He felt his jaw tighten and the same little spot that twitched in his father's cheek when he was nervous now started twitching in the boy's face. The guardians moved in closer. Jedediah was becoming anxious. Had he said too much?

Shaking off his own dark thoughts, Ahaziah stood. "Well, enough thinking about this depressing stuff. Let's go do something. What if we ride out and look for Elijah? Can you imagine how pleased my father would be if the two of us were able to find him?"

Jedediah laughed. "Perhaps shocked would be the word!"

"Hey! I'm a good hunter," Ahaziah protested.

"Yeah, with a retinue of beaters and people to finish killing the beast for you and dragging it back to the palace and so forth."

"You don't think I could find him?" Ahaziah demanded. "Sounds like a challenge to me. Let's go prophet hunting."

"Oh, it's too hot. There's got to be something else to do around here," Jedediah protested.

"Nah, let's go prophet hunting. That could be fun. If you were the prophet, where would you hide?"

Jedediah looked around. What should he say? If he was a prophet, the caves in the Judean hills would be a great place to disappear into. He could hardly mention that, especially knowing that people were hiding there. And he for sure was not going to help Ahaziah search for Elijah. "Well," he said, stalling, "hiding in a small village would be a bad idea because everyone knows everyone. And while there are a few people who will keep their mouths shut or protect you, probably it is unrealistic to count on everyone in an entire village. So if I were a prophet, and I were looking for a place to hide, I would choose a large city and wear a disguise. People there are more used to seeing others they don't recognize, and with any luck no one would pay any attention to me, particularly if I hid alone and without other friends or family."

"Great idea," Ahaziah replied. "It just so happens that we live in such a city."

"Well, if we're going out, we need to take some guards with us."

Life was never safe, but especially now with all the tensions caused by the drought and shortage of food.

"No problem. I'll get us some guards. Let's go prophet hunting."

"Where would you start?" Jedediah stalled some more. "Samaria's huge now. Your father has built it into one of the most awesome capitals in this part of the world."

"I would start in the northern quarter. It's as good a place as any other. We can work ourselves systematically through the city for a few days. Besides that, there may be all kinds of other interesting things out there."

Jedediah reluctantly agreed. The city of Samaria was filled with interesting things, many of which his father had warned him against.

"The marketplace is the most fun," Ahaziah continued. "Traders from all over the world come through here. It's interesting to wander through there looking at all their little stalls filled with rich fabrics and jewels and spices from other lands. And the fruit."

"It's not as interesting as it used to be," Jedediah pointed out. "There's little, if any, fruit in the market now, and the prices are high. The farmers are already selling their cattle and slaughtering them for meat because people are so hungry."

"High prices aren't a problem."

"Not for us, but for the people in the city they are. And the city people are hungry because the farmers aren't bringing in the fruit and grain they used to. There's very little to eat in the market and consequently my father says there are fewer traders coming to Samaria from other countries. They are taking their goods to more prosperous nations where they can get better prices for them. Here in Samaria people are hungry, and any money they do have is going to go for something to feed their families."

"Elijah has ruined our lives here in Samaria," Ahaziah complained. "Nothing is as it used to be since he came through here with his horrible curse."

Jedediah sighed. It was true. Nothing had been the same since then. He wondered if people had returned to worshiping the God of Israel—and if that would change anything. The boy's father had read him some of the promises that the God of Israel had made to His people way back through Moses. Would all of those promises of great blessing still apply if God's people were to worship Him again? He glanced at Ahaziah. No, this was not a good day to suggest that idea, but maybe someday.

"Forget the prophet hunting," he said finally. "Let's go play that Egyptian game that we got. I think I figured out a tactic that will beat you so severely you'll never want to play it with me again."

"You think you can beat me at that game?" Ahaziah countered. "I'd like to see that."

Jedediah grinned at him.

"You ought to let me win sometimes," the king's son complained. "I am a prince, you know."

His friend laughed. "When you are the king and can have me executed for beating you at games, I'll start letting you win once in a while."

Both boys laughed.

"Yeah, you big talker," Ahaziah said. "When I'm king you're going to let me win all the time and you know it."

Jedediah hoped that his friend Ahaziah would someday become king. But Ahaziah was right. It was scary to think of his future here in the land of Israel.

* * * *

"Obadiah!" the two boys heard the king shout as they entered the throne room.

"I'm right here, my lord."

"Oh, I didn't see you. The people are getting restless. They're going to rebel soon if we don't do something. There isn't enough food to feed the people here in Samaria. I think we need to search the surrounding region. Perhaps we will find some grass so that we could at least feed our horses and won't have to kill them."

Ahaziah and Jedediah glanced at each other. This sounded interesting.

"I think we should ride out of the city and then one of us go in a northerly direction and the other head south," Ahab suggested. "If we find some grazing land, we'll send messengers back and bring some of our livestock to that area. Who knows, perhaps we will find a few farmers we can raid."

"Can we go?" Ahaziah asked. "It will allow me to see you conducting royal duties. Please say yes."

The king glanced at the two boys. They stood as tall as they could. "It could be dangerous," he reminded them.

"But, Father, you're going. If you have enough body guards with you to protect you, there should be enough to protect us too. Let us come."

Ahab smiled. "OK, but I need you to be quiet and stay out of the way. And if anything happens, I want you to stay in the center so that the soldiers can defend you."

"Yes," Ahaziah said excitedly. "Don't worry, we will."

The search party rode out of the city until they reached the crossroads.

"Break into two groups," Ahab ordered. "One goes north with me. The other rides with Obadiah."

"Can we go with Obadiah?" Ahaziah asked.

The king frowned. "I thought the reason you came along was to learn royal duties."

"Yes, that's why we came. I'll ride with you, Father. Jedediah can accompany his father. Maybe he'll learn something that will help him serve me when I'm king."

Ahab stared at his son for a moment. "I'm hoping it won't be for some time, Ahaziah," he said finally.

"Oh, of course. I wouldn't want to be king for many, many years."

His father continued to frown. Ahaziah rode over next to him.

Jedediah joined Obadiah. He was glad his father had taught him to keep silent whenever possible. Sometimes Ahaziah would be better off if he learned that too.

Jedediah and his father had ridden for over an hour when suddenly Obadiah reined to a stop. "There's no point in all of us trampling along like a camel train," he said. "Since none of us are royalty it's not as dangerous anyway. So I'd like to break us up into four groups and spread out. We're more likely to find some grazing land that way."

"But we are here to protect you," one of the soldiers protested.

"Yes, I know, but I don't need this much protection."

The soldier reluctantly agreed. The people seemed to direct most of their anger at the king himself. Obadiah faced more danger from the king's wrath for not being able to provide for the needs of Samaria and the palace than he did from the hostility of the people.

"You are right, my lord," the soldier said at last, and he turned to give orders to his men.

"We will meet back here an hour before sunset," Obadiah announced, then he and his son rode off together.

It seemed as if they had been traveling forever when again Obadiah halted.

"What is it?" Jedediah asked.

Obadiah nodded to his left. The boy saw a man approaching them. When he reached them the stranger threw back his hood. Father had already dismounted and was walking toward him. Now he knelt and touched his forehead to the ground. "My master Elijah," he said. "Is it really you?"

Jedediah's chin dropped. Quickly he slipped from his horse and hurried over to his father.

"Yes," the prophet replied. "I want you to tell your master Ahab that I am here."

"Why?" Obadiah demanded. "Why are you doing this to me?" The prophet raised an eyebrow. "You're handing me over to Ahab to be put to death. You know full well that the king has sent spies to look for you everywhere. There isn't a nation or kingdom anywhere in the world where he hasn't sent someone to search for you. Anyone who claimed you weren't there had to take an oath saying they couldn't find you. I'm telling you the truth as certainly as the Lord our God is alive. Now you tell me to go say this to Ahab. The Spirit of the Lord will rescue you and carry you away when I leave you. He protects you. Then I won't know where you are, and if I tell Ahab this and he doesn't find you, he will kill me. Please don't do this. I've worshiped the Lord ever since I was young. I've even taught my sons in secret to worship the Lord."

Jedediah nodded to confirm what his father said.

"My master, Elijah, haven't you heard of the things that I have done for the Lord? Jezebel has been killing the Lord's prophets, but I hid 100 of them in two caves. I've had 50 in each cave and supplied them with food and water all this time. Why are you sending me back to Ahab like this? You know I'll be killed."

"Stop! Stop!" the prophet interrupted. "I serve the Lord who rules over all. You can be sure that He lives, and you can be just as sure that I promise to stay right here. I will speak to King Ahab today. Your life is safe. Go fetch the king."

Obadiah returned to Jedediah. "Let's go," he said.

Jedediah broke into a huge grin and waved to Elijah as they left. He could have sworn he saw a twinkle in the prophet's eye as the man waved back.

It was late in the afternoon when they caught up with the king. Hot, tired, and grumpy, he and his men had found nothing useful.

"Obadiah," Ahab shouted. "Why are you back already? Did you find something good? Shall I bring the horses?"

"I did find something good, your majesty."

"Was it water? Grass?"

"No, your majesty."

"Then what are you doing back here?" the king exploded. "Get out of my sight. Whatever you found, if it wasn't farm crops or water or grass, I don't care. Get out of my sight!"

"Your majesty," Obadiah said calmly, "I found the prophet Elijah."

Ahab stared at Obadiah, then said, "Take me to him."

Jedediah noticed his father becoming more and more apprehensive the closer they got to the meeting place. Would Elijah still be there? He had said that he would. But surely the God of Israel valued him as a prophet and wouldn't just leave him there. As they rounded the last bend in the pathway they saw the prophet there just as he had promised.

"You're the man who has been such a troublemaker," Ahab growled. "You've brought misery to the whole country."

"No," Elijah replied calmly, "you are the one who has caused so much trouble, and you have brought misery to the whole country by worshiping the god Baal. The God of heaven shut up the windows of heaven and gave you no rain for three years. That should prove to you that Baal is not the god of rain."

"So we're having a drought," the king argued. "Let's see your God put an end to it if He can."

"He can. Send for people from all over Israel. Tell them to meet me on Mount Carmel. And bring the 458 prophets of the god Baal and also the 400 prophets of the goddess Asherah. All those who eat at your wife Jezebel's table."

"I will," the king declared. "We'll have a showdown at Carmel, and when we're done we'll kill you and throw your body to the ravens."

Elijah just stood there. "We will meet again—soon."

As they headed back toward the city of Samaria, Obadiah dropped back from Ahab's side and rode next to Jedediah. His son looked around carefully to make sure no one else was within earshot. "Father," he whispered, "have you heard the rumors about the things Elijah has been doing?"

"That depends," Obadiah answered carefully. "Which rumors?"

"Well, I heard that he's been staying with a widow near Zarephath and that as long as he remained with her none of her food ran out. The person I talked to said that they'd been told that her oil jar had more oil in it every day when she went to look and the same with her flour jar."

Obadiah laughed. "I've heard that one, too."

"How could that be true? Do you really believe it?"

The boy's father glanced around carefully, then lowered his voice. "I do. The whole point of this drought is for God to prove that He's more powerful than Baal. What would be greater than for him to demonstrate that He was able to provide even for Baal's own people in Baal's own territory, such as Zarephath? Especially during a time like this when Baal is not acting as god of rain and fertility. People in that town have been starving to death."

Jedediah nodded thoughtfully. "That makes sense. There are so many stories. I even heard that the widow's only son died and that Elijah raised him back to life."

"The God of Israel certainly has a sense of humor," Obadiah chuckled.

"What's funny about that?"

"Think about it. I'm sure that when her son died everyone in the village and everyone who had heard about what was going on would have concluded that Baal struck her son dead because she was harboring the prophet Elijah. What better way for the God of Israel to show that He was more powerful than Baal than to overrule the storm god's revenge and bring the child back to life!"

"Oh." Suddenly Jedediah had a strange feeling in the pit of his stomach. "Then you believe it's true?"

"Right now, there are so many stories circulating. Some of them are just ridiculous. These two sound like something the God of Israel would do, but I suppose we won't know for sure until this conflict is over and people are less afraid to talk about what really happened. Yet I know that our God is able to do such things, and the more the priests of Baal think about it, the more angry they're going to be. Baal really isn't holding up his end for them at all."

"No, Baal hasn't done a thing for anyone for three years."

"I have a hunch we're going to see more action from the God of Elijah and the God of Israel before this is over," his father concluded. "I think great things are afoot."

"I can't wait to see what He does," Jedediah replied.

* * * *

"I'm hot," Prince Ahaziah whispered to Jedediah. "We've been standing out here all day."

Both boys were dripping with perspiration, but not as badly as the dancing priests in front of them.

"I don't see how Elijah is going to be able to be any more success-ful than these guys," Ahaziah continued. "They've been summoning Baal all day and nothing has happened. Now they're cutting them-selves and soaking the ground with their blood. If that doesn't bring Lord Baal, nothing will."

"The mourning dance," Jedediah murmured.

"Yes. Mourning the death of Baal will usually bring about his re-birth and get him active again."

"What's the matter?" Elijah taunted the priests. "Yell louder. Maybe he can't hear you. Perhaps he's on vacation or in the bathroom."

The priests glared at the prophet. Jezebel stomped over to her palanquin and climbed inside.

"No you don't," Ahab hissed to her. "This whole charade is be-cause of you. You need to stay here till it's over. It puts us in enough of a bad light without you leaving."

Furiously Jezebel yanked the curtains closed, but remained.

"This is getting embarrassing," Ahaziah mumbled to his friend Jedediah. "I wish they'd just give up. Elijah isn't going to be able to do anything that they haven't been able to do. They could at least quit and call it a draw."

Jedediah agreed absentmindedly. He wondered whether the God of Israel wouldn't startle the king, the prophets of Baal, and all the people assembled there with another show of His power over Baal. He secretly hoped it would happen. Yet, Elijah looked so . . . well, ordinary, compared to the priests of Baal. And there was only one of him in contrast to the 400 priests.

Finally the Baal priests dropped to the dusty ground from sheer exhaustion.

Ahaziah let out a sigh.

Ahab motioned for Elijah to begin.

"You can come closer," the prophet told everyone.

The boys and everyone else crowded to where they could see what Elijah was doing. The priests of Baal crept closer, wanting to make sure that he didn't hide any fire under his sacrifice or pull any other tricks.

I smiled to myself. They were certainly disappointed that Baal had not answered them, but a show of power is what they had asked for, and it was what they would be getting. The guardians had all of the Satanic forces at bay, not even allowing them to set foot on the mountain. The people wanted to know who was the strongest. They were about to find out.

Elijah took 12 stones, one for each tribe, and built an altar. It was on a spot that had once contained an altar to God a long time ago. But it had not been repaired for ages. Then the prophet dug a trench around the altar. After stacking the firewood, he cut the sacrificial bull in pieces and laid it on top of the fuel.

"Fill the four barrels with water," he instructed the servants, "and pour it on the sacrifice and on the wood."

"Where are they going to find four barrels of water?" Ahaziah asked his father. "Water is hard to come by these days. After all, that's why we're here."

"We're not that far from the coast," Ahab replied. "I'm sure the prophet won't require it to be drinkable water."

Sure enough the servants eventually returned and dumped the water on the sacrifice. "Do it again," the prophet ordered.

A murmur rippled through the crowd. "How does he expect to burn the sacrifice when he's soaking it?" someone inquired.

No one knew.

After the servants splashed the second batch on the altar, Elijah shouted, "Do it one more time." And they did.

The sacrifice and the firewood were soaked. Water ran down the altar and filled the trench around it. Elijah's altar was one huge puddle. No doubt existed in anyone's mind now. It would require a miracle for the soggy sacrifice to burn.

Then the prophet prayed. "Lord God of Abraham, Isaac, and Jacob," he cried in a loud voice, "let everyone know today that You are the God of Israel and that I am Your servant and that I have done all these things because You told me to. Please hear me, God, that these people may know that You are the Lord and that You have turned Your heart back toward them again."

As he finished, with a deafening crack lightning struck the altar. Everyone fell back from the heat. The fire burned the soggy sacrifice and every splinter of the wood. After licking up the water in the trench, it vaporized the altar stones and the dirt around it. All that remained was a smoking pit.

Terrified, the people fell on their faces.

A chant started through the crowd. "The Lord, He is God! The Lord, He is God!"

The prophets of Baal turned pale. Jezebel and her bodyguards had disappeared into the crowd.

"Get the prophets," Elijah exclaimed. "Don't let even one of them escape."

"What are they going to do?" Jedediah asked.

"Execute them, I think," his father replied.

The mob grabbed the prophets of Baal and dragged them down by the brook. They would do anything to avoid offending the God that had just sent fire from heaven.

When Elijah returned, he and many of the people in the crowd were covered in blood and none of the prophets of Baal were with them.

"Get up, your majesty," Elijah commanded. "Have some supper and get home for there's going to be a lot of rain."

Everyone looked around. Rain? Rain! What a wonderful thing! No rain had fallen for three years. Shading their eyes from the sun they scanned the sky. It was completely cloudless.

However, Ahab did as told. The servants put a meal before him while the prophet went up the mountain to pray alone.

Ahaziah cleared his throat and finally spoke. "Amazing! He brought down fire and burned even rock. Do you think he can make it rain?"

"I don't think it's him," Jedediah replied. "I believe it's the God of Israel doing it."

Ahab's son shrugged. "Do you think it will rain?"

"Yes, I believe it will."

Once more Ahaziah scanned the sky. "Well, it's going to have to rain out of a clear sky," he said, "because there isn't a cloud anywhere."

"Do what Elijah said and eat your dinner," Jedediah laughed, "or you're going to be having to go home in the rain on an empty stomach."

"I doubt it," Ahaziah mumbled as he turned to the food the servants had set before him.

Just as they finished the evening meal the prophet's servant hurried down the mountainside. "Look," he said, "there's a little cloud out there toward the city."

The boys stared at a cloud so tiny that if they put a hand up at arm's length, it completely covered it.

"Get into your chariots and head back for the palace or you're going to be caught in a downpour," the prophet commanded Ahab.

The crowd stared at the tiny cloud. Some started moving down the slope toward home. Others just stood around watching.

Jedediah swallowed his last bite and ran over to where the chariots were. "Come on, Ahaziah," he said. "It'd be nice to get home before the rain starts."

They waited in their chariots until the king mounted his and rode ahead of them toward Jezreel. Elijah tucked up his robe into his belt and raced ahead of the chariot.

"How can he run after being here all day?" Ahaziah commented.

"I don't know," Jedediah answered. "Perhaps the Lord who sent the fire kept a little for Elijah." The boys laughed, and then their chariot took off for the palace.

They staggered into the palace in Jezreel soaking wet, having been barely able to complete the journey because of the deep mud and rushing water.

"Mother will be furious," Ahaziah said, shivering from the cold rain. "I sure wouldn't want to be the king right now. He stood by and did nothing to protect the prophets of Baal."

"What else could he do?" Jedediah countered. "The Lord had just brought fire down from heaven. He had to either accept Him as the winner of the power struggle or defy Him. And who would do that? No king in his right mind."

"I don't know which would be worse—to deal with the wrath of the God of Israel or that of my mother."

"She may be angry," Jedediah said, "but I think your father made the right decision. The God of Israel won that one fair and square."

Ahaziah nodded. "Yes, I have to agree with you. The God of Israel is truly amazing."

ZILLAH

re we really at war with Syria?" Zillah asked her father anxiously.

Jedediah paused and looked at his 11-year-old daughter. "Yes. But where did you hear that?"

"I just hear things," she replied haltingly.

"Yes, that you do," he laughed. "You have big eyes and ears and a small mouth, which is very wise when you live in a king's court like this." He put his arm around her. "Don't look so worried, Zillah. Our Lord will take care of us. The God of Israel is stronger than any of the gods of other nations."

"Yes," Zillah said slowly, "but sometimes He allows people to get hurt."

Her father sighed. "Yes, sometimes He does. But you can never go wrong trusting Him. You'll be a whole lot better off than trusting anyone else no matter what anyone in the palace says."

The girl understood that the king and queen had not always followed the God of Israel. She had heard of terrible things that had happened before her birth. Lately Ahab had repented and was trying to obey the God of Israel. However, the queen was determined never to worship the God of Abraham, Isaac, and Jacob, and Ahab was finding old habits dying rather hard.

I continued my duties as a celestial watcher of young people. I was now observing young Zillah, just as I had been assigned to her father, Jedediah, before her. Her Grandfather Obadiah was still greatly honored in the king's court, but spent most of his time away from the city on his farm. Jedediah now performed many of the administrative tasks in the palace that Obadiah had once fulfilled. Zillah's father traveled back and forth between Ahab and Obadiah, because the king still relied on Obadiah for advice and counsel, particularly in serious times such as these.

"Well, as long as you've been listening to everything else," Jedediah told his daughter, "then you'll soon hear this. King Jehoshaphat of Judah is coming here to Israel."

"Is he at war with us, too?" Zillah asked in alarm.

"No," her father replied. "He is coming to make an alliance with King Ahab, and we are going to fight the Syrians together."

The girl smiled. "That's good, isn't it? King Jehoshaphat is a follower of the God of Israel."

"Yes, though he probably considers Him the God of Judah."

"Israel, Judah," Zillah mumbled. "What if we just called Him God?"

"That could work, I suppose." He studied her, then touched her cheek. "So don't be afraid, but do keep your eyes and ears open for these will be interesting times."

I nodded. They certainly would be.

* * * *

Zillah stood behind the lattice work concealing the balcony of the royal throne room. The queen and others used it when they wished to know what was going on in court without actually having to enter where they might not be welcome.

King Ahab and King Jehoshaphat had gone through the usual royal greetings, feasting, and giving of gifts. Finally they were getting down to the purpose of their meeting.

"Your majesty," King Ahab said, turning to King Jehoshaphat of Judah, "when we go to battle against the Syrians, will you accompany us?"

Jehoshaphat nodded. "Yes, as you go, we, too, will go and be part of your people. And those who are at war with you will be at war with us."

"Good. Now we need to get down to serious planning. I've arranged for some prophets to advise on when and where to attack."

"Excellent! So many prophets of God?" he asked in amazement as the 400 prophets filed into the chamber.

"Well, of local gods," Ahab explained. "You know Israel. Not many people worship the old God of Abraham, so I've tried to get prophets of local gods from the villages and places that people are familiar with."

King Jehoshaphat's face creased with concern. Zillah frowned to herself.

King Ahab had been trying to follow the God of Israel since his recent encounter with Elijah on Mount Carmel. What was he thinking?

The prophets to a person all said, "Go, for God will deliver our enemies into the king's hands. We should be victorious."

When they were finished Jehoshaphat turned to Ahab. "Don't you even have one prophet of the Lord here that we might talk to?"

Ahab looked around. Where was Elijah when he needed him? There was, however, another less well-known prophet. The king turned to the Judahite king. "There is one. His name is Micaiah, but he has never prophesied one good thing for me. And every time I bring him into the court, not only does he prophesy against me, but he generally embarrasses me as well in front of everyone."

"Oh, no," Jehoshaphat protested, "I'm sure he won't do that this time. If he is truly a prophet of the God of Abraham, Isaac, and Jacob, then whatever he tells us we need to hear. I would be much more comfortable making our plans after listening to what he has to say."

Ahab squirmed in his chair. "Just as a favor to you, Jehoshaphat," he said, turning to one of his officers. "Quickly fetch Micaiah the son of Emlah."

The officer bowed and disappeared from the throne room.

"Meanwhile," Ahab said, "let's hear a little more what these other prophets have to say. This one's name is Zedekiah. He prophesies for me quite often."

Zedekiah stepped forward. Zillah gazed at him silently. What on earth was on top of his head? It looked like a helmet with huge iron horns sticking out of it.

"Thus declares the Lord," the prophet boomed in a loud voice. "With these ram horns you shall gore the Syrians until you have destroyed them."

Prophet after prophet stepped forward, each saying, "Go up to Ramoth-gilead and prosper, for the Lord shall deliver it into the hands of the king."

Zillah shook her head. She felt relieved that King Jehoshaphat had asked for a prophet of the Lord and that they had sent for Micaiah. But it bothered her that the other prophets were claiming to speak for the true God. Would King Jehoshaphat be able to tell the difference?

It seemed like forever before the soldier that had been sent to find Micaiah returned. He thrust the prophet before the king and hissed in his ear, "Look, Micaiah, all the other prophets have already agreed that he should go to war against Syria, so think carefully about what you say. Encourage the king."

The prophet stared at him. "As long as the Lord lives, I'm going to have to say whatever God tells me to."

Ahab motioned to Micaiah. The prophet frowned as he stood before the thrones where both kings could see him, as well as all the people.

"Micaiah," Ahab began, "should we go to battle at Ramoth-gilead, or should we stay here?"

The prophet looked Ahab in the eye. "Go, and prosper."

Ahab's face contorted into a thundercloud as he bellowed, "How many times do I have to tell you not to say anything to me except what the Lord actually told you?"

Micaiah sighed. "I saw Israel scattered all over the mountain like sheep without a shepherd. And the Lord told me they have no master. Each one of them will return to their home in peace, but without their king."

Ahab turned purple with fury and turned to his fellow king. "Jehoshaphat, didn't I tell you that He would say nothing good to me. He always does this."

"I'll tell you more," Micaiah continued. "I had a vision and saw the Lord sitting on His throne and all the hosts of heaven were standing either to His right or to His left. And the Lord said, 'Who will entice Ahab, king of Israel, so that he will go up and fall at Ramoth-gilead?' Several beings made suggestions and then one spirit stood before the Lord and said, 'I will entice him.' And the Lord asked, 'How will you do that?' And he said, 'I will go be a lying spirit in the mouth of all his prophets.' And the Lord said, 'That will work—you'll be successful. Go and do just that.' This is what has happened, oh King. And the Lord put a lying spirit in the mouths of your prophets. It's your choice whether to believe them or not."

As soon as he finished, Zedekiah, the prophet with the horned helmet, slapped him across the face and said, "So which way did the spirit of the Lord go from me to speak to you? I thought He was still with me."

"You'll see on that day," Micaiah replied calmly. "You'll go into an inner chamber to hide."

Ahab, trembling with anger, shouted, "Guard, seize Micaiah. Take him back to Annon, the governor of the city, and to Joash, my son. Tell them I said to put this fellow in prison and feed him with only the worst of prison food until I return in peace."

"If you return in peace, then truly the Lord didn't speak through me," the prophet countered. "Pay attention, everyone." Then several guards hauled him off to jail.

Zillah shook her head. Grandfather Obadiah had told her that Micaiah was a true prophet of God. So she believed whatever he said would happen. If he was supposed to stay in jail until the king came home in peace, he would be there a long time.

She stared at King Ahab. If he went to war at Ramoth-gilead the way he was planning, would they ever see him again? It made the back of her neck prickle. Why didn't he listen?

I shook my head in frustration. I couldn't understand why, either. Some humans seemed so foolish. Even those who tried to worship the Mighty One. It amazed me that so many could ignore a message so clear.

* * * *

Zillah watched her mother pace back and forth in front of the open window. Grandfather Obadiah looked up from his couch.

"No sign of a messenger yet?"

"No, not yet," the girl's mother said, then resumed her pacing.

"The Lord is able to protect them," Grandfather Obadiah commented quietly. "And should He not, He's still able to care for you."

Mother nodded. "I know that in my head, but this knot in my stomach just won't go away."

Grandfather Obadiah smiled. "I understand. Sometimes our stomachs don't trust the God of Israel nearly as well as our minds do. I've had that problem myself."

Zillah looked up. "Grandfather, what will happen if King Ahab gets killed in battle?"

He patted her on the head. "You don't need to worry about that. You will be fine whether he dies or not. But if our king perishes in battle, then Prince Ahaziah will be the next king."

"I understand that. But if King Ahab does die in battle, then he won't be there to protect us from Queen Jezebel anymore. I think she's still furious at us from way back in the days of Mount Carmel."

Obadiah laughed. "Yes, I imagine she is—and probably always will be. But there will always be conflicts between good and evil and between the people who have chosen the good side and those who have gone to the evil side. Even if Ahab and Jezebel were both gone, there would still be others on both sides."

"That's true," she sighed.

"Besides," Grandfather reminded her, "your father and Prince Ahaziah grew up together, and though Prince Ahaziah does not worship the God of Israel, he is good friends with your father. I don't think the queen will be any danger to you. And until they all come back from the battlefield, you're here in my home and not in the palace."

She sighed again. "That's why I was able to ask these questions."

Obadiah smiled. "Your father has trained you to be very wise. Always ask questions only when you are in a safe place and with safe people."

Zillah knew that in the palace the walls seemed to have ears, and anything said there quickly made its way to those being talked about. One had to be very careful. The many lattices in the palace made it easy for the king's spies to observe unnoticed and eavesdrop on many conversations. The king had to have them for his own security, for enemies lurked even inside the palace.

"Look!" Zillah's mother shouted. "Someone is coming!"

The girl and her grandfather rushed to the window. They saw a rider in a small cloud of dust heading for them.

"Oh, thank You, Lord," Mother said. "Any news is better than this not knowing. And even though I know God can take care of our family, the prophet Micaiah did say that the king would be killed in battle. And with Jedediah being so close to the king . . ." She twisted her handkerchief into a knot.

"Let's go down to the courtyard to greet him," Grandfather suggested. He summoned the servants to prepare refreshments for the approaching messenger.

The courier rode into the courtyard and slipped from his horse. Dropping to his knees before Obadiah, he nnounced, "The king is dead. Long live King Ahaziah!"

There was silence in the courtyard.

So the prophet Micaiah had been right.

"What happened?" Grandfather Obadiah asked.

"The Syrians ordered their soldiers to go just for the king of Israel. They knew that King Jehoshaphat of Judah was fighting with him, and they should ignore him but kill Ahab. Ahab disguised himself as a common soldier, so only King Jehoshaphat was in the royal chariot. The Syrians surrounded it, and Jehoshaphat called out to the God of Abraham for help. That was a sure sign to the Syrians that it wasn't Ahab, and they quickly guessed what had happened. So the battle continued. Even though Ahab was disguised, he was wounded. An arrow pierced his shoulder between the pieces of armor. He had himself propped up in the back of his chariot but died toward evening from the loss of blood. Prince Ahaziah was also disguised and escaped unscathed. He will be returning this evening."

"And Jedediah?" Mother asked.

"He will be returning with Ahaziah," the messenger replied. "Your husband is well."

"Oh, praise the God of Abraham," Zillah's mother whispered.

While she was thankful that her father was safe, the coming changes at the palace made Zillah nervous. Things would be different, and it would take a little while to get used to them.

As if reading her thoughts, Grandfather asked her, "Zillah, would you like to stay here for a while at my farm? There's no reason for you to go back to the palace right now. Princess Athaliah was recently married off to Jehoshaphat's son, so you have no specific duties there. And I would enjoy your company here."

The girl looked at her mother for permission. Mother nodded.

"I would love to, Grandfather."

"Good. I will mention it to your father when he returns."

I was pleased. The palace was not a good place for a young person at the best of times, and the power struggles and political intrigue during a change of rulers made the royal court a dangerous place. I glanced at Zillah's guardian. He seemed pleased, too. While Ahab was an evil king, our expectations of his son Ahaziah were not much better.

* * * *

Zillah stared out the window and stretched. Her back was starting to ache from sitting at the loom too long. But she enjoyed weaving. Grandmother had taught her how since she had come to live with her and Grandfather Obadiah. It was something that most young women in Israel learned to do much earlier. But Zillah, having lived in the palace all her life, had missed some experiences.

She bent over the section of completed cloth, fingering the design. Grandmother had given her a skein of the expensive blue wool and she had woven it into the fabric in narrow stripes near the beginning. Later she would put in matching stripes near the end. Zillah was making a new prayer shawl for her grandfather.

"Someday," Grandmother announced, "these men of ours are going to find you a husband, and when they do, you'll be glad you've learned how to do this."

Zillah, however, was not in any rush for her father and grandfather to get her a husband. She was much happier living with her grandparents. Her stay with them had extended almost two years. But so much was going on at the palace that Grandfather Obadiah's farm seemed a better place to be. She heard that Jehoshaphat and King Ahaziah had also formed an alliance, and they had been fighting against Moab. It always made her nervous when Israel went into battle against the Moabites for she knew her father was with King Ahaziah. Grandfather Obadiah was always especially comforting during those times.

During one battle things had looked particularly grim. Then the Lord had sent rain and all the ruts and trenches in the battlefield turned into water troughs and ponds. When the sun came up in the morning the reflection on the water was bright red. The Moabites mistook it for blood and fled.

"Why?" Zillah asked her grandfather. "Why would God help our military with such a wonderful miracle when our king doesn't even worship Him?"

"Ah," Obadiah replied, "while our king doesn't worship Him, many of his subjects do. And because we have an alliance with King Jehoshaphat, perhaps the Lord was honoring Judah's king and his faith. Or perhaps"—he put his arm around her—"perhaps the Lord did it because He loves your father and was protecting him. The Lord is very merciful even when we have leaders who don't always follow Him. However, such leaders always hurt the country in the long run."

"Does that mean that while the Lord defends our kingdom, He may not protect the king?"

"Only God knows what His plans are. But if I were the king and I were not loyal to God, I would not expect His personal protection, would you?"

Zillah glanced around by force of habit and then remembered at Grandfather's house she could speak freely. She shook her head. "No, but after the God of Abraham made things so clear to everyone so many times, I don't know why anyone would not follow Him."

"I don't know either. But when our leaders choose not to obey God it does make it dangerous for those who do."

A sober expression crossed her face. "I know. At the palace we always had to be so careful what we said."

"It was like that when I served King Ahab there, too."

Zillah's forehead creased into a frown. "It's so hard to know what God expects us to do. We worship Him but never speak of Him when anyone is around. Is that what He wants? What if He wants us to speak out and be brave? How can we tell? Elijah always did. But our family has always been very careful not to say anything when we were unsure of the beliefs of those around us."

Grandfather Obadiah shifted his weight and rubbed his swollen knuckles for several minutes before he answered. "I don't know, Zillah," he finally said. "Working in the palace, I struggled with that issue all my life. Sometimes I felt like such a coward, yet other times I felt as if the only way I was able to do what God wanted me to do and help His people was by maintaining the important position I had."

"Are the rules different for each people?" she asked. "Does God want some people to speak out and others to keep silent?"

"I don't know. I've prayed to Him many times about that. And yet during my years it seemed that keeping silent was the way to do the most good. Because of it I was able to protect God's prophets from Jezebel during the drought. I do believe that is what the God of Abraham wanted me to do at the time, but each person will have to pray and consider that for themselves."

"My father believes the same as you," Zillah said.

"Yes, he does. However, you, my dear granddaughter, will have to pray and make your own decisions as you go along."

The girl returned to her weaving. I knew that the Mighty One had great plans for this youngster and it was important for her to think about such things. And yet, she was so young—only in her thirteenth year. If anyone had told her that the Mighty One was going to use her to bring about major religious and political changes in her world, she would have laughed. However, those of us familiar with the way the Mighty One works would have known that is His way. He often uses the young, the old, and the weak. Because of their weakness it becomes very obvious where the power and strength really lies and it brings honor to Him.

* * * *

Zillah was excited. Her grandparents were returning to the palace for a few weeks to spend some time with the rest of the family. Though Zillah had visited her parents, she had not been inside the main palace for two years. As she walked into the throne room, it was the end of the day and no one was there. She stood with her hand on one of the ornate pillars looking around and remembering how as a little girl she had stood up in the balcony behind the lattices to watch the king and her father making important decisions on how to run the nation of Israel.

Suddenly she jumped and let out a little shriek.

"Oh, I'm sorry. I didn't mean to scare you," a young woman's voice said. "Is that you, Zillah? It's me, Susanna, remember?"

"Susanna," Zillah exclaimed, giving her a big hug. "I haven't seen you for a couple years." She held her at arm's length. "You've grown up a lot."

"So have you. Where've you been all this time?"

"I went to live with my Grandfather Obadiah for a while. After Princess Athiliah moved to Judah to marry King Jehoshaphat's son, I wasn't really needed here although they have younger ladies in waiting in the queen's court, too."

"Yes," said Susanna, "that's where I'm serving now."

"It's been nice at Grandfather Obadiah's house, but sometimes I miss my family and my friends."

Susanna smiled. "You wouldn't believe this place now. If you think things were difficult when Ahab was the king, you should see how they are now."

Zillah quickly glanced around. Her father had always warned her of the dangers of palace gossip. It could get a person in trouble. But Susanna chatted on merrily.

"King Ahaziah must be worried about other people trying to steal his throne because there are spies, and then spies watching the spies, and spies watching the spies who are watching the spies. And nobody knows who is listening to whom and who's going to whom about what they said." She giggled.

Zillah smiled. "Then it would be important," she said slowly, "not to say anything that you wouldn't want repeated to anyone."

"Yeah, that's what my mother keeps telling me. But you can't go through life worrying all the time, otherwise you'd be just like King Ahaziah."

"I'm sure he has a lot of things on his mind to be concerned about," Zillah replied cautiously.

Susanna chatted on. Suddenly they heard a sickening cracking noise behind them and then a crash. The girls spun around. The lattice on the balcony above them had given way and someone had tumbled to the floor. As they rushed over to see if the person was injured, they suddenly stopped, filled with horror. It was the king.

Zillah dropped to her knees. "Your majesty," she whispered. "You're hurt."

"Get help right away!" the king gasped. "I can't move! I can't move my arms or legs or anything."

Jumping to her feet, Zillah ordered, "Stay here with the king, Susanna. I'm going to get help right away!" She rushed out of the chamber. "Guards!" she called. "Father! Somebody help us. The king is hurt!"

Soon a mob of people filled the room and officials hurried the girls out of the way. As they stood outside Susanna whispered, "Do you believe the king was listening to us? Do you think he heard what I said?"

"I don't know. It almost looks like it."

"Right before you came," Susanna continued, "there was an ambassador from Babylon who had been talking to one of the princes. Perhaps the king had been listening to them."

"Perhaps."

"Do you think we'll get in trouble?"

Zillah looked at her for a moment. "I think the king is injured very seriously. And I don't think anyone is going to care what either of us had to say. Right now they're going to be worrying about helping the king."

"I hope so," Susanna said, "because if he wasn't hurt badly, he might be mad about the things I said."

"Susanna, please be careful," Zillah said. "Don't say things like that. We don't really want the king to be hurt badly. After all, he's our king."

The other girl swallowed hard. "I should be more careful. That's what Mother always tells me."

The two girls walked slowly back to Zillah's family's living quarters. Neither of them could think of anything else to say. A feeling of doom seemed to hang over them like a dark cloud.

Later that night when Zillah was alone with her father, she was able to ask a few questions. "Was the king injured as badly as it looked today?"

Her father studied her for a moment. "I think he's hurt very seriously, Zillah."

"Well, he couldn't move his arms or his legs. That sounded pretty terrible to me. How can somebody be king when they can't even move?"

"His injuries are very serious," her father repeated. "We are waiting for a few days to find out whether it looks like a permanent injury or whether he'll be able to regain some movement. He has been very concerned about others trying to steal the throne from him and not to be able to move would make it much more possible."

"Poor King Ahaziah! I will remember him in my prayers this evening."

Her father sighed. "I too pray for the king. Although so far he has chosen not to go to the God of Israel for help. He worships the god Baal."

"Like his mother?"

"Yes, like the Queen Mother. But I still pray for him every night. For even though he doesn't worship the true God, he is still my king, and I am loyal to him."

"I know you are." Zillah hugged Zedediah. "You're a good man, Father, and I think the king should be proud to have you as one of his counselors."

Her father smiled back, but tension filled his eyes and his jaw was clenched.

"Do you think that if someone could find the prophet Elijah, he might ask the God of Israel to heal King Ahaziah?" she asked.

"That's a possibility. He has always had great respect for the requests of His prophet. But Ahaziah hates Elijah, and I'm pretty sure he will not ask him for help."

"It seems like a bad time to have too much pride to ask for help," she observed.

He sighed and frowned. "Let's wait and see what happens."

The next morning Zillah met Susanna in the courtyard as the other girl carried two large baskets. "Here let me help you carry that," she said to her friend.

"Oh, thank you," said Susanna. "There's enough here for two to carry. Have you heard the latest?"

Zillah shook her head.

"The king has sent a group of soldiers with gifts to the Baal in Ekron to find out whether he's going to live or die from his injuries."

"To the Baal in Ekron?" Zillah repeated, her eyes widening.

"Yes. That is the Baal he likes the best. He figured that if the Baal can tell him what is going to happen next, it will help him make some decisions. And he's sending lots of gifts so that the Baal will be in more of a mood to help him."

Zillah did not say anything. To her it seemed that asking for help from Baal was even worse than not asking for help at all. It was like a slap in the face to the God of Israel whom she was sure was the only one who could heal the king of so serious an injury.

"My mother thinks the king is going to die," Susanna continued. "She tells that she's seen soldiers who have been injured like that. Usually it comes from a fall from a horse or being hurt in their necks. And she says once they are paralyzed from the neck down they never recover. Some of them die right away because they can't even breath. Others live for just a little while, but none of them ever get better or walk again. But who knows. I suppose that if you gave Baal enough presents, he might do anything."

Zillah kept quiet. *Is it time to keep silence and keep from getting in trouble?* she wondered. *Or is this a time to speak up and remind Susanna of the true God?* She closed her eyes and shot a quick prayer toward heaven. "Oh, God of Israel," she whispered in her mind, "please tell me when it is right to speak."

The skies were as silent as the throne room in the palace so Zillah said nothing.

A huge commotion in the courtyard caught everyone's attention. Zillah rushed out with the others to see what was happening.

"He was a hairy guy," a farmer, stammering at having to speak in front of such a large crowd, said. "And he wore a camel's hair tunic thing."

"But what about the soldiers?" a guard questioned him.

"He raised his hand and called down fire from heaven. There was a big crack of thunder and fire came and all the soldiers vanished."

"It is the prophet Elijah," Zillah's father interrupted. "We haven't seen him for many years, but I'm certain it's him. He stopped the messenger Ahaziah sent to the Baal of Ekron. The king then sent those 50 soldiers to capture the prophet."

The captain of the guard and Zillah's father headed toward Ahaziah's private chambers. The king was notorious for his temper. Whereas his father used to get grumpy and silent when he was unhappy, Ahaziah was just the opposite. The palace would echo with his shouting when he was upset. Zillah was glad she wasn't the one who had to deliver the message.

Before long a second group of soldiers left to capture Elijah. Zillah shook her head. Did the king really think that 50 of his soldiers were more powerful than the prophet of the Most High God? She felt sure it was a mistake. That evening she could hardly eat her supper as she waited to hear what would happen next.

Sure enough another horrified messenger stumbled into the court. The same thing had happened. Elijah had again rejected the king's arrogant order to return to the palace with them, and again the prophet had called down fire. All 50 soldiers had perished.

Zillah put her hands to her face in horror. One hundred men! One hundred fathers or brothers or sons of families who loved them were now dead. What would the king do now? Was it really worth confronting the prophet of God a third time? She shook her head as she thought of all of the families who would be grieving tonight because of the king's choices and his stubbornness.

It was late when her father returned to his private apartments. Zillah ran to him. "Father, what's the king going to do?"

"He's sending another 50 men in the morning," he said tersely.

"Another 50 to Elijah? Why?"

"Because that's what the king wants to do."

"But they all have families and children. Some of my friends have fathers who are soldiers of the king," she protested.

"Yes, the more responsibility one has, the more innocent people are affected by every decision you make. King Ahaziah has the top position in the land, so his decisions affect more people than anyone else's."

"But—but—"

"Zillah, say no more about this now."

Recognizing the tone of voice, she lowered her eyes.

That evening she tossed and turned on her pallet, but sleep eluded her. Finally she crept out and went up onto the rooftop where she and Susanna used to sit when they had been little girls. The full moon bathed the palace in a silvery light.

"Oh God of Abraham and Isaac and Jacob," she whispered, "we really need Your help. My king needs Your help. My nation needs Your help. Lots of my friends have fathers in the army. Susanna's father is in the army. If the king sends out another 50 men tomorrow and they run into Elijah, please don't send fire down on them again. I know the king wants them to capture Elijah, but all of those families without a father . . . !" Her lips began to tremble and her eyes filled with tears. Suddenly she realized someone was watching her. She spun around.

"It's just me," Susanna said softly. "I heard you. Were you talking to . . . to that God?"

"Yes, I'm a follower of the God of Abraham. I just haven't told anyone because, well, because . . ."

"I know, because officially everybody worships Baal right now."

Zillah nodded. "But if there was ever a time when our country needed the help of the God of Israel, it's now."

"I'm really scared," Susanna said. "My father is in charge of the group that will leave in the morning."

Zillah's eyes widened. "I just was talking to God about that."

"Maybe the God of Israel will listen to you. I can't imagine life without my father."

"He's a merciful God," Zillah said putting her arms around her friend, "but a God of justice. I don't know what He will do."

Then the tears came. Both girls cried and clung to each other.

"If only the king would just ask the God of Israel for help," Susanna gasped. "Then my father would be safe."

"Maybe your father should ask Elijah's help instead of arresting the prophet."

"The king would kill him," Susanna protested.

"Maybe." Zillah shrugged. "I don't know what he should do. It's so hard to know what anybody should do these days. Life is so complicated. I just keep trusting that the God of Israel will take care of us and will have mercy on our country and on our king and on your father."

"Do you think He would mind if I asked Him, too? I haven't ever actually talked to Him before, and He probably knows that I've worshiped Baal."

"He knows," Zillah said. "But I think He would be happy to hear from you. We could talk to Him together." And they did.

The girls spent the next afternoon pacing back and forth on the rooftop of the part of the palace in which they lived.

Suddenly Susanna let out a shriek. "They're coming! They're coming! All of them!"

Zillah looked. Sure enough a large band of soldiers was returning. She strained her eyes to see if they carried a prisoner. They did not. What could have happened?

The girls raced down to the courtyard. It seemed like forever until the soldiers finally arrived.

Zillah's father was there to meet them. Surprise flashed across Zillah's father's face when he saw everybody still alive, but only for an instant. "He did not call down fire on you?" he asked the captain.

"No." Susanna's father leaned toward Zedediah and whispered, "I fell on my knees and begged him for the lives of me and my men. 'We're only soldiers,' I explained. 'We're only doing what we were told.'"

Zillah's father nodded curtly. "And what did he say?"

Before Susanna's father could answer, a voice came from the

rear of the squad of soldiers. Elijah stepped forward. "The Lord says that Ahaziah will die from his injuries," he announced. "Take me to the king."

Impulsively Susanna flung her arms around Zillah. "It's true! It's true! The God of Israel saved my father."

Zillah nodded soberly. "He is very kind and merciful. But King Ahaziah—"

Soon afterward a loud wail tore through the palace from the royal chambers and spread through the palace. Zedediah appeared in the doorway with another individual. "The king is dead," he announced. "Long live King Joram."

The men fell on their knees before the person who until a few minutes before had been Prince Joram, brother of the king of Israel. Now he was the king.

Susanna giggled to herself, then pulled Zillah to one side. "Isn't it going to be a little bit confusing?" she whispered.

"What do you mean?" Zillah asked.

"Well, isn't Jehoshaphat's son named Prince Joram, too? When King Jehoshaphat dies, he'll be king. Then we'll have King Joram of Israel and King Joram of Judah."

Zillah smiled faintly. "And I guess we'll call them King Joram of Israel and King Joram of Judah so that we know who we're talking about."

"I suppose so," the other girl said.

King Joram stood surveying the kneeling men before him. Then he spoke. "We will remove the Baal from the palace," he began. "Under the circumstances, I believe that is the wisest way to start my reign over this nation."

A cheer went up from the soldiers. Zillah smiled and Susanna applauded. Perhaps now it would be easier to be a worshiper of the God of Abraham in the nation of Israel. At least she certainly hoped so.

Change was in the air. I could feel it. Many more guardians than usual pressed close, and we knew that the Almighty had plans afoot. We were all watching carefully to see what would happen.

The Mighty One wasn't the only one with plans, though. Susanna chattered with excitement. "I'm going to be married. I'm so excited. Now I have a chance to have a family. And who knows, maybe one of my sons will be the Messiah."

Zillah hugged her. "Wouldn't that be wonderful," she said. "But I can't imagine you married and a mother. We're still almost children."

"No we're not," Susanna argued, stretching herself up to her full height. "We're women now, remember?"

Zillah put her hand over her mouth and laughed. "Of course I remember. It's just that being a woman after being a child a few days before just doesn't feel that much different to me. I thought when I became a woman I would—well, you know—know everything."

"Yes," Susanna said, "I don't feel very grown up either. But I'm sure not going to let anybody know." She grinned. "You don't have to either. You look wise and wonderful on the outside."

Zillah laughed again.

"I'm going to ask my father if you can come with me to my home as my mother and I prepare for the wedding," Susanna continued. "You've been with your Grandfather Obadiah for a couple of years. I'm sure they wouldn't mind if you came to my house just for a few months to help prepare."

"Yes," Zillah said, after thinking about the offer for a few moments. "In the beginning you and I were here to be companions serving Princess Athaliah. And since she married and moved to Judah, we have had a lot more freedom. Although you stayed here and helped out in the palace."

"Of course. That's where all the fun stuff goes on."

"I was pretty happy with Grandfather Obadiah," Zillah said. "But I would enjoy helping you get ready for your wedding."

After Zillah's parents gave their permission, she joined the group traveling to Susanna's family home. As it rounded a hill on the trail they could see a dust cloud coming toward them.

"It must be some men on horses," Susanna's father said. "They're traveling fast. We should get to the side of the road."

They pulled their donkeys off the trail to make room for the fast-traveling band of men. But it did not continue on.

"Syrians," hissed Susanna. "It's a raiding band."

"Run!"

Some of the men in the band fought the Syrian soldiers. Several servants hid themselves behind rocks. Zillah was terrified. Although she wanted to run her legs wouldn't move, and she just stood there shaking.

The skirmish was short. A soldier grabbed her and threw her across the horse in front of him and galloped away.

It seemed like forever until they at last stopped. A larger group of Syrians waited at the entrance of a small cave with other prisoners. The soldiers were talking, but Zillah did not understand their language. It was a brief rest—just long enough to eat and stretch her cramped muscles. Then the captives and the soldiers sped toward Syria. Raiding bands did not stick around for an army to catch them. *They just dash into Israel long enough to kill people and destroy lives and then escape quickly,* Zillah thought bitterly.

Soon she was so thirsty that she felt as if her tongue was permanently stuck to the roof of her mouth. "God of Israel," she whispered, "where are You? Did You see this? I know that if the prophet Elisha had been there, he could have called down fire from heaven and burned up these guys. But he wasn't there. But You, You can see everything. Why didn't You do anything to help me? I've always been loyal to You."

My heart ached for her. Feeling so alone even though surrounded with extra guardians, she was only a human. She couldn't see or feel their presence. Could she accept by faith that the Mighty One had a plan and that He was always in control? I hoped so.

When they reached Damascus, they first went to a military barracks. As the soldiers and captives milled around in a courtyard, a man entered. Zillah guessed he was important from the way all the soldiers stood to attention and bowed their heads before they spoke to him. Then she heard someone use his name, and she shuddered. Naaman. Even she had heard of him—the commander of the Syrian hosts. The man behind the horrible things that happened to people who were just minding their own business and planning for joyful things such as weddings. Again she shuddered.

Captain Naaman talked to the soldiers for several minutes then inspected the prisoners. When he gestured toward Zillah, the soldier who had captured her shoved her forward. He made some kind of a joke and the other soldiers laughed. Naaman scowled and the room became silent. Then he gave a curt order. They took the other prisoners and departed, leaving Zillah standing before the Syrian commander, eyes downcast. She was terrified.

"You are a daughter of Israel?" he asked.

She looked up suddenly.

"Yes, I speak a little of your language. A good soldier needs to know his enemies well."

Slowly she nodded.

"The raiding band tells me that you are highborn. They thought you might be part of the royal family. Are you a grandchild of Ahab?"

Zillah shook her head. Then finally finding her voice, she said, "No, my father served King Ahab and Ahaziah and now serves King Joram. My grandfather was Obadiah."

"Obadiah! I have heard of him. You come from brave stock."

The girl stared at the floor. She didn't feel brave at all.

"Come with me. You will live in my home."

Suddenly she started to cry.

"Oh, stop that!" he snapped. "I'm taking you as a gift for my wife.

She's young and lonely. I wish you to be a companion for her. Apparently you have experience with that."

Choking back her tears, Zillah gasped, "I was a companion to the Princess Athaliah when I was a little girl—until she was old enough to marry King Joram of Judah."

"That's what my officers told me," he said. "So you will do well once you learn the language. And," he said in a softer voice, "my wife is kind. I think you'll like her. But whether or not, you're her slave and you will serve her well."

As he turned and left she hurried after him.

* * * *

Zillah had been a slave in the house of Naaman for almost a year. Just as the military officer had promised, she was a slave to his wife, and none of the men in the household bothered her. The guardians had seen to that. Naturally bright, the girl quickly learned the language. She found serving Naaman's wife was not all that different from serving her duties with Princess Athaliah, except she liked the wife much better.

Lady Naaman was very young, almost the same age as Zillah. And even though they were mistress and slave, they formed a close bond.

"Are your duties now a lot different," Lady Naaman asked one day, "from what you did in the court of Israel for the princess?"

Zillah thought for a moment. "The things you require are similar. But I enjoy your company more than I did Princess Athaliah. She was very hardheaded with a sharp tongue like her mother, the queen. But of course, I would never say such a thing in Israel."

They both laughed, then Zillah sobered. "You—you are very kind to me, but I'm still a slave."

"Is being a slave so bad?"

Zillah looked at the floor and didn't answer.

"I never really thought about it before," Lady Naaman said, breaking the silence, "but I guess no matter how kind we are to you, it's hard being away from home. And it can't feel good to be owned by someone else."

"There's more," said Zillah, meeting her eyes. "Every girl in Israel hopes to marry and give birth to the Messiah. He's going to come to one of us, and we've all been hoping for Him since the very first human couple."

"But you might still bear children," Lady Naaman protested.

"Yes, I suppose so. But the Messiah will save everyone in Israel. He'll be a great king and rule the earth. And though I come from a noble family and have noble blood in my veins, I can't imagine the Messiah being born to a slave. In Israel I wouldn't always be a slave."

"Really? What do you mean?"

Zillah nodded. "When people are sold into slavery it is only for seven years. Then slaves are supposed to be let go."

Lady Naaman's mouth dropped open. "How wonderful! I did not realize that the Israelite kings were so generous."

"They're not," Zillah said with a giggle. "This comes from the law of Moses. It's our God who is so generous. And the Israelites grudgingly go along with it. Well, some of them. My Grandfather Obadiah served God faithfully and happily, but sometimes he had to do it secretly."

"Yes, I imagine he would have to because for a while when I was a little girl we heard that the royal god of Israel was Baal."

"Under Ahab and his queen Jezebel," the slave girl explained.

"Jezebel is still around, isn't she?"

"Yes, but Joram is king now. He did get rid of the Baal in the palace and has removed others of them from the land. So officially Israel worships Jehovah again. However, I think in the palace it's only officially. It isn't the same as the way my family has worshiped Him. And Joram does not consult the prophet Elisha."

"Tell me about this Elisha," Lady Naaman said, sitting on a mat and crossing her legs. "We hear many stories about him. Are they true? Can he really raise the dead?"

Zillah nodded enthusiastically. "According to my father he brought the son of a Shulamite woman back to life. Other stories about Elisha tell how he was able to cure a whole community of women who were unable to have children by healing the waters they were drinking. And he was able to multiply a widow's oil so that she kept pouring it out of the same flask and was able to sell many, many jugs of it to pay off all of her debts so she wouldn't have to sell her children into slavery."

"How wonderful! If I were King Joram I would want someone like that at court. Think what advantages such a holy man would bring to his kingdom."

"Yes and no," Zillah sighed. "My God requires loyalty and worship, and He doesn't just do miracles on demand. He is powerful enough to, but He is not under the command of any king."

Lady Naaman shook her head in wonder. "Well, I know my husband and Ben-hadad have a fair amount of respect for Him. Apparently He hears things said in secret here in Syria and whispers them in Israel."

The girl thought about that for a moment. "Yes, I guess He could if He wanted to, because He's invisible and can be anywhere."

"What an amazing God!" Lady Naaman exclaimed. "If He is so powerful and if you worship Him, why did He let you be taken captive and become a slave here in Syria?"

Zillah's face fell. "I don't know. I don't understand that at all. But it doesn't mean He's not powerful. It just means . . . I don't know what it means. Perhaps He has a reason."

Suddenly the Syrian woman realized what she had said. "I'm sorry. I've made you sad. Let's go out to the garden. It's too nice a day to think about such things."

As they headed for the door I followed.

Weeks later Zillah stared with concern at her mistress. Lady Naaman's face had been red and puffy for several days now. She looked as if she had been crying herself to sleep every night. Zillah knew that as her slave it was not her place to ask and Lady Naaman did not explain what was the matter.

They sat in silence in the garden. Suddenly the tears started to flow again.

"My lady," Zillah whispered, "it breaks my heart to see you so sad. Are you ill?"

Lady Naaman glanced at the slave girl kneeling at her feet. "I can't tell you," she said, fighting back more tears. "I can't tell anybody."

Zillah nodded, then lowered her eyes.

"But I have to tell somebody. Please promise me you won't tell anyone what I'm going to share with you."

"I promise."

"It's Naaman," she whispered.

Zillah's mind spun quickly. What could be the matter? Naaman was home right now. No major wars were going on that she knew of. Had he been mistreating his wife? No, she couldn't ask that.

"He has leprosy," Lady Naaman blurted.

"Leprosy!" the girl said in shock. "That's terrible."

"Yes." The young woman started to sob. "I don't know what we're going to do. Right now we're going to just keep it a secret. But we won't be able to ignore it forever. What's going to happen to us? What's going to happen to me without my husband?" She buried her face in her hands and sobbed.

Zillah jumped to her feet. "I wish he could go to Israel," she burst out.

"Israel?" Lady Naaman demanded, jumping to her feet. "Israel! You mean to get killed?"

"No," the girl protested.

"Your people in Israel don't treat lepers that well, either, you know. I've heard that they have to live off by themselves and would starve unless their families bring food to them."

"Sadly, those things are true. But I was thinking of Elisha."

"Has the prophet healed any lepers?" Lady Naaman asked more thoughtfully.

Zillah shook her head. "I've never heard of any, but surely healing leprosy would not be as difficult as raising a dead boy to life."

Both sat in silence for a few minutes.

"It would be dangerous for him to go to Israel," Naaman's wife pointed out. "Even though we're not at war right now, there are still all kinds of border raids."

"I know," Zillah said sadly.

Lady Naaman put her hand over her mouth. "Of course you do. I'm sorry I forgot. It's that I just feel as if you've always been here."

I smiled gently. Lady Naaman might forget occasionally, but I was certain that Zillah never did, for even though she had great affection for Naaman's wife, I often saw her when she cried at night out of loneliness for her family.

"I will talk to my husband. Life as a leper is a hopeless one. If there's any possibility in this, it would be worth at least finding out." She thought a moment. "I'm going to talk to him right now."

Zillah stayed in the garden. "Oh, God of Israel," she whispered, "I hope You can hear me. I believe You're everywhere and that You can even hear me here in Syria. My father and my grandfather and his grandfather all served You loyally and loved You. But they knew when to keep their mouth shut. Should I have kept my mouth shut, too? Have I just made a terrible mistake that will cause the death of Captain Naaman? Or is this different? Was this a time to speak?

"Grandfather Obadiah said that You would let me know when it was time to speak and when it was time to keep silent. But the words just came right out of my mouth. Is this part of Your plan? Oh, God of Israel, I don't like being a slave. I'm homesick for my country and my family. But Lady Naaman has been very kind to me, and I don't want her husband to be killed for something I suggested. Please help him make the right decision."

The girl took a deep breath. Her family had always left the final decisions up to the God of Israel. She would leave this one with Him, too. Slowly she returned to the house.

* * * *

The feast was huge. Everyone was there, even the king. Zillah and the others hurried to bring more food and refill goblets. The king had offered sacrifices in the temple of Rammon earlier that day—sacrifices of thanksgiving for the healing of Captain Naaman. The celebrations continued deep into the night. By the time all the guests had left, the sky was streaked with pink. Although the slaves were exhausted, they still had much cleaning up to do.

But Zillah, the head house slave, called to them. "Everyone, we need to meet in the gardens. Captain Naaman has summoned all of us. Yes, even you kitchen slaves. Everyone to the garden."

Every slave in Captain Naaman's huge house and estate had assembled beneath the palm trees of the garden. The huge containers of soil that Naaman had brought back from his trip had been dumped in the center of the garden and formed into a little altar.

"This altar in the garden is to the God of Israel, for He is the God who healed me of my leprosy," Naaman reminded them.

A murmur rippled through the group of slaves. Word had traveled quickly, and by the time Naaman had left on his trip everyone knew of his illness. They had heard the story of his healing again and again as he told it during the recent celebrations.

The king of Israel, terrified when Naaman had showed up in his court, ripped his clothes and told him no one could heal him of leprosy.

Naaman's laughter rang out as he repeated the story once more to the tired slaves. "Apparently, my wife's slave girl knows more than the king of Israel. We were starting back home, feeling embarrassed and humiliated, when the servant of the prophet of Jehovah came to us and told us the prophet would see us. When I reached his house, he didn't even come out, but just gave me another message through his servant to go bathe in the muddy waters of the Jordan. I thought surely the Israelites just intended to humiliate me further. I almost didn't go. And yet Dathan"—he slapped his bodyguard on the back, playfully— "Dathan here, talked me into trying it. What harm was there? What could I lose? As if I would have any dignity left as a leper!

"I dipped in the Jordan River seven times just as the prophet had instructed me and the God of Israel removed all of my leprosy. It had to be the God, for the Jordan is a filthy, muddy little river. Ours are so much better." He laughed. "Yet this prophet would not accept any of my gifts. I took great wealth along with me to give him—the ransom of a king—for I am a rich man and my life was worth it. Yet he would not accept it. He said my healing was a gift from the God of Israel. So I brought back soil from Israel to build an altar, and I and my household will now worship the God of Israel in this garden as long as I shall live."

Zillah was delighted. Surely Jehovah had heard all of her prayers. As Captain Naaman now offered a sacrifice on the altar, she knelt with the other slaves and quietly poured her heart out to God in thanksgiving and praise. Surely He was the God of all the entire earth.

Then Naaman's voice interrupted her prayers. "There is more," he said. "Those of you who come from the land of Israel and who worshiped Jehovah God before arriving at my house will stay here in the garden. The rest of you may return to your tasks."

Most of the slaves stood and walked back to the house. Zillah looked around. Six slaves remained before the altar. Her mouth dropped open. She had known there were slaves from Israel in the house of Naaman, and she had spoken to some. However, no one had mentioned whether they worshiped Baal or the God Jehovah. She smiled shyly at the other five.

Suddenly a cold chill swept over her and a terrible feeling formed in the pit of her stomach. What was Naaman going to do? She knew that some of the surrounding countries still practiced human sacrifice. Was he going to offer them back to their god?

"The God Jehovah has been so good to me, and I wish to make a gift to Him even if His prophets won't accept the wealth I brought to give Him," Naaman said.

Zillah started to shake.

"Trust Him," I whispered in her ear. "Trust Him. Jehovah has taken care of you all this time."

The girl took a deep breath.

"My wife tells me that slavery is not a lifelong thing in Israel. This has been my year of jubilee. I was delivered from a terrible illness. Now I'm going to give you six back to your God by offering you your freedom and returning you to the land of Israel. He may not need my wealth and my riches, but I believe He will appreciate my treatment of His loyal followers. We will leave tomorrow and take you to the borders of Israel. You will be free."

Shrieks and cheers rose from the garden. Lady Naaman beamed at Zillah, but the tears welled up in her eyes. Suddenly she flung her arms around her. "Oh, Zillah, I know you are my slave, but you have been such a friend to me, too, and I will miss you so much. But you'll get to go home. You'll get to marry and have children. Maybe even your hoped-for Messiah. You deserve it."

In a state of shock Zillah hugged her mistress back. She couldn't believe it—she was going home! Then she took a deep breath. The God Jehovah did have a plan for her the whole time. There was a reason for everything, and He did let her know when to speak and when to keep silent. A huge smile swept across her face. If the God Jehovah had been in control through all of these amazing events, He could do anything. For the rest of her life she could trust Him with anything.

I smiled too, for Zillah was right.

AARON

 aron woke to the sound of his mother sobbing. He could hear his father's deeper voice, low and calm, trying to comfort her. What could be wrong?

"I can't bear it! I can't bear it again!" he could hear his mother say. "I lost my first husband and now you!"

The boy sat up. He and his older brother had been sleeping on the flat roof of their home. Now they looked at each other. "What does Mother mean?" Aaron asked.

Adam shook his head. "I don't know. You know that my father, Mother's first husband, died?"

"Sure, otherwise Mother wouldn't be married to my father."

"Right."

"But if Mother's crying about losing her husband again, why would Father still be downstairs talking to her? It doesn't make any sense."

"Maybe we need to listen a little longer," Adam suggested.

Although they strained to hear, Mother's sobbing revealed no more details.

Aaron awoke early as the sun peaked over the horizon. His father was already in the courtyard. He was packing a small bag on the family donkey and Mama was baking bread and fixing a basket of provisions.

"Are you going on a trip, Father?" the boy asked.

His father gave him a tired smile. "Sort of. We need to talk. You and Adam come sit with me over here while we have some of this wonderful bread your mother's making."

Mother tried to smile, but didn't quite make it.

"I have to go away," Father said slowly after they sat cross-legged in front of him.

"Where are you going? May we come?" Adam asked.

"No," Father replied.

Aaron shrugged. Father went on trips frequently. Their family served the king, and he often had to make important journeys.

"Where's the king sending you this time?" Aaron asked. "Or is it a secret?"

Suddenly Father looked tired and old. "The king isn't sending me this time. And it's not going to be a secret."

Mother put her hands over her face and lowered her head. Suddenly the morning air seemed cold. Aaron shivered and folded his arms across his chest. "What are you talking about, Father? What's the matter?"

"I went to see the priest yesterday," Father began. "I've had this rash for a while and it's been getting worse. The priest says that it's leprosy."

"Leprosy!" Adam exploded. "Oh, I would talk to another priest."

"I already have. It's leprosy."

Mother started crying softly.

"Well, what are you going to do?" Adam demanded.

"I'm going to do what every leper in Israel does—I'm going to move outside the city walls and live in a leper colony so that I don't give the illness to you boys and to your mother."

"You're leaving us? You're never coming back?" Aaron gasped.

Father nodded slowly. "But you need to understand that I'm leaving because I love you and because I can't bear the thought of giving this disease to you boys. Adam, you're a man now. Aaron, you're close enough to be one. I've tried to be a good father to you. I've taught you everything you need to know. And I've trained you to take good care of your mother. I expect you to continue to do that. Your uncle

Jedediah will take care of you, too, so you won't want for anything. You will be well provided for. But I can't do it anymore."

"But I don't want you to go," Aaron protested. "This—this doesn't make any sense. And—and what about all the stories cousin Zillah told me?" The boy knew that the Syrians had captured her and that she had been a slave to Naaman, the Syrian military commander. She had persuaded Naaman to come to Israel to ask the prophet Elisha to heal him.

"Elisha healed Naaman," protested Aaron. "Remember he dipped seven times in the River Jordan and was healed. You could go to the Jordan, Father."

His father sighed. "That was a miracle, Aaron. They don't happen every day. Naaman was a very important person."

"You're very important," his son protested.

His father smiled sadly.

"Miracles happen," Adam said slowly. "Remember when I was at the School of the Prophets back when my father died and Mother and I were so poor?"

"I know things were very hard for you," his stepfather said.

"Yes, but remember when I was out chopping wood with the other students? I had borrowed an ax from our neighbor and was trying so hard to chop extra firewood to take home to Mother. Suddenly the head of the ax flew off and fell in the river."

His stepfather had heard the story several times.

"I was so upset," Adam continued. "Mother and I had nothing, and it was a borrowed ax. I knew the neighbor would be furious and that he could have us sold into slavery to recover the loss of the ax head. Then Elisha prayed and God made the ax head float right on the water—an iron ax head! That was as big a miracle as curing leprosy. Something that heavy wouldn't float by itself."

"God can do anything," Father said, "and sometimes He does miracles, but usually He doesn't. We don't always understand why God does or doesn't do miracles. Your mother and I have prayed to God for healing. But the leprosy is still here." Father pulled back his sleeves. The boys could see that it still marred his skin.

"Doesn't God love us as much?" Aaron asked.

"Of course He does. We are His 'anyway' people."

"'Anyway' people?" Adam repeated. "What do you mean?"

"Well," Father explained, "how much faith does it take to love God after He's healed you of leprosy or made your ax head float?"

"How could I not love Him."

"All right, He did wonderful things for you and it's easy to love Him. But what about people who haven't had any miracles and who have bad things happen in their lives and who love Him anyway?"

"Oh."

"Well," Father continued, "I plan to love the God of Israel anyway. I have served Him all my life with my healthy body, and I plan to love Him now with my sick body as long as there is breath in me. I am one of God's 'anyway' people."

Mother's quiet crying turned to sobbing, and she ran into the house.

"Adam," Father suggested, "why don't you finish up that bread that your mother was working on so it doesn't burn?"

"'Anyway' people, 'anyway' people." The phrase echoed through Aaron's mind again and again. His father was going to be one of God's 'anyway' people. He would be, too.

During the next few months Aaron missed his father terribly. Mother was quiet and didn't sing anymore. And although Uncle Jedediah was now the head of the house, it just wasn't the same.

The leper colony was just outside the city walls. Only a few lived there, for during the previous winter a fever had swept through it and most of its members had died. While the boys were not supposed to go anywhere near the lepers, Aaron couldn't help it. Missing his father so much, he would slip outside the city walls and sit on the big rock near the caves where the lepers lived. There he would whistle in the special way that his father had taught him, and Father would whistle back. Then he would come out. Father would never let him sit very close or touch him, but he would sit on the big rock and they would talk. Often Father would tell him stories about times when things had been hard before and how God had always taken care of His people. Aaron couldn't see how God was caring for them now. Just having Uncle Jedediah providing for their needs hardly counted. What he wanted was his father.

Aaron thought his visits to his father were a secret. However, as he set out one day for the city wall, Mother grabbed him by the arm. "Are you heading outside the city again?" she asked him.

He nodded guiltily.

"Well, take this. You might want to leave it out there on a rock or something." She shoved a basket into his hands.

Smelling the fresh bread and fruit, he broke into a huge grin. "Sure, I'll leave it out there. You never know when a hungry person might appreciate it."

Mother smiled for the first time in weeks. "Yes, it could be a hungry person's favorite things. Might cheer him up a little bit."

"I'll bring the basket back," Aaron assured her.

Mother winked at him and turned back toward home. Aaron's heart felt lighter as he scampered toward the city wall.

The gift delighted his father. The boy had spread a piece of cloth on the big rock, fixed a bountiful meal, and then taken his basket and backed off as Father and his friends gathered around it.

"Oh, my favorite," he told his son. "Your mother's good bread drizzled with honey and sprinkled with cinnamon—there's just nothing as good as this."

After they ate Father's leper friends retreated back into the cave. Aaron sat on the ground talking to his father. "I don't understand the king," he said. "He got rid of the Baals in the city and in the palace, but he doesn't pay much attention to God. He practically ignores the prophet Elisha."

"Yes," Father said, "that's how it has been. It's as if he got rid of the Baals, but never replaced them with the true God, so in a way we're still a heathen nation."

"Why?" Aaron demanded. "How many more miracles does God have to do to show the king that He wants to be the God of our country?"

Father shook his head. "I don't know. But when the national leadership does not follow God, the rest of the country doesn't either. And when bad things happen, they blame God for not helping."

"But they don't ask Him for help," Aaron protested.

"That's right."

"From the stories that you've told me," Aaron said, "the king's whole family has been like that. It seems as if God has done everything He could possibly do to get their attention to prove He was more powerful than Baal and to show them how much He cared for them, and yet they're ignoring Him. What more could He do?"

"I don't know. But I do know that if a family continues to ignore God, despite all the ways that He tries to care for them and to get their attention, eventually He takes away their power and the family is destroyed."

"Are you saying that might happen to the royal family?"

"I believe it has been already prophesied," Father said slowly. "Those are things I can say now as a leper. Nobody can do anything to me now for it. You must never repeat this inside the city. But I want you to know it. I want you to understand that people who love God and worship Him are His people and He takes care of them. And people who ignore Him eventually perish. None of us can live without His care."

"He's not taking care of us," Aaron protested.

"Sure He is," his father insisted. "Look around you when you go back into the city. How well off are you compared to most boys your age. God is taking very good care of you even if your father is ill. And think about it. I may be ill, but you still come out and see me, and even though I can't touch you, we talk. Your half-brother Adam couldn't do that after his father died."

"Yes, I suppose that the God of Israel has been good to me," Aaron admitted reluctantly. "It's just that sometimes I wish things were different."

"Talk to your cousin Zillah about that," Father suggested.

"Why? Zillah's father is fine."

"Yes, he is. But think about this: There were probably many times when Zillah felt as if the God of Israel was not paying attention to her and many times when she wished things were different. And yet it was all part of a great plan that He had devised.

"And Captain Naaman came to worship the God of Israel," Father continued. "Who knows, perhaps my leprosy is part of a plan that will be a blessing someday."

"I don't see how," Aaron muttered bitterly.

"I don't either," Father sighed. "And there are days when I feel very discouraged. But whether it's part of the plan or not, our family worships Jehovah."

Aaron squared his shoulders. "Yes, we do and we will. And I will go talk to Cousin Zillah."

* * * *

Adam burst into the courtyard. "Mother," he shouted, "Mother, we're under siege. The Syrians are attacking us again."

Cousin Zillah came out of her quarters. "I can't believe that," she protested. "What are they doing now? Captain Naaman surely wouldn't be attacking us."

"No," Adam said, "it's not Captain Naaman. I think it's Ben-hadad."

"Oh, of course," Zillah muttered. "Ben-hadad was never very impressed with Naaman's healing. There's some kind of power struggle between those two."

"Well," Adam said, "regardless of how Naaman and Ben-hadad feel about each other, Ben-hadad is marching on us with a huge army. It's split into three parts, and it looks as if they're going to be surrounding the city."

Zillah shook her head. "Don't they ever get tired of fighting?"

Uncle Jedediah entered the courtyard. "Is it true, Father?" she asked him.

Her father nodded. "Yes. I believe the Syrians are planning to put Samaria under siege. Our soldiers have already closed all the gates and barred them and we are moving reinforcements up on the walls."

"What's going to happen to Father?" asked Aaron.

"Probably nothing," Uncle Jedediah replied, "at least that's what I hope. Syrians avoid lepers just like we do. They don't want to get the sickness either, so they probably won't bother your father and his companions. I think they'll be OK. But they will be outside the wall and we will be inside, so we probably won't know too much until the siege ends."

"But how will I—I mean, how will he get food?"

Jedediah turned and looked at his young nephew for a long moment. "He'll get food the same way as he always did. Lepers scrounge for food outside the city walls. They eat wild berries and things."

Aaron blushed and his mother stared at the ground. Neither one wanted to confess how much they had given Father.

Uncle Jedediah smiled gently and said, "They'll receive fewer gifts during the siege, but the Lord will look after them."

Aaron glanced up and met his uncle's eyes. Uncle Jedediah knew, too?

"Think about this," his uncle continued. "God will take care of your Father. And He will take care of us, too. Remember when the

Syrians put Dothan under siege?"

Zillah started to laugh and the boys joined in.

The prophet Elisha had prayed and God had struck the invading soldiers blind. The prophet had led them clear down to Samaria where the people fed them and then sent them home. The most humiliating thing that could have happened to the Syrian soldiers, it was much worse than being killed in battle. No wonder they were so angry and wanted to besiege Samaria.

Cousin Zillah shook her head. "Syrian honor. It's so important. Those men went home just fuming. To be helpless before the enemy and then be fed and sent home and not even be worthy enough to be killed must have infuriated them."

Aaron perked up. "Maybe God will do that again."

His cousin started to laugh. "God does miracles sometimes, Aaron, but it's not as if every time Israel ever has an enemy God strikes them all blind. Sometimes we have to trust Him anyway."

"You sound like my father," the boy said.

"Of course," Zillah agreed, "he's my uncle. We were all raised to trust the God of Israel. Sometimes it's harder than other times to trust Him. It was extra hard being a slave in Damascus in Naaman's house, yet the God of Israel took care of me, and here I am back in Israel and betrothed to be married."

"You won't be able to go marry your husband with Samaria under siege," Aaron said. "How would he get you out of here?"

"He won't," she replied. "But I plan to continue my preparations, because when the siege is over I have a wedding to go to."

Aaron fidgeted. He loved God, but he wished that he could feel as confident as his cousin Zillah or his uncle Jedediah. Sometimes bad things happened to people who loved God. What if this was one of those times? What if God wasn't planning to take care of them? What if his father couldn't find enough food outside the city? What if . . . Aaron's stomach twisted into such a knot he had to stop thinking about the what ifs.

I hovered near young Aaron, wishing that I could just wrap my arms around him and fill him with hope and strength and confidence. Yet I was not allowed to interfere. Each human must make their own choices and trust or not trust as they choose—to concentrate on the power and goodness of the Almighty One or worry about their problems. Yet I felt confident that Aaron—with his family around him who trusted the God of Israel even in a city full of those who had forgotten Him—would be OK.

* * * *

It seemed as if the siege had gone on forever. The skinny street urchins were now starving to death. Even the wealthy could find little to buy. Aaron walked across the courtyard to the kitchen area where his mother was stirring a pot of soup.

"What are you preparing?" the boy asked.

"Don't ask," his mother snapped.

Aaron shook his head. He knew his mother was irritable because she wasn't able to get the things she was used to fixing. But at least their family had food. Both his father and Uncle Jedediah had been fairly wealthy and what little food was available in the market, they were able to buy.

He went and perched on the low wall next to his older brother, Adam. "Mother is really upset today," he commented.

"The siege is getting to her," Adam said. "It's getting to all of us."

"No it's not," Aaron replied. "We still eat every day. It's the people outside our family compound that are really suffering."

Adam sighed. "They're starving to death. But the reason Mother is upset is because she's making donkey head soup."

"What?" Aaron asked incredulously.

"You don't believe me, go look in the trash pile behind the kitchen."

Aaron hopped off the wall and went to investigate. His brother was right. There were the boiled bones of a donkey's head. "That's disgusting!" Aaron exclaimed. "What about all of our rules from Moses about clean meat and unclean meat?"

"We're under siege," his brother reminded him. "It isn't so much an issue of clean meat or unclean meat as whether we starve to death or not."

The younger boy shuddered. "I guess I would have been happier not knowing."

"That's why Mother told you not to ask."

Aaron make a face.

"Do you know what the worst thing about it is?" Adam continued. "Not that we're eating a donkey's head, but how much it cost."

"We paid money for that?"

"What do you think? Everyone is starving. We paid 80 shekels of silver for that donkey's head."

"Eighty shekels!" Aaron exploded. 'Don't most workmen get a shekel for a month's work?"

Adam sighed. "Yes," he said. "This would have cost the average workman his earnings for 80 months."

Aaron shook his head. He couldn't imagine spending six and a half years of a grown man's earnings on just the head of a skinny old donkey that was probably as hungry as the people who had slaughtered it. Had God forgotten about them? Again he shook his head and squared his shoulders. If Father could be an "anyway" person with his leprosy, then he could be an "anyway" person and still love God even if he did have to eat donkey head soup.

The siege dragged on. While Aaron's family managed to obtain some food, it was not the kinds of things they used to eat. And he was always sorry when he asked what it was.

The laws of Moses about diet had long since been forgotten. His family was now just struggling to survive. What little they had they ate slowly so each meal would last as long as possible. But they were still better off than most families in Samaria.

"If things are this bad here," Aaron said to his brother one night, "what do you think is happening to Father?"

"I don't know," Adam replied.

Aaron rolled away from his brother. Suddenly the whole siege and everything associated with it was just too much to bear. He put his head in his arm and cried silently until he finally fell asleep.

The following afternoon Uncle Jedediah entered the courtyard. "Aaron," he said, "come with me."

Glad to be able to be somewhere besides the family home, he asked, "Where are we going?"

"Up on the wall."

Weak from malnutrition Aaron followed his uncle. He was thankful that the walls of Samaria were strong and thick. They were wide enough for several people to walk abreast across the top.

"Adam tells me you've been worrying about your father."

The boy stared at the ground. He had hoped that his stepbrother hadn't seen him crying the night before.

"Yesterday we saw several lepers outside the wall over toward their colony. I thought it would make you feel better to come up here and see. In fact, someone spotted your father yesterday. And although they don't come out much because they're avoiding the Syrians he's still there. See, right over there!"

Aaron knew where to look. He raised his arm and waved. The man standing outside the caves waved back. His father was still alive. Suddenly Aaron's heart felt lighter. God was taking care of his father. He could even survive the donkey head soup and other terrible things he had to eat as long as he knew his father was all right.

"Do you think the siege will be over soon?" he asked his uncle.

Uncle Jedediah looked grim. "Yes, it'll be over soon. But things aren't going well, and it may not end the way that we had hoped."

"Oh," Aaron whispered.

His uncle put his arm around him. "The Lord takes care of His people even when they lose battles. It's going to be OK. I'll walk you down from the wall, and then I want you to go back home. The king and I have some things to discuss."

Aaron turned to go, but paused. The king and his men were ascending the wall. He stood respectfully waiting for them to pass. Just as he started to leave a woman shouted, "Your majesty, your majesty, help me!"

"How can I help you?" the king snapped. "If the God of Israel isn't paying attention and isn't going to help you with anything, what do you think I should do about it?"

"You could at least guarantee me fair treatment from my neighbor," she whined.

The king gave a loud sigh. "What's the problem?"

"Last week," she said, "we agreed that we would boil and eat my son. This week we were going to eat her son."

Aaron felt himself begin to retch.

"When it was her turn, she'd hidden him. I don't know where he is. It's not fair."

The king shuddered. Had it really come to this in his own capital city?

"What do you think I can do if God isn't helping anyone?" he shouted angrily. "I swear that by this afternoon the prophet Elisha is going to pay for this with his life."

He turned to Jotham, his right-hand assistant. Aaron frowned. He knew Uncle Jedediah didn't like that individual at all. The man did anything the king asked him and agreed with him whether the king's ideas were good or not. Privately, Uncle Jedediah referred to Jotham as the king's pet toad, but, of course, that wasn't something he would ever say out here on the city wall.

"Jotham," he said, "go get the prophet Elisha. We'll make him pay for this with his life."

Aaron's mouth dropped open. Surely the king would not kill God's prophet.

"Elisha is in his quarters with the elders," Uncle Jedediah interrupted. "He has said that we should wait for word from the Lord, and that whatever God says we will do."

"We've waited long enough for the Lord," the king exploded in anger. "He's the one that has sent this calamity in the first place." He turned to Jotham. "Go kill him!"

"Yes, your majesty." And off he went.

Uncle Jedediah frowned, then glanced at Aaron. "Go home," he whispered. "Go straight home, and don't come out again until you know it's safe."

Aaron headed down the steps from the wall. He meant to go home, but his feet took him closer and closer to where the prophet was staying. What would Elisha do? Would the king's servant really kill him? He was just rounding the corner when Jotham banged on the door of Elisha's house.

"Open up in the name of the king," he shouted.

Then Aaron heard the prophet's voice from inside. "Look," he said, "here's a messenger from the king. Grab him and hold him here. His master should be following him shortly."

The men with Elisha opened the door and grabbed Jotham. Aaron grinned. Served him right!

Just as the prophet said it was only a few minutes before the king rounded the corner. "This has got to stop. The Lord has refused to intervene and help us. Why should we wait any longer?" he muttered to his guards.

"I have a message for you," the prophet interrupted. "Here is the word of the Lord. This time tomorrow a whole container full of fine flour will sell for only a shekel and two containers of barley for a shekel in the gates of Samaria."

"Even if the Lord made windows in heaven and dumped it on us, this couldn't happen," Jotham replied sarcastically.

Elisha turned to Jotham with a cold stare. "You," he said, "will see it with your eyes, but you won't taste a single mouthful."

Aaron shuddered. Uncle Jedediah stood next to the king. Suddenly he caught sight of Aaron and glared at him. The boy ran home as fast as he could.

"Adam, Adam," he called. His brother, weak as he was from malnutrition, was trying to clean out what had been the stables. The family no longer had any animals in them. "Adam, the prophet Elisha says that this time tomorrow we'll be buying barley and flour—fine flour—in the gates of Samaria. The siege is going to be over."

The older boy grinned. "I told you," he said. "God will fix things."

"But Adam, I was up on the wall with Uncle Jedediah this afternoon. There are as many Syrians as ever out there. What do you believe God will do to 'em all? Do you think he'll strike them blind again?"

Adam laughed. "I don't know. But Jehovah can do anything He wants to, and I'll be delighted to watch whatever it is."

I smiled. It was refreshing to find someone in Israel who still believed the Almighty could do anything He wanted.

That night Aaron couldn't sleep. He tossed and turned. Finally, just as pink began to streak the sky, he pulled his cloak around him and slipped down to the courtyard. No one else in the family was up yet. Carefully he lifted the heavy bar on the gate and crept out. Wanting to see if he could spot his father again, he hurried to the city wall. Only a few guards remained from the last watch and they ignored him. Climbing slowly to the top, Aaron followed the wall around to the side that faced the cave where the few lepers lived. Weak from hunger, he had to rest several times. A guard shuffled over and smiled at him kindly. "I knew your father." Aaron looked at him. "He's a good man. And he's still out there. We see him pretty often."

The boy smiled despite himself.

"The siege has been hard on them too. We think there's only about four left over there. I guess they're as hungry as we are."

The guard's comment sobered the boy. He hated the idea of his father being hungry. Somehow he had been hoping that his father was finding something better to eat than donkey head soup. He looked in the direction of the caves but saw no one.

"He's not over there," the guard explained. "He's up by the wall, over there."

"He is?" Aaron asked. "What's he doing up by the wall? That's dangerous." Hurrying as fast as his strength would allow, the boy went to the section of the wall nearest his father and peered down at him. "Father, it's me, Aaron."

His father looked up. "Aaron, I've got wonderful news! You've got to share it with the rest of them."

"What?" the boy asked.

"There's no one in the Syrian camp."

"No one! It still looks as if they're all there."

"Well, the tents are all there. But there's nobody in them."

"How do you know?"

His father laughed. "My friends and I, we've been over there."

"You did? Weren't you scared?"

"Of course. Because we haven't had anything to eat for days, we were talking last night about what we should do. We couldn't stay the way we were. If we came up to the city, chances are we couldn't get in. And if we did, there's no food in there anyway. So we decided to surrender to the Syrians and see if they would give us anything. Only when we got there, everybody was gone."

"Everybody?"

"Honest. The four of us ate and ate, and we brought back things and hid them in our cave for later. Everything in the Syrian camp is there. Their tents, their horses, their donkeys. They left everything behind."

The soldier who had talked to Aaron now crowded next to him. "Are you sure?" he called to Aaron's father. "You know sometimes during sieges they pull back long enough for us to open the gates, and then they attack and break into the city."

"Believe whatever you want," Aaron's father said, "but look at this." He held up a bag of silver and a gold platter. "Aaron, I want you to lower a basket, and I'll send food up."

"Don't bother," the guard said, "until we talk to the guards at the gate. Come meet us by the gate."

Aaron's father walked toward the gate on the outside of the wall. The boy noticed now that his father's three leper friends accompanied him.

"You go to the gate too," the guard told Aaron. "I need to call the king."

It was not long before the national and city leaders had all gathered at the gate. "It's a trick," the king declared.

"Who cares?" another countered. "What if we got out there and got some of that food and managed to make it back before they were able to ambush us?"

Uncle Jedediah spoke up. "Your majesty," he said, "why don't you let me take some men and the five horses we have left. We'll ride out and check it out. If it's an ambush, they'll kill us but the rest of you will be fine."

The king nodded. "Take a couple of chariots and scout it out."

As Jedediah and his party rode out the gate it slammed shut behind them. Aaron staggered back up the steps to watch from the top of the wall. What would happen? Would the Syrians pounce on his uncle? Would he be able to bring some food back before they captured him?

As Uncle Jedediah headed toward the Syrian encampment, Aaron held his breath. Less than an hour later Jedediah returned.

"It's true," he reported. "They're gone and have left everything. The road toward the Jordan River is full of clothes and weapons that they dropped or threw away as they ran. Something must have terrified them."

The king stared down over the wall. "Did you four lepers scare them away?" he asked.

Everyone watching from the wall roared with laughter.

"Open the gates," the king ordered.

The crowd on the wall rushed down the steps. Below, the gate-keepers pulled the gates open, and the swarms of people listening in the streets poured out.

Jotham scrambled down as fast as the rest of the mob. As the mass of people surged through the gates he tripped, and the starving horde trampled right over him.

"Help, help!" he cried, his voice lost in the animal-like roar of the starving mob as it thundered on. Aaron stared, but could not see Jotham anywhere. Finally the boy pushed his way through the mass of people to where his father sat happily in the sunshine watching the city's inhabitants pour out to loot the Syrian camp. Halting, Aaron stared at the ground shyly.

His father grinned at him. "I told you there was a reason," he said. "If I wasn't out here being a leper, we'd all still be in there hungry as could be, thinking that it was a Syrian trick while all this food was waiting for us."

The people swarmed back from the tents with full stomachs and carrying as much as they could. And just as Elisha had predicted, people sold flour and barley cheap in the gates of the city, for they found it everywhere in the tents of the Syrian army.

Later the king looked around. "Whatever happened to Jotham?" he asked his attendants

"He's down here," called a gatekeeper who had overheard.

"Well, send him up," the king ordered.

"He won't be going anywhere," the man replied. "The people trampled him to death."

Aaron's mouth dropped open. It was just as the prophet Elisha had said. Jotham had seen everything with his own eyes, but never got a taste of it. The boy shook his head. The God of Israel had done it once again. He was proud to be an "anyway" person.

Miriam

y newest assignment took me away from the kingdom of Israel. Heaven had assigned me to a young woman named Miriam in Judah. She was the daughter of the current high priest in Jerusalem, Jehoiada, and his wife Jehosheba. These were violent and exciting times, and I knew it would not be a quiet assignment.

I was also thrilled because one of my previous young charges had now married the brother of the high priest Jehoiada. Young Zillah had finally received a husband. The Almighty had rewarded her for her faithfulness, not only by restoring her freedom and giving her the husband who had been arranged for her (and whom she loved very deeply), but had also brought her into the priestly family where she could live on the grounds of the Temple and spend the rest of her life not only spiritually, but now also literally, under the shadow of the Almighty.

However, her niece Miriam was my charge now. Miriam, 12 years old, had strong views on everything, though not always backed up by logic that made sense to me—a condition not unusual among humans. My new charge had an inquisitive streak and was determined to find out everything. However, like many of her fellow humans, she often jumped to highly creative conclusions before getting the facts.

I drew near to observe her as she stood in the doorway of the family apartments. Miriam pursed her lips and made a quiet humpf noise.

"What is it?" Yoshebel, her best friend, asked.

The girl shook her head. "Just my aunt."

Yoshebel glanced over and watched Miriam's Aunt Zillah crossing the courtyard carrying a mended robe she had just finished.

"What about her? She seems like a nice enough lady."

"Lady's hardly the term I would use," Miriam replied.

"Really?" Yoshebel said, genuinely interested.

Miriam shook her head. "It's one of those family secrets."

Yoshebel nodded. She knew all about secrets. Miriam and Yoshebel had been young when Jehu had ridden into Judah and killed King Ahaziah, but not too young to learn rapidly that life was full of things that one could not say out loud in public where anyone could hear them. Living in the Temple area with both of their fathers working there made them especially aware of such secrets. A few they learned— things that they needed to know because they were part of the priestly families. Many other things remained secret, though both girls were itching to find out.

Miriam's mother was the sister of the murdered king. As if that wasn't traumatic enough to the family, Queen Athaliah had killed all the other royal heirs, leaving only herself as the royal heir to the throne.

Just thinking about it made Miriam shudder again. It was disgusting. Judah had always remained loyal to God. After all, His Temple was here. But Queen Athaliah had been imported from Israel where they could never make up their minds whether they really served God, or not. Doubly disgusting was that Queen Athaliah had never claimed to serve God at all. Her mother had been the high priestess of Baal,

Jezebel, who had helped lead Israel and King Ahab into such sin. But one could never discuss such things—not at home, not in the Temple, and not anywhere else.

The girl shook her head. How had God ever allowed a mess like this to happen in Judah? And right here near His own Temple? *He must be punishing someone for something really bad,* she thought.

"So what is it that you dislike so much about your Aunt Zillah?" Yoshebel asked. "My mother says that she seems to be a very kind person. She acts the same whether she's talking to rich and important people or to the lowest slave."

"Yes, well, she would," Miriam said in a mysterious tone of voice.

"She would? Why?"

Miriam lowered her voice. "I heard that Aunt Zillah used to be a slave herself. I don't know who thought it was appropriate to bring an ex-slave into the family of the high priest for a wife. But I guess if you've been a slave, you can relate to them. She'll probably always have a slave mentality."

"Are you sure?" Yoshebel whispered. "I mean, couldn't she just be a really nice person?"

"I suppose she could be nice. Or there could be more to it."

"How did you find this out?"

"I've learned that it's better not to reveal my sources," Miriam replied mysteriously. "Let's just say that occasionally I hear things when people think that I'm asleep. So now, not only do we have an imported queen from Israel, but I have an imported aunt from Israel and an ex-slave at that."

Yoshebel shook her head. "I wonder how she became a slave and how she was able to get such an important family to accept her as a wife?"

"I don't know, but I intend to get to the bottom of this. Want to help me?"

Her friend nodded. "Sure, I'm always ready for a mystery. Nothing ever happens around here. This should liven things up."

"Well," Miriam said, "let's both keep our eyes and ears open, and let's think of some good questions we can ask when the grown-ups have their guard down and will give us honest answers."

Yoshebel looked hard at Miriam. "My parents always give me honest answers. Sometimes they tell me that they can't tell me. But that's honest."

Miriam nodded. "Well, yeah, my parents are honest, too, but you know what I mean."

The two girls put their heads together to plan their strategy. As they did, Aunt Zillah waved to them and proceeded across the courtyard.

* * * *

"Miriam," Yoshebel called as she bounded across the courtyard.

"What? You look excited."

"I found out some more stuff—about your Aunt Zillah."

"Really? What?"

"Well, I just out and out asked my mother if your Aunt Zillah really did come from Israel. She said it's true. But Mother says that your Aunt Zillah was from a very important family in Israel who had served for several generations in the palace of the royal family. Your aunt Zillah used to be a companion to Queen Athaliah when she was a little girl."

"And she's part of our Temple family now?" Miriam spat out with disdain.

"Well, my mother claims that your aunt Zillah's family was always faithful to God, even back in the times of Ahab and Jezebel. My mother also says that your Aunt Zillah's grandfather was Obadiah."

"*The* Obadiah?" Miriam demanded. "The one who hid 100 prophets of God during the time of no rain in Israel?"

"The very one. So she comes from a family who loved God and was loyal to Him, and she was highborn. So she doesn't sound like such a bad choice for a priest's wife."

Miriam sniffed disdainfully. "So what about this slavery part? And how did somebody so highborn and important end up a slave? I asked my father last night if it was true that Aunt Zillah had once been a slave. He said yes and that we didn't talk about that anymore. When I asked him why, he said there were a lot of things I would understand when I was older that he didn't want to discuss with me right now. You know what that *always* means?"

"What?"

"Oh, you know, adult stuff and things that they think we don't know anything about."

"Oh, *those* things. But I don't understand. That doesn't fit with your Aunt Zillah at all."

"Well, who knows," Miriam said. "But I'm going to find out. I think I'll start following her all the time and just see if I can find any clues in the things she does. She's so quiet. There's obviously something mysterious about her still. And whatever it is that we aren't supposed to know about, I'm going to discover it."

"Me too. I'll tell you everything I learn if you tell me everything you do."

"It's a deal."

Usually Miriam stayed in the family dwelling near the Temple. Jehoiada, now the head of his family as well as being the high priest, had a large family compound. It was not uncommon in Jerusalem that each extended family had its own quarters around a common courtyard. It was an easier place to keep track of the children than the Temple apartments, though priests when they were on duty also had those available to them.

Now, with Miriam's new interest in tracking Aunt Zillah, she followed her everywhere. She noticed that both her mother, Jehosheba, as well as Aunt Zillah, went frequently to the Temple apartments. One of them visited there every day. *Why?* Miriam wondered. While the high priest had duties at the Temple every day, he didn't stay there, except when important events were going on. Usually he returned home to the family compound. Servants did the necessary cleaning. What was it Aunt Zillah was doing over there? Her husband was not involved every single day in Temple activities since priestly duties went on a strict rotation.

Miriam followed Aunt Zillah to the Temple apartments. She stood behind a pillar until Aunt Zillah entered them, waited a few moments, then slipped inside. At first she didn't see her aunt. Cautiously she peered around the corner into the private sleeping chamber. Then she spotted Aunt Zillah standing near one wall. A second later the woman vanished through a door into a storage room. "What on earth could she be doing?" the girl muttered to herself.

Carefully Miriam slipped to the storage room and slowly cracked the door open. What she saw made her breath stick in her throat. In the light of several flickering lamps Aunt Zillah stood holding a little boy.

"Here," she heard the woman say, "I brought you some lunch, and here is a new robe for you. You're getting so tall."

The boy was just a little child. He had scrambled into Aunt Zillah's arms and was hugging her around the neck.

"I know," she said, "you get so lonely in here. But it's how things have to be right now. I can stay with you all afternoon. And later Uncle Jehoiada will come by."

"He always tells me stories," the little boy said.

Aunt Zillah hugged him. "He is a good storyteller."

Having seen enough, Miriam closed the door and crept out of the room. She sat in the courtyard back at home trying to figure out what Aunt Zillah's secret could mean. Obviously she had a child that no one was supposed to know about. But someone knew. Could her father really be in on it? He was a wonderful storyteller. But why would he be a party to Aunt Zillah hiding a child in a storage room?

Then another thought struck her. The little boy looked to be 6 years old. Aunt Zillah had only been married to her uncle for three years, so where had the child come from? If it wasn't her uncle's son, whose was it? And why was Aunt Zillah hiding him?

Suddenly an idea crossed her mind. It must be Aunt Zillah's child from her slave years. After all, he had called her father Uncle Jehoiada. No wonder the family wanted no one to see him. But how would they keep such a child secret forever? And wasn't it cruel to hide anyone away from the rest of the world like that? How would he ever grow up knowing what life was about? Wouldn't it be better for Aunt Zillah just to admit whatever the truth was? Of course that would just prove how inappropriate she was to be a wife in the family of the high priest.

Miriam shook her head. She disliked Aunt Zillah more and more every day. How disgraceful! And to be hiding her child right in the Temple, a holy place! Did she think that God wouldn't know?

Suddenly Miriam felt herself filled with righteous indignation.

I stood and watched and shook my head. *Sometimes,* I thought to myself, *humans need guardians to protect them from themselves and their curiosity as much as they need protection from the evil one.*

Miriam followed her mother into their private quarters. "Mother," she asked, "may I ask something?"

"Sure, anything. What do you want to know?"

"It's about Aunt Zillah."

"Yes."

"Is it true that she used to be a slave?"

Her mother nodded. "Yes, for several years."

"How did someone from such a wellborn wealthy family end up being a slave? Did they have to sell her to pay their debts? How did it happen?"

"Oh, no," said her mother. "Aunt Zillah's family was quite wealthy. She was not a slave in Israel—she was a slave in Syria."

"Syria!" Miriam exclaimed.

"She doesn't talk about it often. Those were some hard years for her. She was very young when taken there."

"But how did she ever end up here?"

"That's a story your father likes to tell," Jehosheba laughed. "You should ask him tonight."

Her daughter nodded. She certainly would.

She hurried down the narrow street to meet her friend Yoshebel.

"Syria," Yoshebel exclaimed, "she was a slave in Syria! Heaven knows what happened to her there. Syrians are horrible."

"One of their raiding parties must have captured her. I've heard that Israel had a lot of trouble from them back then."

Yoshebel nodded. "Well, maybe some of the things you don't like about her are just traits she picked up in Syria. Being a slave over there, who knows what type of bad habits she could have learned."

Miriam nodded. Then another thought struck her. Slaves often had children without fathers. But how did Aunt Zillah manage to marry a priest? "I'm going to figure this one out," the girl determined.

"Father," Miriam asked that night, "Mother said I should ask you the story about Aunt Zillah coming to live here. I heard that she was a slave in Syria. Since Syrians don't ever let their slaves go free, not like us with the year of jubilee, how did she end up here? Did you buy her for Uncle?"

The high priest burst into peals of laughter. "Oh dear me, no; but it is a wonderful story. You've heard of the prophet Elisha?"

"Of course. Everyone's heard of him."

"Well, then, do you also remember the story of Naaman, the Syrian military commander that came to Elisha for healing?"

Miriam nodded.

"Zillah was a slave in the house of Naaman. She was the one who spoke to Lady Naaman about sending her husband to the prophet for healing. The Naaman family tried to give great wealth to the prophet in exchange for healing, but Elisha said it was a free gift from God. Captain Naaman made a gift to God by building an altar and worshiping Him at his home in Syria. He also set free any of his slaves who had come from Israel and who worshiped the God who had healed him. So your aunt Zillah was set free and returned to her family."

"How did she end up married to Uncle? Did he feel sorry for her?"

Her father burst out with his big infectious laugh that Miriam just loved. When he laughed, pretty soon everyone was laughing, whether they knew what it was about or not. "I don't think feeling sorry is what your uncle felt for Aunt Zillah," he said, his eyes twinkling. "She was a celebrity. They are very devoted to each other. And it was a fine match. She comes from a noble family and . . ."

"Yeah, I've heard that part. What about all her years as a slave? Didn't that affect how Uncle felt about her? Was she really a good match for someone in a family as important as ours?"

Father laughed again. "Zillah's family is as important in Israel as ours is here. And she is close to the royal rulers in both nations. She was quite the catch. Your uncle was delighted and honored to take her as his wife."

"Humpf," Miriam said to herself, trying to digest it all. The pieces just didn't fit. They didn't make sense. "Does he know all her secrets?" she asked bluntly.

Father's chuckling stopped. He looked into her eyes very seriously. "Which secrets would those be?"

The girl was silent for a long time. Then she asked, "Did you know there's a child in the private chambers in your Temple apartment?"

Her stared at her in what seemed like a growing horror, then said in a voice that had never been more serious, "You will never speak of this again. And you will never go there again!"

"Why? Why are you being part of that secret?"

A stern expression on his face, he took both her hands in his. "Miriam, you must not ask any more questions. Sometimes you just have to trust. Do not speak of this to anyone. It is not just a secret to tickle the ears of people who want to know. It is a life or death issue.

It could bring destruction to our entire family."

I bet it could, she thought. *What a scandal it would turn out to be.*

"You must promise me you will never mention this again to anyone. Promise me, Miriam."

Reluctantly the girl nodded and looked at the floor. *How could this be?* she thought. *How could even my father be a part of it and refuse to be honest with me about it?* She felt angry at everyone in her family and now realized that she hated Aunt Zillah.

* * * *

"Miriam," Yoshebel called. "Miriam wait for me. What is the matter? You've been avoiding me for two days. Have you found out anything new?"

"I can't talk about it," the girl said sullenly. "I asked too many questions, and now my father has sworn me to secrecy without explaining anything at all or given me any reasons for the secrets I have found out. I'm disgusted with them all. I don't know how God puts up with them. Right there in His house. Pretending to serve Him and be so holy and righteous and still keeping secrets like that."

Yoshebel shook her head. "Miriam, maybe there's more to it that we don't know. Or maybe it's not what we think."

"A likely story!" Anger sharpened her words. "But what can you expect after she grows up with someone like our queen. And then, as if that wasn't bad enough, she spends time in Syria, picking up who knows what else. And she obviously has divided loyalties. Who would want the captain of the Syrians to be healed? Both Israel and Judah would be a whole lot better off if all of the captains of the Syrian army died of leprosy."

"But our God did heal him through the prophet Elisha so He must have meant for . . ."

"Don't defend her," Miriam snapped. "I'm ashamed of my whole family."

Yoshebel sat with her in silence. But after realizing that her friend was going to spend the afternoon pouting, she left and returned home. She had more important things to do.

Miriam's sullen attitude continued for weeks and then months. She felt anger at her entire family, but especially at Aunt Zillah. The girl avoided the woman as much as possible.

One day her mother sat down to speak with her. "I don't know what has happened to make you so angry," she told her daughter, "but whether you're going to be happy or not, you still need to do your chores. You're still a part of this family, and I still expect you to treat the other people in this family with respect. When Aunt Zillah or I try to teach you something, you need to pay attention and learn. You won't always be a spoiled child in the house of your father, the high priest. Someday you're going to marry. You may have to do chores, you may have to cook for your family. Or should we be able to arrange a marriage into a wealthy enough family for you that you have servants to perform all of that, you'll still need to know what they are doing in order to supervise them."

Miriam grunted a noncommittal reply.

"You can be as angry as you want to," her mother continued, "but you're going to have to behave appropriately. You're going to have to be a part of this family, and you're going to have to treat the rest of us with respect."

Her lips tightly pressed together, Miriam nodded.

"Now, we have a lot of baking to do. We're going to have a family celebration a few days from now, and we need to get as great an amount of supplies in as we can prepare and store in our compound."

"What's the celebration?" Miriam asked.

"It will be a surprise. But we need your help."

The girl knew there was no point in arguing when her mother

used that tone of voice.

The next few days they spent shopping in the marketplace. Servants bustled all over the courtyard as they fixed numerous delicacies seasoned with spices and honey. Whatever it was Mother had in mind, it was going to be a spectacular party.

"Put on your best robes, Miriam. Get dressed. We're going to go to the Temple today, and there's lots to do."

"Today?" Miriam said. "My best robes?"

"Yes. Those special ones that we've been working on with the new gold embroidery."

"Why are we going to the Temple today?"

"To worship," said Mom.

"Is something special happening?"

Busy braiding her daughter's hair, Jehosheba didn't answer at first. "Don't ask too many questions, just come," she said finally. "It will all make sense shortly."

Miriam, her mother, and her aunt entered the Temple grounds early and hurried back to the high priest's private apartments to wait. Mother and Aunt Zillah were so excited that their eyes just sparkled. When they entered the high priest's apartments they headed straight for the storage rooms.

"Come on, Miriam," Aunt Zillah announced. "You won't want to miss this."

Both women went to the entrance to the storage room and opened the door. Miriam suddenly heard her father's voice coming from inside. "Look," she heard him say to someone, "here are your aunts now. They have a new outfit for you."

When she entered the room Miriam stared at the boy standing in the circle of lamplight. He was a little taller than when she had seen him last. Mother and Aunt Zillah quickly undressed him, then pulled a purple robe out of a bag.

"Royal purple?" Miriam asked incredulously.

"Royal purple for a royal boy," her father replied. Then he placed a circlet of gold on the child's head. "This is what we're going to do out front," he explained to the child. "There will be lots of shouting, but they're cheering for you. The whole nation will love you."

"They will?" Miriam said, trying to understand what was going on.

Her father lifted the gold circlet back off the boy's head, then turned to his daughter. "Miriam, meet his majesty, Prince Joash."

"Prince?" she echoed. "I thought Queen Athaliah killed all the princes."

Her father nodded. "That's what she believed too. Your mother rescued him. He was tiny then. She hid him in her own bedchamber. And we have raised him in secrecy here in the Temple, as close to the shadow of the Almighty as a little prince could be."

The child nodded. "I've been hiding under His wings."

Miriam's mouth dropped open. "Prince Joash? But . . ." Suddenly it all made sense. Of course, he would refer to the high priest as his uncle because her mother was the sister of King Ahaziah, so her father would be Uncle Jehoiada. The boy was not Aunt Zillah's child.

Suddenly terror filled her. "But what about the queen?" Miriam asked. "When she finds out . . ."

The high priest knelt before his daughter and took her hands in his. "Remember when I told you that you had to keep this a secret?"

She nodded. "It was to protect our family."

"Yes, the queen will be very angry. But we are going to crown Prince Joash king today. That's what all the celebration preparation has been for. We will have many soldiers around the gates of the Temple—soldiers that are loyal to God and will be to Prince Joash when they find out that he exists. It's going to be all right.

Sometimes you just have to trust."

Feeling dizzy, Miriam stared at Aunt Zillah. "Could you ever forgive me?" she finally asked.

"What for? Oh, of course." She smiled. "I can understand how you could jump to some pretty strange conclusions without knowing the whole story. It just wasn't safe to let anyone know."

"It's time," Miriam's father interrupted. He took Joash by the hand.

"I'll see you later, Cousin Miriam," the little boy said over his shoulder as the high priest led him away.

The girl smiled at him. "Yes, Your Majesty, you will."

She hurried out to where she could see as her father guided the tiny king-to-be out to the steps of the Temple and presented him to the worshipers. The ram's horn had summoned the people.

Suddenly Miriam's stomach seemed to leap into her throat as she heard a huge commotion at the outer gates. Queen Athaliah burst into the Temple grounds.

"Treason!" she screamed. "Treason!"

The crowd outshouted her. "Long live the king! Long live the king!"

"Treason!" she continued. "Kill him! Kill the priest. Who is loyal to me?"

Miriam's father stepped forward. "Who is loyal to Jehovah?" he shouted. "And his majesty, King Joash?"

The crowd roared. Then he pointed to Queen Athaliah. "Take her outside the Temple grounds. Do not defile God's ground with her blood."

The soldiers grabbed Queen Athaliah and dragged her, kicking and screaming, from the Temple precincts. The cheers and the roar of the crowd was deafening. Miriam felt herself shaking from head to toe as she shouted with the crowd. "Long live the king! Long live the king!"

DAUD

aud leaned against a large wine amphora on the docks and watched the people milling around. He had to be careful. The dock hands knew who he was but didn't bother him as long as he didn't steal from them. That was OK because they didn't have much anyway. It was the strangers coming into the port of Joppa that interested him.

The shouting attracted his attention, and he slipped over where he could get a better view. The short, angry man was arguing with a boat captain.

"I'm willing to offer a fair price. What's the furthest you can go?"

"Tarshish," the captain replied. "That's the furthest west anyone goes. If one goes out through the straits beyond there, it's just open sea and nothingness. There could be sea monsters or one could fall off the end of the world."

"Yes, yes, yes," the other man insisted. "Take me there."

"How much are you willing to pay?"

Their voices lowered. Daud smiled. *A perfect customer,* he thought.

The man wore clothing that only a rich person could afford. His hands looked soft, and his nails were manicured. Obviously he was not someone who had done a lick of work in his life.

The boy smiled. That was fine with him. It probably meant that he wouldn't be very athletic and would be unlikely to catch him once the chase started.

Daud walked over to the man. "May I help you load your things?"

"Yes, yes," the rich man said irritably. "I just have those two bags there."

Picking up one in each hand, Daud started for the boat. The rich man was still talking to the captain. As soon as he passed the pile of amphorae and other cargo, he made a sharp left and started to run. He raced down the dock and back to the beach. There he shoved both bags under an old fishing boat rotting on the sand and rolled under it with them. Would the rich man even notice?

Sure enough, a few moments later he heard shouting on the beach.

As long as he didn't steal from the locals, Daud knew that they would not tell the rich man where he was unless he offered them a lot of money. From the heaviness of the bags Daud hoped that most of his gold was in one of them.

The boy stayed under the boat until it began to get dark, then he crept out. He pulled his ragged cloak up over his head—more to hide his face than to protect him from the evening coolness.

I shook my head. Most of the young people I had been assigned to were worshipers of the Almighty, and, even though they made mistakes, at least they loved Him. This scruffy little ruffian knew nothing of the God of Israel and likely would care even less if he was to learn anything about Him.

It made me feel sad to see humans like this who had been unloved from birth with no family or protector. No wonder they were the way they were. I knew that our heavenly King looked on them with compassion, although they seemed fairly unredeemable to me.

Daud made his way back to where the ship was that the rich man had been boarding. It had sailed. He sat down on the edge of the dock, swinging his feet. "So I got away with it," he mumbled to himself.

One of the dock hands gave him a gentle kick and said, "Hey kid, do you know who you were stealing from today?"

The boy spun around. "No. But he looked rich."

"That he was. He is the prophet who lives in the palace with the king and gives him messages from God. The one who tells him what the Syrians are going to do before they ever do it."

Daud grew pale. "That was *the* prophet? Jonah the prophet?"

"The very one."

Suddenly the boy felt a knot forming in the pit of his stomach. Of all the bad luck, he had stolen from a prophet. Would he curse him? He remembered the story of the street gang that had threatened the prophet Elisha and how the man had cursed them and God had sent two bears that had mauled them. A shiver ran through his body. Joppa had no bears. It was a coastal town. But who knew what other kinds of curses this prophet might have up his sleeve.

The dock hand laughed. "I wouldn't get too scared. The prophet was blistering angry, but he seemed more anxious to leave on his trip than to chase you down. I don't know what he had in the bags you stole, but he certainly had a lot of gold on him. Enough to pay for his passage."

"Do you think he'll be back?"

"Most likely. But I wouldn't worry about that too much because it's about a three-year trip to Tarshish and back. Besides," he laughed, "he may not even return on that ship. He may have business in Tarshish for a while. Who knows. Maybe he had an argument with the king and had to flee. I wouldn't worry much now. You can't change a thing anyway. But next time you might be a little more careful whom you steal from."

Daud shivered again. Suddenly the evening seemed cold. Jumping up, he headed back for his hiding place. Perhaps he would find something from the prophet's things to trade for food. He hadn't eaten yet that day. Maybe that would make his stomach feel better.

* * * *

Daud walked down the beach whistling. Restless waves from a storm far out at sea sloshed against the sand. It had been several days since the unnerving discovery that he had stolen from a prophet of the God of Israel, but so far nothing bad had happened to him. *They're all a bunch of fakers anyway,* he thought to himself. *People are so superstitious around here. They make up and exaggerate all kinds of stories. Those bears were probably a coincidence anyway.*

I shook my head at his ignorance, but continued to follow him.

The prophet Jonah's bags had contained wonderful things and Daud had been able to trade some for food every day. For the first time in as long as he could remember he went for long walks down the beach just to watch the ocean instead of looking for ways to find food.

A thrashing in the water caught his eye. Some kind of huge fish seemed to be in distress. Daud strained his eyes. It didn't look like anything he had ever seen before, and he had seen every kind of fish brought into the port. This was huge. "It must be a monster," he murmured to himself.

Suddenly his knees turned to jelly, and he crumpled to the sand. This was it. The God of Israel had sent a monster. It was going to crawl out of the sea and eat him for stealing from His prophet.

Sure enough the huge fish monster swam through the breakers and onto the beach. Daud didn't move. What was the point of running away? The huge monster opened and closed its mouth. "God of Israel," the boy shrieked, "if You spare my life, I'll do whatever You want. Anything."

The monster opened its mouth wider, and suddenly with a roar and a rush of the most foul smelling stuff it threw up on the beach. Daud collapsed on the sand, quivering. The creature thrashed its tail and with a struggle that churned up the sand and surf into great whirlpools and eddies, finally turned itself around and disappeared into the sea.

"I thank You, God of Israel," Daud in a shaky voice. "Just tell me what You want me to do."

"Well, you could start by helping me a little bit here," a grumpy voice declared.

The boy nearly jumped out of his skin. He had thought he was alone.

The voice was coming from the foul-smelling pile of sea garbage the fish had vomited on the beach. Suddenly it unfolded itself and sat up.

Daud couldn't stop the piercing scream that escaped his lips. The God of Israel hadn't spared him. He had just used this great fish to vomit up a sea demon, and now he was going to die.

"Oh, shut up," the creature ordered, "and give me a hand here."

Shakily Daud did as he was told.

"I know I must look terrible to you," the being said, "but I'm just a man, so don't act as if you've seen a demon or something. My name is Jonah. I am the prophet of God."

"Jonah." Daud fell to his knees. "I'm so sorry. Really I am. I had no idea. I didn't know you were the prophet of God. I would never have . . ."

"Oh, stop it," the prophet snapped. "I'm not interested in listening to your petty confessions. I'm cold. I'm hungry. I'm ill. I've been in the belly of that fish for three days and have had nothing to eat. Now I would appreciate some help with some of those problems, rather than listening to your babbling."

Daud helped the prophet up the beach to a more comfortable spot to sit.

"There's a little stream that comes down very close to here," the boy said. "You can wash and get a drink there. And while you do that, I will get you something to wear and some food. I'll be right back."

The prophet nodded dismissively, not even saying thank you, and headed for the creek.

While Daud was not sure there was enough water in all Israel to cleanse the stench off of the man, he figured any washing at all would be better than none. Meanwhile he would go back to his hiding place and bring the prophet back some of his own clothes.

By the time the boy returned the prophet was wet and cold and hungry, but smelled much better. Daud set a bag in front of the prophet. "Here," he said, "these are your clothes anyway."

The prophet opened the bag and drew out an expensive warm woolen robe, under things, and a mantel. "So you're the little thief that stole my things at the dock."

The boy nodded miserably.

The prophet shook his head and laughed for the first time. "Perhaps this was all God's plan. He knew I'd need these things. Where's the other bag?"

"It's gone. I sold some of your things for food. Some for me over the past few days and this stuff I brought now." He opened the basket he was carrying. "I got you some bread and some roasted meat and some dried fruit and this goat's skin of milk curds."

"Excellent," the prophet said, then began to eat hungrily while Daud stood on one foot and then the other.

Finally the prophet finished eating, wiped his mouth on his sleeve, and looked up. "Well, what are you waiting for?"

The boy started to put the food back in the basket.

"Where are we going to sleep tonight?" the prophet asked.

Daud shook his head. "I don't have a home. Usually I sleep on the beach."

"On the beach!" The prophet scowled. "Where does your family live?"

"I don't really have a family," Daud said, staring at the ground. "Although some of the dock hands are pretty nice to me."

The prophet scowled more, finally grasping the situation. "Have you eaten?"

"Not yet."

"Well, finish this stuff up." He pulled the food back out of the basket.

"I usually sleep over there." Daud pointed to a place where the rocks made a natural enclosure. "There isn't a cave, exactly, but the rocks shelter me on three sides, so it's less windy. When it rains I sleep under a boat down closer to the docks."

The prophet nodded. "We will sleep in your enclosure and then I need to be on my way in the morning."

"Where are you going?"

Jonah scowled. "Nineveh."

"Nineveh!" the boy exclaimed. "But that's the opposite direction of Tarshish."

"Yes, I know," the prophet growled.

"The traders who come through here say it takes at least a whole month to get to Nineveh by caravan."

The prophet nodded. "Do you know of any heading that way?"

Daud shook his head. "No, the last one left a few days ago. And it will be a long time before the next one. Not that many go there. It's a long ways."

"Yes, I know," Jonah sighed.

"Why do you need to go to Nineveh?"

"For a boy, you ask a lot of questions. Why don't you mind your own business and go to sleep."

With a shrug Daud headed for his sleeping place.

The next morning he awakened and glanced around. Suddenly he sat up with a start. In the light of day the prophet was the most frightening looking person he had ever seen. His unruly mop of black curly hair had turned completely white, as well as his beard, and his skin was white, too. It was not the pale, easily sunburned skin of the northern people, but bone white, like death itself, a total absence of color. Daud shuddered.

"It's about time you woke up," Jonah snapped. "I need to be leaving soon. I've looked through the things in this bag. There were two bags. There's no way you could have used or traded away everything in the other bag. I want you to take me to where you have it hidden and whatever is left of those things we will sell for provisions for my journey."

Without a word Doud got up and headed back for his hiding place. The prophet followed him. Silently the boy pulled out the other bag and the rest of its contents.

The prophet nodded. "Excellent. We can get provisions with this. Now take me to where you do your trading."

Daud did as he was told.

The prophet bartered his belongings for dried fruit, fine flour, and other provisions for his trip. The last item drawn out of the bag was another fine woolen robe. "Here," Jonah said, tossing it to Daud, "wear this. Your clothes are terrible."

"I can't wear something as fine as this," the boy protested. "Everyone will know it's stolen."

"Well, here, I'm giving it to you, so now it's not stolen."

Daud smiled. *In spite of the harshness of the prophet's words, there must be a streak of kindness in there,* he thought. "Thank you," he said simply. He pulled the robe over his ragged clothing. It felt soft and warm and comfortable and too long.

"Here," the prophet said, tossing him a sash, "hitch it up around your waist and then tie the belt like this. There you go. Now you won't fall over your own robe and hurt yourself."

The boy had never felt so handsome in all his life. As he strutted along next to the prophet he held his head high and hoped that all the dock people noticed his rich robe.

"Now," said the prophet, "I have my bag, I have my provisions, and a new walking staff and new sandals. Now I need to be heading off."

"May I come with you?" Daud surprised himself by asking.

Jonah stared at him. "Why would you want to do that?"

"What is there for me here?" The boy paused. "I know I'm just a common dock thief, but I promised the God of Israel that if He spared my life, I would do whatever He wanted me to."

For the first time the prophet's face softened. "I made a promise like that myself," he said slowly.

"Really? When did the God of Israel ever threaten your life?"

The prophet laughed. "I suppose you've forgotten about the big fish that vomited me onto the beach?"

"Oh, I thought that God sent you to me through the fish to punish me for stealing your bags."

"No," Jonah sighed, "I was in the big fish because I was being punished for disobeying God."

"You were disobedient?" Daud asked in surprise. "What did you do?"

"Well, as you observed, I was heading for Tarshish, the opposite direction of Nineveh."

"So?"

"God told me to go to Nineveh. I'm supposed to tell them all that they're terrible sinners and that He's going to destroy their city in 40 days. Would *you* want to do that?"

The boy violently shook his head. "Does God know what the people of Nineveh are like? They'll skin you alive and hang you up on the wall and other terrible things."

"Yes, I know," Jonah frowned, "so I didn't want to go there either."

Suddenly Daud understood. Tarshish was the furthest place from Nineveh that anybody could go in the civilized world. Jonah's reaction made sense to him.

"Now do you still want to go?" the prophet asked.

Shuddering, Daud took a deep breath. "I promised. I wouldn't want the God of Israel to chase me down with a great fish too."

"Well, that makes two of us," the prophet added. "It sounds as if in spite of our great differences, we have something in common. And if I have to walk all the way to Nineveh without even a caravan for protection, I guess I should be glad for a traveling companion, even as young as you are."

Regardless of what might happen when they got to Nineveh, at least the trip would be a great adventure. Together they turned and headed east.

* * * *

The walk to Nineveh was much longer than Daud had expected. It seemed to take forever. However, I enjoyed it immensely. I delighted in listening to Jonah telling stories of the Creator to Daud and watching him drink every detail in like a thirsty sponge. By the time they reached the outskirts of Nineveh, Daud had fallen as deeply in love with the Creator as any Jew had ever done, and in telling the stories of the Mighty One's goodness, Jonah's love for Him had been rekindled, too.

However, it still made me shudder when they discussed Nineveh's destruction.

"Can you imagine how fabulous that will be?" Daud chortled to Jonah. "With the capital city of Israel's enemy destroyed in one blow without any soldiers from our side dying or even having to go into battle. That will be just like Jericho and those other cities!"

Jonah nodded. They both eagerly looked forward to watching the Ninevites roast.

Topping the crest of a slight rise, they suddenly caught their first glimpse of the city. It took their breath away. Perched alongside the Tigris River, it had beautiful gardens and a high, thick wall.

"Now, remember," Jonah reminded, "we'll go in there to do our preaching, but we're going to sleep outside the city gates every night. That way we can watch it go up in flames."

"Don't worry," Daud assured him, "I won't lose track of the days. I don't want to accidentally be inside when that happens."

"Good lad. Now, let's go tell them what's going to happen and then we'll find out if we'll still be alive in 40 days."

"I think that if God could protect His people through all those stories you were telling me, that He could take care of us if He wanted to. If He went to all the trouble to have you rescued out of the middle of the ocean by a fish, He can certainly keep you safe even in a big city like this."

Together they entered the city.

* * * *

Daud picked up the food basket. "I'm heading down to get our food for today and a few extra things for our trip home."

"Good," the prophet replied, "but don't take too long in the city. Today is the day."

With a nod Daud started toward Nineveh.

He and the prophet had built a small shelter up on a rise where they could watch the city. A little vine had mysteriously sprung up overnight and crawled all over the shelter so that it was shady and relatively cool from the blistering summer heat.

God had been good to them. They had preached in Nineveh and no one had killed them. In fact, the king himself came out to hear the prophet's declaration of doom. He had called his wise men and asked them what they thought. After slaughtering several animals and closely examining their kidneys, livers, and entrails, they agreed that the signs were ominous. Everyone knew that the God of Israel was powerful and that if He wanted to destroy, He probably could. The king had gone into mourning. The people of Nineveh knew enough about Israelite customs to put on sackcloth and ashes. They even put them on the animals just to be safe. Having heard that the God of Israel stressed justice and repentance, everyone from the highest to the lowest in the city had repented and prayed to the God of Israel for deliverance.

The inhabitants of the city had seemed so sincere that it didn't seem near as exciting to Daud now to see Nineveh destroyed. In fact, he felt sorry for the people. However, Jonah's attitude did not change. "It's not a real conversion," he snapped the night before when they had been talking about it. "These filthy heathens are polytheistic, and just because they accept that the God of Israel may be more powerful than their gods, doesn't make them His people. Although they may acknowledge God's power, they still deserve to be destroyed for everything they've done. Besides, they're our enemies."

The boy had remained silent. It wasn't his place to argue with Jonah, and he wasn't sure what he would say anyway. The God of Israel was a deity of justice, but in the stories He seemed so merciful, too. It was all terribly confusing.

Daud knocked at the gate of the court kitchens.

"Enter, servant of the prophet of the God of Israel," the steward said. "You've come for provisions for the day?"

"Yes," the boy said.

The man took his basket and started loading it. "Ironic isn't it," he laughed. "We're all fasting and praying while you and your prophet are eating well."

"Servants of the God of Israel have no reason to be afraid of Him," Daud commented.

The steward nodded. "Hopefully He will accept our repentance and let us be His servants, too."

The boy just stood in silence.

"The king would have been happy for us to cook for you and provide all your provisions."

"Yes, I know," Daud mumbled. "That's very kind of him, but . . ."

"I understand. You Jews eat such strange things and have such strange restrictions."

"Our God asks us to. The prophet told me all about it. It's in the laws of Moses."

"Really?" the steward said. "I would like to learn more about that."

Daud thought about the man's question. Here was a whole city full of people wanting to know more about the God of Israel, yet after tomorrow there would be nothing here but charred earth. The boy shook his head. He just couldn't think about it right now.

"Here you go," the steward said, handing him the basket. "The king has asked that you also take royal greetings back to your master, and tell him that his offer is still open to become a royal adviser."

"I will tell him," Daud replied, edging toward the door.

"The king's advisers live pretty well," the man pointed out. "Your master would become a very wealthy man. Much more wealthy than being a royal adviser in the court of the king of Israel."

"I'll tell him," Daud repeated. "And thank you for the food."

"It's the least we can do. Perhaps you and your master will put in a good word for us with your God."

Although Daud thought it very unlikely, he said nothing.

The boy and the prophet had sat up all night and all day watching and nothing had happened. Now it was sundown and Nineveh still stood. Even from their distance they could hear the sounds of rejoicing and feasting and music as the people celebrated the mercy of the God of Israel who had heard their prayers of confession.

Secretly Daud felt relieved. But Jonah was furious and paced back and forth. The boy sat hunched over inside their little vine covered hut, trying to make himself as small and inconspicuous as possible. Jonah's reaction frightened him. The prophet seemed to be talking to someone that Daud could not see.

"You've made a fool of me," he shouted, then a pause. "Yes, You have. You sent me here to tell them they would be destroyed in 40 days. I told them just like You said I should, and what happened? Nothing. Not a single thing." Another pause. "Yes, I know You're merciful to those who worship You, but these people don't worship You. Yes, I know they confessed with sackcloth and ashes, but what does that have to do with it? They're Assyrians! They're heathens!" Another pause. "Well, let's just say You're a pushover, You can be bought!"

Daud cringed. How could this man talk this way to God? Even if he was a special prophet? I cringed, too. How could any human make such accusations against the Creator?

"Oh," Jonah said after a pause, "yes, I am thankful that You listen to prayers of repentance, and yes, I am fortunate that You are easy on sinners who repent, but—" He groaned as he kicked at something and stubbed his toe. Limping into the little shelter, he barked at Daud, "We may as well get some sleep. We'll leave here tomorrow."

"What are we going to do?" the boy asked.

"I don't know. Go home, I guess."

Daud awakened with a start. Something was different. Then he realized that the sun was in his eyes. Had he fallen asleep outside? He looked above him. No, the structure of their little hut was still there, but the vines were all gone. He jumped up and took a look. The plant had shriveled up and the sun was beating on both him and the prophet.

The prophet sat up. "What did you do?" he snapped. "All our shade is gone."

"I didn't do anything," Daud protested. "Something's happened to the plant. It died."

"Well it couldn't perish that rapidly!"

Daud just raised one eyebrow. Jonah was right. It didn't make sense that the plant had died so quickly, but obviously it had, so what was the point of him arguing about it? He knew that to point out something like that to the prophet would only make him more angry, so he just stood and said nothing.

Jonah poked around the roots. "Ah, look at this. A worm ate through it right here." He kicked the stick supporting the corner of the booth and the whole hut collapsed. Then he strode off to his praying place. "This is all Your fault," he shouted to the cloudless sky. "You could have prevented this vine from dying. You're the Creator. You can do anything. You could have had mercy on a poor little vine."

"Yes," he said after a pause. "Yes, people are more important than vines. Why?" "Yes, I suppose that 120,000 people are more important than a vine. Are you saying that I care more about the vine than people?" "Oh, You are. But they're Assyrians, they don't count." "Are You sure that they count to You, God of Israel?"

Finally Jonah returned. "I guess we've been giving Him the wrong title," he said.

"He's not the God of Israel?" Daud asked in surprise.

Jonah grimaced. "He's the God of the whole world. The God of the universe. He created everyone, even the Assyrians. And now He's had mercy on them. The plan has changed."

"What are we going to do now?"

"I guess we're going to go down to Nineveh and live with them at least for a little while. If God really cares this much about these people, I guess as His prophet I should too. I will accept the king's offer to be an adviser and teach them a little more about the God of Assyria." He said it so slowly, as if it was almost painful for him to say out loud.

Daud jumped to his feet. "That's great! Some of them are really nice people, and the steward in the palace has been very kind to me and . . ."

"Yes," Jonah interrupted. "The Lord God told me that those who have received His kindness and mercy should show kindness and mercy to others. The king is offering that to us, and since both of us have received God's kindness and mercy and forgiveness, I guess we can show it to the king, too."

Daud grabbed his basket, and Jonah picked up his robe and his walking stick, and together they entered the city.

Delighted, I followed them. It was amazing to me how the Mighty One was able to use these stubborn and grumpy humans to bring blessings and mercy to others. He never ceased to amaze me with His goodness. It had been a good assignment after all.

JOSHUA

ather burst into the family quarters, brimming with excitement. He grabbed Joshua and swung him in the air. "You are so lucky to be alive at this time in history," he said, setting him down gently. "The most amazing things are happening."

"What? What?" Joshua sputtered.

Father's excitement was contagious.

"Grab your mother and your sisters. I want to tell you all at once," Father said.

By this time everyone had gathered to see what the exciting news was.

"As you know, King Ahaz has not been feeling real well lately, so he is making Prince Hezekiah a coruler with him."

"But that has happened before with other kings."

"Yes, but that's not what I want to tell you about. I would never be excited that my king was feeling too ill to rule by himself. The exciting thing is that Prince Hezekiah is much more interested in the old religion. King Ahaz has pretty much ignored the God of Abraham as have many other kings before him. But Prince Hezekiah has studied the old ways. He has sent envoys to King Hoshea of Israel inviting anyone from Israel who still worships the Lord God to join us here in Jerusalem for the Passover. To celebrate the Passover at all right now is very exciting. It hasn't been done in years and years. But to have all of Jehovah's worshipers from both kingdoms celebrating Passover at once—well, nothing like this has happened since the glorious days of

King Solomon. And we are right here in the middle of it. People will be traveling here from all over the place. And we live here!"

"Do people still remember how to do Passover?" Joshua asked.

"Moses wrote everything down," Father explained. "We have all of our records. And we even still have some priests and Levites. Although with the Temple being unused, they've had to do other things for a living. Now they are going to tidy it up so that we won't be embarrassed when everyone shows up for Passover."

"That's wonderful," his son exclaimed. "Do you get to be part of it? Do you get to work in the Temple?"

Father shook his head. "No, we are from the tribe of Judah. Our family has been serving the king and the king's family for many, many years. That's what we do. People from the tribe of Levi take care of the Temple. They have divided their duties up among the different families. Those descended from Aaron became the priests, those from Korah sang in the choir, and those descended from some of the other Levites took care of the Temple—the actual maintenance and polishing and all the other jobs that go with it. But we will go there to worship. And when I take messages from the king to there, I will take you with me so you can see how things are progressing."

"That's great!" his son shouted, jumping up and down.

Even though he was still a little boy, he knew he would be a man eventually, and he could hardly wait to serve the king like his father.

Joshua's family worshiped the Lord God, but they had done it secretly in their home because King Ahaz did not.

Father had told his son many stories about Moses and how their ancestors had been slaves in Egypt. When he described the Red Sea splitting apart and the water piling up on either side, Joshua could feel its cold, wet spray on his face and sensed the urgency with which the Israelites must have rushed to cross before the walls tumbled back in, covering everything with water.

"I'm going down to the Temple later today," Father told him, "so keep your eyes open and be ready when I come by for you."

"Can we go, too?" Joshua's little sisters asked.

"No, I'm afraid not. But we will all be a part of the big Passover celebration." The boy smiled at his sisters. "Someday you'll be old enough to do more things like me. But you must remember that you're women and you just can't do everything we men can."

Father smiled and winked at his son. Joshua felt very important and grown up, even though he was only 7 years old.

Later that day as he rode on his father's shoulders through the streets, they came upon a great commotion. Men were using two large poles as levers to topple the Baal image on the corner, and then people were pounding it into bits with stone hammers and wooden clubs.

"What are they doing?" he asked his father.

"They're destroying the Baals," Father replied happily. "King Hezekiah has men going through the entire city and destroying all the Baal altars with their pillars and incense stands. Also, they will cut down all the Asherah poles and the groves where idol worship takes place. We're going to make Jerusalem God's city again."

"Does this mean that it doesn't have to be a secret anymore?"

"What?"

"That we worship the God Jehovah. That we don't like Baal."

"Yes," Father explained, "that's what it means."

Joshua clapped his hands. "Father, let me down. May I help hit the Baal?"

The pillar and its incense altar had already been shattered into pieces, but Joshua and his father stomped on several fragments and broke them further. Soon many of the shards were just small pieces of grit to be tracked around the city on the bottoms of people's sandals.

"That's what happens when you're only made of stone or clay," Father said.

"Jehovah God isn't made of clay, is He?" his son asked.

"No, Jehovah God is a spirit. No one can touch Him or hurt Him physically no matter what they do. He is more powerful than the strongest warrior on earth."

"I'm glad."

As they neared the Temple they heard a great deal of shouting.

"Who is it?" Joshua asked, pointing to the man standing by the statue of the Nehoshten, the bronze serpent that God had Moses make during the wilderness wandering.

"It's the prophet Isaiah. He's a cousin of the king and a friend and adviser to Prince Hezekiah."

"You have made this thing into an idol," Isaiah proclaimed. "This was only supposed to be a symbol to direct your attention to the God Jehovah."

"Is that true?" Joshua whispered, tugging on his father's robe.

"Remember the story I told you?" he said, leaning down to speak in the boy's ear.

Joshua nodded. He remembered his Father describing how Moses had led the rebellious Hebrew ex-slaves of Egypt. Poisonous snakes had swarmed through their camp and bitten many of the people. Hundreds died. Moses had made a snake out of bronze and wound it around a pole. Then he held it up. God wanted the people to look at it, and if they did, they would be healed. The ones who did had not died. Joshua could never understand why something as simple as looking at a bronze snake could heal them. Even harder to understand was why somebody would not look when it would be so easy. His father had explained to him that no matter how simple God made it for people to turn to Him, some people just refused His offers of healing and blessing and protection.

"Sometimes people are just stupid," he had remarked to his father.

I had to agree. It seemed that humans were that way. And certainly they had acted that way about the bronze serpent. For though Moses had created it to draw people's attention to God and His willingness to heal them, and though it was a symbol of someday the Son of God being lifted up on a pole at the cross so that everyone could look to Him and be saved, the people had missed the point. Over the years they had treated the bronze serpent with great reverence. Now it even had a name, Nehoshten, and they were burning incense to it.

With a mighty thud the prophet Isaiah chopped down the pole the serpent was on. Then he lead the people in destroying it. The pieces of bronze that remained were melted and used for something else.

Joshua was confused. "Is that right for him to do that?" he asked his father.

His father just looked at him. "He is God's prophet," he said, "so I suppose that is what the Lord wants."

"But Moses made it. Doesn't that make it sacred?"

Father laughed. "Moses was a great leader. He was the one who led us out of Egypt and helped transform a bunch of ignorant and badly abused people into a mighty nation. But that didn't make him a god. The Lord told us not to worship any graven images. I suppose that includes this one. If people had not worshiped Nehoshten instead of God, I guess it could have remained forever as a reminder of what the Lord did for them in the wilderness. But it is better not to have it at all, than to have people worshiping it."

"I guess so," Joshua mumbled, although he thought it was sad that something that old and that special with such a story behind it was gone.

"I want you to remember all of this," his father told him. "Remember Nehoshten and what happened to it. Remember this Passover. It hasn't happened since the time of Solomon and it may not happen again. You must remember. Someday you will serve the king just as I do and perhaps even be an adviser to him."

The boy nodded solemnly. "I will."

* * * *

The years passed quickly. Joshua had officially become a man and took his place at his father's side serving in the palace. King Ahaz had finally died and been buried in Jerusalem. And now Hezekiah was king in his own right.

Terrible things had happened to the nation of Israel to the north. The Assyrians had completely destroyed it and taken many of its people captive. The Assyrians scattered their conquered peoples throughout their kingdom so that they totally lost track of their families and tribes. And no one in Judah knew where to contact all of them, for there were little pockets of them everywhere. It was the Assyrians way of assimilating them and making sure that there weren't enough people of Israel anywhere to lead a rebellion. Israel as a nation was gone and destroyed as the prophets had predicted through all their years of idolatry. (Fortunately, though, many others from the northern kingdom had left Israel and settled around Jerusalem so they could worship the God of Abraham, Isaac, and Jacob.)

"Our nation must turn to God," Hezekiah told Joshua and his father.

"Yes, your majesty," Father said, "it has. You've destroyed the Baals and the groves and the Asherah poles and the altars and the high places. We celebrated one last Passover with the people of Israel before they were destroyed."

Hezekiah nodded. "The Lord God said that if His people would humble themselves and pray, that He would heal their land. Right now we're still threatened by the Assyrians just like everyone else in the world. But I feel that if our whole country put its whole heart into worshiping Him and serving Him and turning away from all of the mistakes that we have made and the evil things that we have committed, then perhaps He would keep us safe. One of the things I have been really concerned about is the Temple.

"While it is open now and we are having services again, it's in very bad physical shape. The years have not been good to it, and it does not appear that many repairs have been done since the days of Solomon. I would like to put you and your son in charge of the repair program. The doors on the Temple look terrible. They need to be repaired or replaced. The gold leaf has crumbled away in many places. And we need to replace some of the furniture."

"The furniture?" Joshua asked.

"You know the big bronze altar over in the side of the courtyard?" When Joshua nodded, the king continued, "That used to be in the center. Solomon had it built for the sacrifices. But my father found another altar that he liked better and had it put it there. But that one is actually a pagan Assyrian altar. I would like it removed and replaced with the original altar. I want everything that God Himself did not ask for in the writings of Moses now removed. And I want everything repaired. I want His Temple to be perfect and just as He desires it so that He will feel delighted to reside in Jerusalem with us."

Joshua's father turned to him. "Will you draw up some plans? We will discuss them with the king tomorrow."

Though young by some people's standards, Joshua had already shown excellent organizational skills, and making plans for maintenance and repair of the Temple sounded more exciting than anything he had ever been asked to do.

It delighted me to be recording the life of someone so enthusiastically committed to worshiping our Creator. So many of my in-between assignments that I've not included here had been sad and discouraging.

* * * *

"Wake up, Joshua," his father said, nudging him.

"What? What is it? Have I overslept?"

"No," his father laughed. "You're the first one up every morning. But we need to go to the palace. The king has summoned me, and I want you to come along."

"What's the matter? Is the king upset with something?"

"No, but he's getting worse."

Joshua threw off his sleeping cloak and stood. He knew the king hadn't been feeling well lately and that he had some kind of open wound. But he hadn't paid much attention to it. After all, his primary concern had been with the reconstruction and repair of the Temple. And though the work had gone well for several years, Joshua was a perfectionist and spent most of his time at the work site. He loved just being near the Temple, feeling that it was the closest place in the whole country to the physical presence of the God of Judah.

Soon he and his father hurried to the palace. As they entered the king's chamber, Joshua recoiled from a horrible stench.

Joshua's father glanced at him. "It's the wound on the king's leg," he whispered. "It has become infected and the poison has gone through his entire body. The king is dying."

Although Joshua remained near the doorway because of the overpowering smell, Father approached and touched the king's hand.

"Ah, my good friend," the king said faintly. "You are here."

"Yes," Father murmured. "Your majesty, you know that I would do anything in my power to help you. Is there anything I can do?"

The king closed his eyes a moment, then opened them. "Send for the prophet."

Joshua's heart leaped at the request. Of course, God could take care of this. He could take care of anything.

Father turned to his son and their eyes met. "I'll go," Joshua said, rushing out the door.

He knew where the prophet Isaiah lived. Isaiah often came to the Temple. During breaks Joshua would go over and listen to him. Although he didn't always understand the things the prophet said, he liked Isaiah and considered his poetry beautiful. As Joshua hurried down the corridor and rounded the corner a sandaled foot stuck out from a doorway and tripped him. Sprawling in the hallway, Joshua skinned the palms of his hands and knees and banged his chin hard on the stone pavement. His face reddening, he rolled over and looked up into the laughing face of the king's son, Manasseh.

"Prince Manasseh," Joshua said slowly, "I didn't see you there."

Manasseh laughed harshly. "Well, of course, that was the point, wasn't it? Wouldn't have been any fun if you had seen me."

Joshua made a mental note that he hadn't noticed it being fun anyway, but said nothing.

"You think you're important strutting around the palace here doing all these repair jobs for my father," the prince sneered.

Joshua stood to his feet and looked at him calmly. "I do feel very honored to be doing these things for the king," he said slowly, "and I can't think of anything more important than pleasing the God of Judah and making His home a place where He wants to be with us. It's important not just for our religious life, but for the safety of our nation. I believe that if He dwells here with us in Jerusalem and we make Him welcome, then we won't have to make the Assyrians welcome."

"Ahhhhh, the Assyrians. What a bunch of cowards you all are," Manasseh exploded. "You know we could fight them if we had to."

"Yes, we could," Joshua replied. "But the prophets have told us that if we don't return to God we'll be destroyed."

"The prophets I could deal with—if my father wasn't so dependent on them. You all make me sick."

Abruptly he turned and headed back to the royal apartments. Joshua shook his head. He knew that Manasseh would be king when Hezekiah was gone, so it would be wise not to antagonize him if he could help it.

"Oh, God of Judah," he whispered, "please be with the king and preserve his life and help him live a very long time. At least long enough for Prince Manasseh to gain some wisdom."

I wondered when that would be and whether any human could ever live quite that long. Manasseh, though still very young, was also extremely headstrong and was already making his choices very clear. With a shudder I hoped that King Hezekiah would live a long time, too.

Now Joshua ran through the dark streets and banged on Isaiah's door. It only took a few moments for the man to grab his cloak and follow him back to the palace.

The prophet approached the king's bed.

"Isaiah, my old friend," Hezekiah said.

Smiling, Isaiah took the king's hand. "Neither of us are that old," he said.

Hezekiah sighed. "Perhaps. But today I feel ancient."

The king was silent a moment.

"I asked you to come so that you could ask the Lord if I could be healed, or whether I'm going to die."

Sadly Isaiah looked down at the king. He seemed to struggle for words, then swallowing hard, declared, "The Lord God of Judah says that you will die."

The king made a sound as if someone had punched him in the stomach. All his breath come out in one gasp. "Die! The Lord says I'm going to die!"

Tears filled Isaiah's eyes. "I'm sorry," he murmured.

The king turned on his side and sobbed. Everyone in the room became uncomfortable, though the king seemed to forget that they were even there. "Oh, Lord God," he cried, "I've tried so hard to serve You. I've done everything I could think of to make Judah a better place and to make my people worship You. I have used my wealth to restore the Temple and to make this a place that You would want to come. I don't want to die. I want to live here and be Your king."

As Hezekiah continued to sob and pray the prophet slipped out of the room and headed for home. Several of the others present in the room also left and stood outside.

Joshua felt the tears welling in his own eyes. He didn't want the king to die either. Finding a place to sit in a nearby courtyard, he watched the dust motes drift in a beam of sunlight.

Suddenly he became aware of someone next to him. "It's my father, isn't it?" Prince Manasseh demanded.

Joshua nodded, not sure if his voice would work.

"I heard someone say that he's dying. Is that true?"

Again Joshua nodded. "The prophet Isaiah was just here. He inquired of God and God said it was true."

"That means I'm going to be king. Joash became king when he was 7, so I'm plenty old enough."

Turning, Joshua stared at him. "But what about your father?"

"Well, he's dying—that would make me king, right?"

God have mercy on Judah, Joshua thought. With Prince Manasseh as king, the nation would need God's mercy abundantly.

Just then the prophet hurried back across the courtyard toward the king's chamber.

"He's back," Joshua murmured to himself. "Maybe God changed His mind."

"Jehovah God doesn't change His mind," Manasseh said scornfully.

"He has a few times in history."

"No, no," the boy persisted. "My father's dying. It's time for me to be king."

"Let's go see what the prophet has to say," Joshua said, not wanting to argue.

Isaiah burst into the royal bed chamber and, without waiting to be acknowledged, strode to the side of the sobbing king. "Your majesty," he began, "the Lord God has heard your prayers and is going to grant your wish. You will not die, but live."

Hezekiah rolled over on his back and turned his tear-stained face to the prophet. "I will?"

"God will add 15 years to your life."

"Fifteen years," the king repeated. "Oh, thank You, God of Judah."

"Now," Isaiah continued, "we need to do something about this leg. Someone bring me some dried figs."

While the servants hurried away to get the items the prophet requested, he spoke further with the king.

"Are you sure?" Hezekiah asked. "I don't feel any different."

"Of course, I'm sure. You asked me to inquire of the Lord and I did."

"Well, do you think He would give me a sign?"

Isaiah shook his head in frustration.

I couldn't blame Him. Humans were such doubters. They would make huge requests from the God of the universe, and then when He granted them, ask for proof. Fortunately the Almighty is much more patient than either Isaiah or myself.

"Yes," Isaiah said, "He will give you a sign. The Lord will make the sun stand still and move the sundial back 10 degrees."

Everyone knew how proud the king was of his special sundial in the royal garden. He had built two staircases in the gardens, a copy of one constructed by astronomers in Egypt. When the sun shone on the stairs, it also told the time.

No one had ever heard of the shadow of a sundial moving backward before. In fact, it seemed impossible. Certainly if the Lord did this, it would be a sign. Yet the prophet nonchalantly assured him that God would do it.

* * * *

Joshua stood and stretched. It had been a long day. His steps quickened as he walked toward his family's apartments in the palace.

It didn't seem as if it had been that long since he had been a little boy following his father around and listening to the advice that he gave to King Hezekiah.

Hezekiah was still king, though Joshua's father had died during the summer fevers the month before. Some days Joshua felt lost without him. Father had been a tower of strength to him during the siege and the problems with Sennacherib and then during the king's sickness. Now he was gone and Joshua knew that the 15 years the Lord had given King Hezekiah were almost up, too. Joshua now had his own family and two little sons, yet he still missed his father.

He was just entering the main gates of the palace when a servant ran up to him. "The king wants to see you right away. Some ambassadors from Babylon have arrived."

Joshua turned and headed toward the king's chambers.

"Babylon," Hezekiah quickly explained to him, "is a city also subject to Assyria. It has great astronomers. They saw the sign of the sundial that the Lord gave me back during my illness."

The foreign ambassadors bowed. "We have journeyed here to find out more. And about the power of a God that can change the courses of even heavenly bodies."

Hezekiah smiled. "Not only did the Lord extend my life, but He has honored my kingdom with great wealth. I will show you everything that He has given me."

Joshua realized that he needed to make sure that everything at the Temple was perfect, for surely the king would bring the ambassadors down there to see what Judah had done to honor its God. And though they could not enter the Temple, surely they would at least want to see the Lord's dwelling place in Judah.

Busy entertaining the ambassadors, the king dismissed everyone else. Joshua returned to the Temple to talk with the priests before he headed home. It had been a long day, but he wasn't tired anymore.

Early the next morning Joshua checked in with the priests.

Everything was right on schedule and the daily sacrifices had started. He walked around the courtyard. Though it was busy and noisy with the bleating of goats and sheep as they were brought in for sacrifice, nothing appeared out of place. The bronze altar and the huge laver had been polished to a high sheen. Satisfied, he went on his way.

Toward sundown a servant found Joshua and announced, "The king is holding a banquet for the Babylonian ambassadors. You are invited."

Joshua turned and looked at him. "Were the ambassadors impressed with the Temple?"

"Yes, but they spent most of their time in the Temple treasury and the palace."

"The treasury?" Joshua asked in surprise.

"The king showed him all his riches," the man explained. "After all, he's one of the wealthiest kings we've had since Solomon."

"Yes, I know. But why would he show that to strangers from another country? It seems unsafe."

The servant shrugged. "I'm sure our king had his reasons."

Joshua shook his head. "I thought sure that Hezekiah would want to spend more time at the rest of the Temple. But I will come to the palace."

As Joshua walked slowly back to the palace, he felt bitterly disappointed. Ever since his youth the Temple had been the most important thing in his life. He had assumed that it was just as important to King Hezekiah. And since it was the God of Judah who made the shadow on the sundial retreat backward, surely that's what the astronomers from Babylon would want to know more about. He couldn't understand his king's behavior.

I also shook my head. It made no sense to me either. But I felt an even greater danger looming than Joshua did as the king continued to show off his wealth.

BEULAH

eulah sat in the corner of the room under her heavy veils, as frightened as she had ever been in her entire life. The wailing and screaming around her drowned out any thoughts she might have, and she sat numb with her fingers pressed firmly against her lips. What would happen to her now? She felt lost and even more afraid than when her father had brought her here and left her to be the wife of Jobab. Only 8 years old, she had clung to her mother and cried and begged to remain in her home.

Her father just laughed and pulled her away. "I'll never get another dowry offer like this. And you'll be the wife of a palace servant. You'll have a much better life than staying here with your mother and me, and"—he smiled to himself—"I'll do well by it myself."

"Besides," her father continued, "if 8 years old is old enough to be king of Judah, it's certainly old enough to take a husband."

It was true. King Josiah had become king at age 8 when servants had killed his father, King Ammon.

He must have felt like this, the girl thought. But then she shook her head. Hardly! That death had made him king of Israel. This death left her a young widow with no children and no rights, little better than a slave in the house of her in-laws. No, it wasn't the same. No one could understand how she felt.

The day passed in a blur. The burial finished and the mourners left. Then the arguing began.

"According to the ancient law, now she's mine," her brother-in-law, Elam, suddenly announced. "I get her. That's what Moses said."

Her mother-in-law, Ada, stood in the middle of the room with her hands on her hips. "Yes, but bear in mind that she's just a little girl. She was too young to be married to your brother, and she's too young to be married to you. Besides, she's a widow right now. Give her some time."

"What does she need time for?" he protested. "Staying busy will be the best way to get over it. Besides she and Jobab weren't married long enough for her to become very attached to him."

Beulah sat motionless, listening. It was true. She had hardly known Jobab. Her father had sold her to get her off his hands. While her mother-in-law had lectured the girl's husband about how young his wife was, and although he had been kind to her when he was around, still he had spent little time with her and mostly ignored her for, after all, she was just a little girl.

"Well, then, Elam," his mother snapped, "think about this. If you take your brother's wife, as Moses' law says, and have children with her, the child will be your firstborn, but he will inherit only Jobab's properties and not yours."

Ada could see a light dawning in her son's head. She shook her head. *When all else fails, appeal to their greed,* she sighed to herself.

"Oh well," he said, "she'll be more attractive when she's a little older anyway." And he stalked out of the room.

The woman turned to the young girl. "Elam was right about one thing. Staying busy will be the best way for you to get through this. I am going to keep you with me all the time and train you to be my assistant. It will give you a little more security in your life. And hopefully it will keep you out of the way of these men."

As she sat down her voice softened. "A woman has no value if she is widowed and has no sons. And you are so young. Yet a skilled midwife is treated well. And later, when you're older, you can bear children. For now you can stay with me and assist me. As you know I'm the midwife to the royal family. There are so many of them that it will keep us busy and you will learn much."

The girl didn't know what to think. She had been afraid to get married, afraid of leaving her mother. Jobab had been kind to her and yet he had been a very short-tempered man, which was what had triggered the brawl that left her a widow.

"Thank you," she said gratefully to her mother-in-law. "I will work very hard and do whatever you want."

"I know you will," Ada smiled back at her. "We will work well together."

Beulah took a deep breath. Somehow she sensed that it was the beginning of a whole new chapter in her life.

True to her word, Ada kept the girl with her all the time. She immediately started instructing Beulah in the art of assisting with birth. The woman taught her about the stages of normal labor and some of the problems that could occur as well as about a few of the herbs and simple remedies that eased some of the pain for the new mothers.

But no amount of coaching could have prepared Beulah for her first birth. She was fascinated and horrified and delighted all at the same time. Fascinated with the process, horrified at the amount of suffering crammed into those few hours, and delighted with the miracle of life at the end.

"Beulah," Ada said as the little one nursed drowsily with his mother, "in our pack is a package of salt. Get that out and when this little one is finished eating, we'll rub him with that to help clean him. Then we wrap him in this long piece of swaddling cloth. That will make him feel secure so that he'll rest better. And it will make his limbs grow strong and straight."

The girl rummaged in the bag and pulled out the coarse salt. Her mother-in-law took the infant and held him in her arms, facing the light from the doorway, her lips moving. Beulah could barely make out a word her and there. Something about a rod of Jesse and the Messiah. She would have to ask later.

"Have you and your husband talked about what you're going to name him?" Ada asked as she turned and started rubbing the baby with the salt.

The new mother smiled. "We've considered several names, but we haven't decided on anything yet. I suppose we'll still be discussing it right up to the day he is circumcised."

"It happened that way at our house, too," Ada said. "It's hard to come up with the right name and meaning when it can affect their whole life."

Names were very important. Baby boys were circumcised on the eighth day, and that was the time for the naming ceremony.

As Ada and Beulah walked toward home, the girl asked, "What were you doing when you were holding the baby and whispering?"

Ada glanced at her sharply. "Oh, you heard that?"

"I did. I heard something about a rod of Jesse."

"Well, ever since Eve, every baby boy that has come into the world has been an exciting occasion for its mother. I always pray that this new baby will be the hope of Israel."

"Yes, I've heard of that before," the girl said. "But what's the Jesse thing?"

"When I was a little girl, a prophet named Isaiah visited the palace quite a bit. He prophesied that a rod would come out of Jesse and that it would lead to a government that would last forever."

"The Messiah?"

Ada nodded.

"So who was Jesse?"

"Jesse was King David's father. And, as you know, the royal family of Judah is descended from King David, so anyone who is related to the royal family could give birth to the Messiah. I always pray for the babies that one of them might be the hope of Israel and Judah, the Messiah, and that He will take away all of these horrible things around us."

"That would be wonderful," Beulah said. "But what happened to the prophet? Is he still around?"

Ada frowned and shook her head. "No. When I was a little girl the king was named Manasseh. For most of his life he was a very evil man. He even brought a big wooden idol into the Temple and people actually worshiped it right there in God's holy place. Idol worship was everywhere. Jerusalem was not a safe place to be. The prophet Isaiah spoke out against all of these things and so, of course, the king hated him."

"Did the king do something to him?"

The woman sighed. "He had him stuffed inside a log and sawed in half."

Beulah shuddered. "That's horrible."

"Yes, it was. But horrible things happened to King Manasseh, too. The Assyrians took him prisoner and dragged him to Babylon with a hook through his nose."

"Through his nose!" the girl exclaimed.

"Yes, if he got too tired or fell down, it just ripped out and they stuck it back in again."

Beulah shuddered. "That is horrible, but it sounds as if it served him right."

"In the end, God is always just and fair. But while he was in Babylon, Manasseh repented and he actually returned here to Judah. Unfortunately, all of the people who worshiped idols with him back in his rowdy days continued to worship idols. He came back pretty much a broken man. When he died his son became king, and we were hoping for some strong godly leadership."

"But Ammon wasn't king very long," Beulah replied. "I know that story."

"Well, the reason he wasn't king very long," Ada whispered confidentially, "is because he was so evil. Israel couldn't afford to have another 55 years of evil leadership. Your husband and his father, my husband, were involved in that. But that's a family secret you must never share. His servants assassinated King Ammon when he had been king for only three months. That's how King Josiah got to be king so young. Now we are watching closely to see what kind of a king he is. So far he hasn't been too bad. But I still pray over every baby that he will be the Messiah and that Judah will go back to worshiping the Creator-God. I pray for Josiah every day, too, as he grows up."

"I will, too," Beulah announced. "Being the king of a country has to be a difficult job. And the king is the same age as I am."

"He is. But there's no age limits on whom God can use in His plans. He uses anyone who makes themselves available to Him."

"Even people from a family like mine?" the girl asked hesitantly.

"Of course. You're a daughter of Abraham and a child of the tribe of Judah. And besides, you're in *my* family now, and we serve the Lord."

Beulah smiled. "I'm glad. I want to, also."

* * * *

Breathlessly Beulah hurried along at her mother-in-law's side. They were on their way to the palace. The girl had helped with several births now, but this was her first royal birth. The others had been lesser members of the royal family or their servants. Today the queen was in labor. The hours dragged painfully by. The progress of the young queen's labor was slow.

"It often is," Ada explained, soothingly, pushing the damp hair off of the woman's forehead. "Your next child will be much easier."

The mother-to-be queen just moaned softly.

Beulah's mind wandered to the discussion that had taken place on the rooftop the previous night after dinner.

"Those potions you give these women, Mother," Elam, her brother-in-law, said, "don't you think you're defying God? Women are supposed to suffer with childbirth."

Ada's eyes flashed. Elam loved starting arguments with his mother. "I don't think it is ever the plan of the Mighty One for His people to suffer," she replied. "Especially when giving new life."

"Of course it is," he continued. "We've read you Scripture. It was God's curse to women for bringing sin into the world."

"Yes, you've read me from the Torah. Isn't that the same Scripture that says that men will have to work by the sweat of their brow in order to provide bread for their families?"

Her son nodded uncertainly.

"Well, does that mean that if you serve at the court where you're indoors and have some slave fanning you that you are defying God's wishes, because you aren't perspiring enough?"

He shifted uncomfortably in his seat.

Jeremiah, whom Elam usually referred to as the weird cousin, laughed out loud. "She's got you there," he said.

"I refuse to argue the scriptures with an ignorant woman," Elam snapped. "These kinds of discussion are best suited to men who have studied such things."

Ada laughed and put her hands on her hips. "That's Elam's usual response when he doesn't have an answer and doesn't want to admit he's lost an argument."

Jeremiah chuckled again.

The woman turned to her nephew. "It's good to hear you laugh, Jeremiah. It doesn't happen much these days."

"There's not much to laugh about," he grimaced.

"Nonsense. Things are going well. We have a king who loves God and Judah is prosperous."

"Judah is nearing disaster," he said slowly. "Remember all the prophecies? How many kings have been told that great disaster is coming, but because of their faithfulness to God it would be put off until they died and it would then happen to their children and their children's children? Do you think that will continue forever?"

His aunt put her arm around him. "You worry too much. And I think you spend too much time at the Temple. At your age you should be involved in other things. Have some fun."

Jeremiah shrugged. "I am having fun. Studying the Lord's Word is the most important thing I can do with my life."

"Well, it sure has made you too sober," Elam said. "I don't know what your problem is, but I think maybe some of Mother's herbal remedies that she gives women could really help you."

Jeremiah colored and said nothing. Beulah felt really sorry for him.

"Hey, Mother, don't you have a preparation you give women when they reach a certain age and start getting introspective and miserable?"

Ada glared at her son.

"A little bit of that might help Jeremiah."

"That's enough," she snapped.

"Oh, I think you could all benefit from some," Elam growled as he stalked down the stairs. "I'm going somewhere where the company is better."

Now Beulah watched the young queen moaning softly between contractions. She hoped the birth would come soon. They had been there 14 hours now, and the young expectant mother was becoming exhausted.

"Lord God of Judah," she whispered, "please have mercy on our queen. Please help the babe to come soon. I don't believe it is Your plan for women to suffer so in childbirth. I believe You were just telling Eve one of the consequences of sin and how hard life would be. I don't know for sure, though. And whatever Your plan is, I'm willing to accept it. But please help our young queen."

Ada folded the covers back. "Your Majesty, it's time to start pushing. We'll have this babe here in no time."

Beulah hurried over and took her place behind the young woman's back, supporting her shoulders and allowing the queen to lean against her as she pushed.

"Thank You, God," Beulah whispered.

"It's a boy!" Ada shouted triumphantly. "Your majesty, meet the new crown prince."

The infant wailed in protest as Beulah toweled him off vigorously and rubbed him with salt. Then holding the child close to her chest, she whispered, "Oh, Lord God of Judah, let this be the hope. Let this be the Messiah. We need Him so badly."

My heart twisted with compassion. I wanted to fling my arms around the young woman and whisper, "Not yet, not yet." This young prince would be king some day when he was only 25 years old, but his reign would only be 11 years and it would not end well. Sometimes it was best humans not know what awaited them in the future.

* * * *

Ada was right. When it came time for the queen to give birth to her second child, her labor was much shorter, and while one could hardly call it easy, it certainly was not as traumatic as the first delivery.

Beulah wrapped the second wailing prince and prayed again. "Oh, Lord, let this one be the hope."

I shook my head. This one would not be the hope, either. And while he would be a king of Judah, his reign would last only three months and the Egyptians would haul him off as a prisoner.

As Beulah continued to learn, she was becoming respected as a skilled midwife like her mother-in-law. Spring was in the air and it seemed as if every family was experiencing at least one birth. Many of the royalty, many of their servants, and even Jeremiah's mother was pregnant.

"Beulah," Ada told her, "we're expecting many births shortly. You and I may need to attend some of the women separately should they labor on the same days."

"By myself?" Beulah asked anxiously.

The older woman nodded. "It will be OK. You always pay attention and have learned well. I've taught you almost everything I know. The only thing you lack now is just the years of experience I have. And this is how you get them. In a few weeks I'm going to go stay with my sister for the birth of her child."

"Your sister? I didn't realize you had one," the girl blurted.

She laughed. "Where do you think Jeremiah came from? My sister lives in Anathoth. Her husband is a Temple priest, but she does not come up to the city with him. She prefers to stay at their home in the village, feeling more comfortable there. I will go and attend her birth."

Then Ada became serious. "She had a terrible time giving birth to Jeremiah. Some women have difficulty birthing, and I'm concerned for her. I will stay with her until she has safely delivered, then I shall return. I've told the women of the palace, and they will do anything you ask them to to help you assist with the other births. And perhaps I'll be back quickly enough that we can do them together. But you never know. Babies come when they're ready, not necessarily when you are ready to catch them."

It was true—babies had no respect for convenient scheduling.

"I'll do my best," Beulah said nervously.

"I know you will. You've been doing this with me for several years now."

"I know I'll be fine," the girl sighed. "I just hope the mothers and their babies will be."

Ada put both hands around her assistant's face. "The Lord is with you, Beulah, and He will give His blessing to the women under your care."

The girl closed her eyes and received Ada's blessing. "Thank You, God of Judah," she whispered silently. "I will need You."

And she was right.

As Jeremiah lifted the food bag onto the basket on the mule, Ada told Beulah, "Remember, everything will be all right. The queen mother is going to attend the lying in of all three of her daughters.

She's been through this before, too, and she will give a lot of support. And the Lord is with you."

She patted Beulah's shoulder.

"Travel safely," the girl said, hugging her mother-in-law.

"I'll be fine. I have Jeremiah with me."

"Yeah, a lot of help he'll be," Elam mumbled.

His mother glared at him. "You just make sure that you're a help. Remember that you're the man of the house and, except for the servants, it will just be you and Beulah."

The girl stared at the ground and said nothing.

"Elam," said his mother, sharply, "you will not mistreat her or you will answer to me."

"And me," Jeremiah startled them by adding.

"And you?" Elam demanded.

"And my father," Jeremiah quickly added.

"Don't worry," Elam said between clenched teeth, "you've already given me enough threats. We'll be fine."

Ada was still frowning as she turned to leave.

Although Beulah knotted her fists up at her side, she remained silent. What was there to say? Whatever Elam chose to do, under the law it was his right as her husband's brother and now her protector.

As she hugged the girl, Ada whispered in her ear, "Don't be afraid. Elam's greed will outweigh his lust. He'll wait till he has an heir before he bothers you."

Still staring at her feet, Beulah managed to nod. She had such mixed feelings. While she was afraid of Elam and didn't like him, she did want to have children someday. And without sons she would have no protector and could not have use of her husband's property later on. Closing her eyes, she prayed, "God of Judah, I will have to leave this one with You. I don't even know what to ask for. I'm afraid of all of it."

The God of Judah did not reply, so she took a deep breath and turned toward the house.

* * * *

After drawing water from the well, the girl walked slowly back toward the kitchen area. She felt restless and worried with Ada away. It was true that Anathoth was only a few miles distant, but Ada might be there several days, depending on how her sister was doing. It wasn't that Beulah couldn't take care of things if any babies chose to come at this time. Rather it was just that she preferred to do things with Ada. She felt more comfortable with her mother-in-law. Beulah hoped that Ada would be back in time for the royal births.

As she neared home she realized that was not going to happen as a royal messenger emerged from the gate of the family courtyard.

"Oh, there you are," the servant called. "Come quickly. You're needed at the palace."

"Let me grab my things," the girl replied. "I'll be right there."

Taking a deep breath, Beulah drew herself up to her full height. She had been learning from Ada for several years. And though she was just in her teens, the women in the royal family trusted her.

"Please be with me, God of Judah," she whispered. "Don't let me make any mistakes that could harm the little ones coming into the world." Then she hurried to the palace.

It was a long labor since it was a first birth. The queen mother hovered anxiously in the background. But the infant emerged to wail his protests at being thrust into the world.

As she held the baby, Beulah whispered her prayer to Yahweh as the child continued to cry and flail his tiny red fists.

The queen mother beamed. "Beulah, you did a wonderful job. Ada will be so proud of you."

The girl smiled. "The little prince doesn't seem to think so. Look how furious he is."

"Ah," the queen mother observed, "a prince with a strong will."

"Hopefully he will use it to Yahweh's glory."

The new mother raised up on one elbow. "His father is going to name him Daniel," she said.

"Well, Daniel," Beulah commented, "you take that strong will of yours and channel it in the right direction, and no one will be able to stand up to you."

In spite of her kind words, Daniel continued to howl. Beulah wrapped him in swaddling bands and tucked him in with his mother where he settled down to nurse.

The queen mother laughed. "He's going to be a fine strong one. Isn't it funny to have all three of my daughters expecting at the same time? Do you think Ada will get back soon?"

Beulah shrugged. "I don't know, but I certainly hope so. I miss her terribly."

"I'm sure you do," the queen mother agreed. "But she would be very proud of the job you've done."

"Well, at least it's done. I'm going to go home and get some rest."

"Yes, all of us could use some after this little one keeping us up all night," the queen mother sighed.

The young midwife headed for home. She felt as if she had only slept a few hours when a servant jostled her awake. "You are needed at the palace again."

"Already?" Beulah protested.

The servant nodded.

Beulah grabbed her things and pulled a cloak over her shoulders. She had slept through the day, but still felt exhausted. Evening was approaching. *Could it be the other princess?* she wondered.

When she arrived at the palace another servant hurried her into the queen mother's quarters.

"Is it one of the princesses?" Beulah asked. "Or is something wrong with the baby we delivered this morning?"

"No, no, it's one of the servants. She's been in labor for two days, and the servant midwife was helping her, but nothing is working. I'm afraid the mother's going to die."

Beulah accompanied the queen mother to the servants' quarters. The servant girl looked extremely young, perhaps even younger than Beulah. She was pale and exhausted from her ordeal.

Carefully Beulah examined her the way that Ada had taught her. Then she turned to the queen mother. "You are right, there are serious problems, and I am concerned for the life of your servant. I think we must do whatever we can to help deliver her of the baby."

"What about my baby?" the girl asked in a weak voice.

Beulah took the servant girl's hand in hers and looked into her eyes. "I am so sorry. I don't believe your child lives. The labor has been too difficult and I feel no movement. What I need now is for you to work with me to free you from the infant, so that you can live and have other healthy children in years to come." She squeezed the servant girl's hand. "What is your name?"

The girl closed her eyes and tears trickled down her cheeks. "I've known it," she said between gasps. "I've known it for days."

Beulah wiped her face with a cloth. Then the girl opened her eyes.

"Hannah," she said. "My name is Hannah. What do you want me to do?"

It was far into the night before Hannah's child was finally delivered, and Beulah had been right. The infant was dead.

"Thank you for coming," the queen mother said afterward. "You have spared the life of one of my favorite servant girls, and you won't go unrewarded." She turned and left the room.

Hannah reclined on the cushions, exhausted.

Beulah washed and wrapped the child. "Would you like to see her?" she asked.

The girl nodded.

As Beulah brought the baby over and placed it in Hannah's

arms, tears spilled down the girl's face as she rocked the little bundle. The young midwife stood and caressed the girl's hair as she wept over the dead infant.

"I don't understand. I don't understand. Why? Why?" she kept murmuring.

"I don't understand either," Beulah whispered.

I nodded. Neither of them did. Would it have comforted them to know they didn't have to understand in order to be part of the Mighty One's chosen people? They just had to choose to be loyal to Him.

My heart was heavy as I watched the two girls weeping. Sometimes my job is just painful.

When Beulah awoke the next day she heard someone in the courtyard. Pulling on her cloak, she rushed outside.

"Ada, Ada, I'm so glad you're back." She flung herself into her mother-in-law's arms, then suddenly became aware that the woman was holding something.

"Careful there, Beulah. I'm happy to see you, too." The woman backed away and held a bundle toward the girl. "This is Hannaniah."

"Oh, he's beautiful," Beulah exclaimed.

Hannaniah, however, did not appreciate his boisterous welcome and raised his voice in protest, flinging his tiny fists back and forth in the air.

"Is this your sister's baby?" Beulah asked.

Her mother-in-law's eyes filled with tears.

"Ada, what happened?"

"She died. I could not stop the bleeding after the birth. Hilkiah had no relatives in Anathoth who had given birth recently. There was no one to wet nurse him. I brought him back here where we had a better chance of finding someone."

Beulah caught her breath. "Of course, Hannah." Quickly she told Ada about the events of the night before. "Do you think the queen mother would let Hannah come stay with us and nurse Hannaniah?"

"I don't know, but we could find out."

"She mentioned that Hannah was one of her favorite servants."

"Perhaps that's why she called you for aid," Ada suggested. "And you did help her give birth successfully."

"Yes, I'm so thankful that she didn't die, too."

Her mother-in-law sighed. "It is more difficult for a woman to birth a dead child than a living one who is fighting to come into the world."

Beulah fought back tears. "It was terrible." Suddenly a thought occurred to her. "Could it be that the God of Judah intended for me to be there so that I would know about Hannah? So that I would know where to find someone to nurse little Hannaniah?"

"I don't know," Ada said slowly. "It could be."

A few evenings later Beulah was startled to see a priest enter the family courtyard. *Who is he?* she wondered. *And what does he want?*

But Ada rushed past her and threw her arms around his neck. "Hilkiah, how good to see you."

Beulah's mouth dropped open. This must be Hilkiah, the priest whose wife had just died giving birth to Hannaniah a week before.

"Are you well?" Ada continued.

"I am, but I've come to ask your help."

"What is it? We will do anything."

"It's Jeremiah."

Ada sighed knowingly. "It's a difficult age, and he's just lost his mother."

"No, there's more to it than that. Truly it is a difficult age, but he has always been one to think his own thoughts and keep them to himself. I've never understood him. Lately, even before," he paused, "well, even before last week, he had been behaving strangely. He believes the Lord has called him to be a prophet."

"A prophet?" Ada asked in surprise.

Beulah's eyes widened, but she said nothing.

"He's not old enough to be a prophet. He has to be 30 before he's even allowed to serve as a priest. And he must be the same age as Beulah here—in his late teens and so officially a man and a son of the law—but so young!"

Hilkiah nodded. "Yes, but since he believes the calling is from God, he has been preaching to the other priests in Anathoth."

"Oh," the woman laughed, "I bet that goes over well."

"Not at all," Hilkiah frowned. "They are ready to stone him for speaking treason against the Temple and the city."

"Treason?" she asked in puzzlement. "Josiah has been knocking down the altars and bringing about some reforms. Our king is trying hard to bring Judah back to the God we once served a little more enthusiastically than we do now, but we're making progress."

Hilkiah took a deep breath and shrugged. "I don't know what to do with him. My rotation for serving in the Temple is coming up and I'm afraid that the men in Anathoth will stone him, especially if I'm not there to protect him. May he stay with you for a while?"

"Oh, certainly. But I'm afraid that if he felt a need to preach to the priests in Anathoth, he's going to really think the inhabitants of Jerusalem are heathens."

The priest smiled ever so slightly. "That's because they are," he said softly.

"I know," she replied. "Josiah is trying, though."

"It's just been such a long time that people no longer know how to worship the God of Israel. They're going to have to learn all over again."

"Better that than being punished until they remember who He is," Ada suggested.

"Now you're sounding like Jeremiah. I thank you greatly and will bring him tomorrow."

Ada bowed to him. "Would you like to see your other son? He has grown so much just in the few days he's been here."

The man's face lit up. "Yes, where is he?"

The family compound was full again. The queen mother had given Hannah to Beulah and Ada in gratitude for their midwifery services. Hannah shared Beulah's quarters with the infant Hannaniah. Elam had taken a wife and they were expecting a young one soon. So as to have some privacy, he had built for Jeremiah a room of his own. And Hilkiah frequently visited and stayed in his son's quarters.

Jeremiah was a shy boy who rarely smiled. Some evenings he would come and sit by the cooking fire with Beulah and tell her stories from the scriptures. One time he described how God had called him to be a prophet, and how he had protested that he was too young. And the Lord had told him not to say that again. Beulah had to smile to herself for it sounded just like what Ada had said when she had recruited her into midwiving as a young widow, even though she was barely old enough to marry and knew nothing of birthing babies.

"Perhaps," Beulah said, looking into his dark eyes, "perhaps it's only people that care about age. Perhaps Jehovah chooses whom He will as long as they love Him and are willing to do what He asks of them."

Then they both smiled shyly, realizing that they shared a common bond.

"I pray for the Hope of Israel over every male baby born," she said.

Jeremiah glanced up. "You do?" he said in a surprised voice. "I thought I was the only one praying daily for the Hope of Israel."

She shook her head. "He's coming, you know. We just don't know when. He could be any one of these little ones being born this year. Ada taught me some of the prophecies of Isaiah. It's very exciting."

"That they are. Yet it concerns me that most of the people in Judah now pay little attention to our God. If they were to keep His Sabbaths and worship Him, this would be the most prosperous place on earth. It would be like a paradise. But I don't think it can be that way."

"You don't?"

"No. All through our history God has required loyalty and obedience. The people in Judah now just want to ignore Him or worship Him only when it's convenient and when they can fit Him in around their other activities or their other gods. I feel that unless our people sincerely turn back to Him, terrible things are going to happen."

"Oh, Jeremiah," she whispered, "if you say that out loud, people will be very angry with you."

He laughed bitterly. "They already have been. I've been accused of treason against the king, treason against the Temple, and treason against the city of Jerusalem."

"Aren't you afraid?"

"No. When the Lord called me, the same time as He told me not to keep complaining about being a child, He also assured me that He would protect me. That while people would be extremely angry with me and would do bad things, He would always take care of me."

"That's amazing," Beulah said. "Do you realize how special you are to be personally protected by the Almighty God of Abraham, Isaac, and Jacob?"

Jeremiah smiled. "I always feel happier when I'm near you."

I smiled. It was true. Beulah always had a positive outlook because of her simple trust in God. And Jeremiah was highly honored to be so protected by One who had the entire universe to care for.

Over the next year two more little princely cousins entered the world. Their parents named them Mishel and Azariah. Beulah went almost daily to the palace to check on her little ones, and they all adored her. Jeremiah referred to the children that she had helped deliver as the "Hopes," short for the Hopes of Israel, because of the prayers she said over them.

Even though none of those babies were the hoped for Messiah, they were Beulah's hopes. They were the happiness and the fulfillment that the Lord had given her, instead of the sad and difficult life she could have had.

One day Jeremiah strode into the courtyard and sat near the fire.

"Are you hungry?" she asked. "This pot has some of the best lentil soup I've ever had."

"I'm starving." He tore some bread apart and dipped it into the pot. "Hmmm, this is good," he commented. "So how are the Hopes today? I saw you playing with them at the palace."

Beulah laughed. "They're growing so fast. And they're so much fun. I saw you at the palace, too. You were talking to King Josiah."

"Yes, the priests may not care for me much, but I have the ear of the king. And he is really sincere about bringing our people back to God. Another prophet has been here in Jerusalem this week. His name is Zephaniah, and he is also calling Israel to repentance."

She clasped her hands together. "Jeremiah, that's wonderful. Then all those things that you have been so worried about aren't going to happen."

He stared into the fire thoughtfully. "They will happen. But Josiah is a good and loyal king, and I don't think that any of these things will take place as long as he is king or as long as those who follow him continue to pursue the God of Jacob. But I haven't told you the most exciting thing. Josiah has decided to repair the Temple. He is collecting funds for it, and we're going to get it all cleaned out and rebuild the broken places and make it back into a beautiful house of worship for the Mighty One."

"That's even more wonderful!" the girl exclaimed. "He removed the idols when I first got married." A cloud crossed her face at the memory, then she shrugged it off. "That is truly wonderful. I am so glad."

"You wouldn't believe some of the trash in there," Jeremiah continued. "They did take the idols out, but there is a lot of junk just dumped and stored in the Temple. It will really take work. But with the king behind it, I think that we'll be successful."

Beulah stared into the fire. "We are greatly blessed to have a king who wants to pursue the heart of God," she whispered.

"Yes, and we are even more blessed to have a God who wants to pursue the hearts of His stubborn people and woo them back to Him like a lover or a loving parent."

If only they knew, I thought. If only they knew how much, how the Mighty One's heart yearned and ached after them, how much He loved them. How could humans ever resist if they had any clue? It was beyond me.

Jeremiah returned home that evening in great excitement. He couldn't wait to talk to Beulah. But when he arrived at the family compound it was not to be. He caught sight of her out near the tall jars where they kept water.

"What's happening?" he asked.

"Elam's wife is having her baby," she gasped, "and things aren't going well. You need to go somewhere else for a while. This isn't a good place for men right now."

Feeling disappointed, Jeremiah turned and wandered back toward the Temple. He had wanted to talk to Beulah, to tell her some exciting news. But he supposed that at a time like this he should be praying for the child of his cousin Elam. Jeremiah had never liked Elam, and Elam only barely tolerated Jeremiah's presence in their home. Somehow he couldn't imagine the Messiah being born from a father like that. Still, the father's attitude was not the child's fault, and he hoped that the little one would enter the world healthy.

It was the next evening before he had a chance to speak with Beulah, and by then she had already heard the news he had tried to bring her the day before.

"Isn't it wonderful about the scroll Shafan found," she bubbled as soon as he entered the courtyard.

Jeremiah enjoyed the way she always got so excited over everything. "Yes," he said, "Shafan gave it to Hilkiah (not my father, but the high priest) and Hilkiah took it to the king. Now the king has contacted the prophetess Huldah, and she has confirmed that it is the law of God."

"Do you think it's an actual scroll that Moses wrote?" Beulah interrupted.

"I don't know, but if it isn't, it's a copy. People have memorized his teachings and passed them down through the generations by word of mouth, but now we can read what he actually said."

"Perhaps this will be a great time of turning back to the Lord," she suggested.

"That would be a wonderful thing. It truly is a time of hope and of change."

"As long as there are people who are willing to return to the Lord, there's always hope, isn't there?" Beulah asked.

He smiled. "The Lord is always faithful to those who are faithful to Him. Every morning He comes up with new mercies for us. He is good."

She returned his smile. "I was over in the compound of your friend Baruch today," she said, "and helped one of his cousins birth another little hope. They're going to name him Ezekiel when they take him in on the eighth day to be blessed. Baruch was so excited."

"Yes, he's another one like you. He always gets such pleasure out of the little joys in life."

Beulah laughed. "The Lord needs people like Baruch and like me to help balance those who worry about all the difficult things."

Jeremiah sighed. "It is unfortunate that the Lord needs people like me to continually remind others what will happen if they don't pay attention. I think I'd rather be like you."

"The Lord wants you just the way you are, Jeremiah. He knew you from before you were born. Perhaps even planned for me. Whoever we are, and whatever part we have in His plan, isn't He good?"

As Jeremiah nodded, I nodded, too. And my heart filled with hope. As long as there were people like Beulah and Jeremiah, there would be worshipers of the Mighty One in spite of the calamities that were to come so soon.

JONADAB

onadab slammed the door to the slave courtyard, grabbed a dipper of water, gulped it down, and then flopped down by the cooking fire. "Don't even ask," he snapped at his friend Shamma.

"I didn't ask," the other boy said. "I could tell. Why didn't you ask how my day was?"

"'Cause I don't want to know."

"Still in one of your pleasant moods, huh?"

Jonadab rolled his eyes. "You know, I had connections. They could have given me a more responsible job than this. But, no, I get thrown in with the peasants."

"Oh, is that still bothering you? That your friends from when you were a little boy have government positions and you are just a slave?"

"Well, you would think the Babylonians could tell who had potential and who didn't," Jonadab growled.

"Maybe they could just tell who was pleasant and who wasn't," his friend observed. He dodged the half-hearted blow Jonadab shot in his direction. "Personally," Shamma went on, "if I were you, I would be glad that you were with the regular slaves. We can have children and eventually the Messiah may come through our line. If you had ended up being a palace eunuch, well—"

Frowning, Jonadab said nothing.

"Not only that," Shamma pointed out, "if we do ever get to go back to Jerusalem—and that depends on which prophets you believe—people who have been mutilated aren't even allowed in the Temple. Your friends who are so important here in the government wouldn't even be able to go there to worship. Maybe you should be thanking the God of Judah that you're here with us lowly people."

"Oh, shut up. You have no idea what it's like for me."

"I have a pretty good idea. I was out there working on the plain just as you did today, trying to get ready for that stupid festival coming up."

"Yeah," Jonadab said, "so what do you suppose my high-placed friends are going to do during it?"

"Oh, probably have a good time," Shamma suggested. "Why?"

"Well, the reason King Nebuchadnezzar is having the festival is sort of a call for loyalty. He's invited all of his government officials from top to bottom to assemble there and bow down to this image of him. I believe it might have something to do with the insurrection he just put down a few months ago. There were some people plotting against his life. I think he's asking for absolute loyalty."

"So? Kings do that kind of thing."

Jonadab's eyes narrowed. "Yes, they do. But can you imagine my four snooty friends kneeling to a Babylonian king?"

"Oh, I see what you're getting at. You don't believe they will."

"Well, what do you think? They wouldn't even eat the food from the king's table and refused the stuff that he was drinking as if it wasn't good enough for them."

"But the king knows their loyalties. Maybe he's sent them on other assignments this week."

"Maybe." Jonadab thought a moment. "I know that Daniel has gotten close to King Nebuchadnezzar ever since he interpreted that nightmare the king had. I just couldn't believe it when Daniel asked for all of the wise men to be preserved and rewarded when he was the one to interpret the dream. He could have had them all killed off. The death decree had already been given for all the wise men, and then he would have been the only one left. If he had had any political savvy, he would have done just that."

Rolling over, Shamma stared at his friend. "Kind of a cold-blooded old creature, aren't you?"

"Maybe—or perhaps I just have more political potential than my overly conscientious ex-friends."

Shamma shook his head. "I think you're just jealous of them. You're pitiful."

"I just don't understand," Jonadab said, ignoring him, "how they can continue to be so faithful and pious about a God who isn't even capable of taking care of them. I mean, they're here, aren't they?"

"Yes," Shamma shrugged, "but it sounds as if you're upset that He's taken better care of them than He has of you." On impulse he pulled his blanket over his head. Sometimes listening to Jonadab spout off was entertaining, but today it was just annoying.

I had to agree with Shamma. Not all of my assignments were as pleasant as others. And Jonadab was turning out to be one of the noisier, more ungrateful ones the Almighty had placed me with. The boy reminded me a lot of his father, Elam of Jerusalem, although those days seemed far away to them now.

The siege of Jerusalem had been terrible and many had died during its fall. I felt grateful that my last charge, Beulah, had died in childbirth several years before this. It would have broken her heart to see her "hopes" bloodied and beaten and carried off into captivity to

Babylon. Sometimes the Mighty One's actions seem severe at the time and yet they really are merciful in the end.

Jonadab and the other slaves continued to work daily out in the plain erecting the huge stelae with the golden image on the top. The work was back-breaking and the desert plain was hot enough without having to stoke the fires in all of the brick kilns. It was unbearable and the death rate among the slaves was high.

Lying on the floor in the slaves' quarters that evening, Jonadab continued to complain.

"I can't believe the God of Judah could let us end up here doing this. Spending the last dregs of strength we have erecting images to some pagan king."

"Then maybe you should have listened to His prophets," Shamma finally exploded when he could no longer take Jonadab's complaining.

"Listened to the prophets? What do you mean?"

"You know exactly what I mean. My family wasn't important, but we knew who you were in Jerusalem. The prophet Jeremiah even lived in your home for a while."

"Oh, Jeremiah," he said dismissively.

"Yeah, Jeremiah. If you and the rest of the important people in government had listened to Jeremiah, perhaps we would still be in Jerusalem now."

"Well, you don't understand how it was," Jonadab protested. "At the time we just thought he was mentally unbalanced and becoming more unhinged as he went along. He had always taken a very pessimistic view of everything. It seemed to us that you could either believe the prophet Isaiah or you could accept what Jeremiah said. But they couldn't both be right."

"No," Shamma said slowly and thoughtfully. "I understand that the prophet Isaiah said that some of the princes of Israel would end up being eunuchs on the court of a heathen king. So not everything he prophesied was positive."

Jonadab made a face. "I guess that Jeremiah could have been right. But God didn't have to make it so confusing. How were we supposed to know?"

"Don't ask me. I'm just a lower-class person. So if you believe in the prophets and you believe in the God of Judah, does that mean that you are going to refuse to bow to King Nebuchadnezzar at the festival?"

"Don't be stupid!. You think I wanna die?"

"That's what I thought."

The day of the festival dawned early. It was as clear and blistering hot as every other day had been out on the plain. The slaves were out before sunrise making sure everything was perfect and ready. It took most of the day for all the processions to arrive. They came in reverse order of their importance.

The musicians had all arrived earlier along with the slaves and were all in formation, ready to provide the entertainment. Finally everyone was in place and the king arrived fashionably late.

Then the announcement went out. When the music started everyone was to demonstrate their allegiance to the king by falling on their faces before the image. And should there be anyone in the crowd who was still contemplating treason, they could feel free to remain standing, but they could count on a one-way trip to the brick kilns.

Shamma glanced over and caught the eye of Jonadab and then looked away. Would he remain standing? Not likely.

The music started and the plain shook with the sound of falling bodies as everyone rushed to prostrate themselves before the king and his image. Suddenly a murmur rippled through the crowd.

"It's them," Jonadab hissed. "I knew it. I knew they would do this. They are such an embarrassment to the rest of us."

"What are they doing?" Shamma asked, his voice muffled and his forehead firmly placed on the ground.

"Three of them are standing there."

"Three? Aren't there four?"

"I don't see Daniel. My cousin Hannaniah thinks he's so important but he's no different than me. He lived in our compound. And look at him there. Now they're being called up to the king. They're in for it now."

"What's happening?" Shamma persisted.

"I can't tell. They're just talking to the king."

Then the heralds shouted an announcement. "Everyone may stand. You will have one more opportunity to . . . Never mind! Remain kneeling!"

Jonadab and Shamma may not have been able to hear, but I could. The three Hebrews had respectfully explained their position to the king. He could have struck his servants for pointing their disobedience out, and himself for forgetting to give them "urgent business" elsewhere that day as he had for Daniel. Now he offered them one more chance. They countered, "Our God is able to take care of us and deliver us from your gods and even your fiery furnace if He decides to. If He doesn't, we still choose to serve Him, and while we respect you, oh King, His wishes take priority." I felt my wingtips quiver with pride at their loyalty. Would the Mighty One save them?

"What do you think that was all about?" Shamma whispered.

"My guess is that the king was going to give his pets one more chance but they told him not to bother. They are still standing there in front of him and he looks as if he is about to turn a new shade of purple. They have embarrassed him in front of everyone here."

"I'm going to turn a new shade of purple if I have to stay in this position for much longer," the other boy mumbled.

"Furnace slaves! You three get over there and stoke the furnaces up seven times hotter on the king's command!" a soldier barked. He gestured to Jonadab and two others on the other side of him.

Hmm, Jonadab thought. *Those furnaces are already so hot that to get close enough to add more fuel and stoke them up anymore will probably kill us. And how will anyone be able to tell when it is really seven times as hot as it was before?* But it didn't matter. Just obeying the king as fast as possible was all that was important—if one wanted to live!

Shamma raised his head a little, just enough to see what was happening. Poor Jonadab. Now he would really have something to complain about! Then Shamma caught his breath as he saw Jonadab fall to the ground in front of the furnace. Nobody made any move to rescue him.

My heart sank as I watched life leave the motionless body. How often the Mighty One had given opportunity after opportunity to this stubborn human. Now there would be no more chances. I would have grieved more but there was too much happening at once.

Now the soldiers were tying the hands of the three Hebrews and dragging them toward the furnaces. A ripple of amazement swept through the crowd as the soldiers collapsed at the mouth of the furnace. The three bound captives just stepped over them and continued on into the furnace.

By now Shamma had inched his head up higher. So had everyone else. Was the heat playing tricks on him or were there four in the furnace? The fourth one definitely did not resemble Daniel.

"Get them out of there!" the king bellowed. Soldiers leaped forward to do as he commanded and passed out in the heat on top of the others. "I sent three men into the furnace, but now I see four!" the distraught ruler screamed. "And the fourth one looks like a son of God!"

The four men who were walking and talking inside the inferno now glanced out at the king. "Come out!" he bellowed. They one by one stepped out and over the bodies in their way. The ropes had burned away but their clothes remained in perfect condition. They seemed calm and totally unharmed and not even slightly singed. But now there were only three of them.

Shamma was now in a half crouched position with his mouth hanging open, gaping like the rest of the people assembled on the blistering plain. "God of Israel and Judah," he whispered. "You did it! You really can take care of those who are loyal to you. I am only a lowly slave in Babylon—even more insignificant than when we lived in Jerusalem (and that was pretty lowly), but if you want me, I am willing to give my highest loyalty to you, just like those three."

I swooped through the air in delight. Another victory for the Mighty One! Proof to the whole country that the God of Israel was stronger than any Babylonian deity. And just as valuable and exciting, the heart of a lost son of Judah had turned to his Maker. I had the best job in the universe!

ELIAH

liah shouldered the heavy wine pitcher and entered the opulent chamber. It was 147 feet long and the only room in the palace large enough for such a feast. The oil lamps and torches flickered and reflected off the three walls that were covered with glazed brick. The fourth wall was smooth white plaster. At the midpoint in the room against the white plaster wall was the dias where the king sat.

By now no one in the room needed any more wine. They had been drunk for some time and were getting more and more unruly. The boy was glad that his mother had been moved into the other palace to care for the queen mother where she wouldn't have to see what went on tonight.

Carefully Eliah refilled people's wine cups. *I may be here in body,* he thought, *but my heart is in Jerusalem.* Ever since he was a tiny boy, his parents had told him about Jerusalem. His great-grandparents had lived there before King Nebuchadnezzar had brought them as slaves to Babylon. It was the hope of many Judahite slaves that they would go home to Jerusalem one day.

The lad continued to fill wine cups. "Any time now, God," he whispered, "I would be delighted to go. It wouldn't even hurt my feelings to miss the last half of this party. Whenever You're ready, my family and I would love to go back to Jerusalem. Don't forget us here."

In spite of the chaos of the room, he felt a little glow of peace in his heart. The God of Judah wouldn't forget them. Even the prophet Jeremiah had promised that God would bring them back to Jerusalem again some day. He wondered if Jeremiah would be there, then shrugged. Probably not. He had been an old man even way back then and someone had told Eliah that Jeremiah had gone to live in Egypt where it was safer for him.

His wine pitcher empty, the boy returned to the kitchen for a refill.

Everybody was making toasts and speeches. Eliah shook his head. The Babylonians loved the sound of their own voices. But he didn't have to listen. He ignored it as he began filling cups again, starting at the opposite end of the room.

Suddenly he perked up his ears.

"And in honor of Marduk we will display the holy items from the temples of the lands he has conquered," the coregent shouted, his words slurred.

Holy items? Could he mean the sacred things the Babylonian armies had stolen from the Temple in Jerusalem? Surely not the Lord God's Temple vessels!

Eliah bit his lip.

The Babylonians worshiped Marduk, but they generally tried not to desecrate objects belonging to other gods. Nebuchadnezzar had even acknowledged the God of Judah and Israel, but not Belshazzar.

"Boy, are you gonna give me more wine or not?"

"Yes, sir," Eliah answered, snapping back to attention and continuing to pour.

A spattering of approval arose as the priests of Marduk carried in the sacred things stolen from the Temple. Eliah lowered his eyes. He couldn't bear to even look at them.

"All of these vessels are from conquered gods of conquered peoples," Belshazzar proclaimed. "So what if we lost the battle at Opus last week. Marduk is still the most powerful god in the world and he can still conquer anyone else. Next week we will fight the Medes and their Persian lackeys. But tonight we will celebrate and remind Marduk of his great power and how much we worship him."

The clamor and cheering rose to a crescendo.

"What are a few Medes and Persians to a god like Marduk?" the ruler proclaimed.

Eliah stood still and set his wine jug down. "God of Judah," he whispered without moving his lips, "can You hear this? Are You going to let him do this? Please do something. Show him that You're not the conquered God of a conquered people. We're a conquered people because we sinned and forgot You. But You're the most powerful God in the universe. Show him, please."

Suddenly the room fell silent. Something was wrong and Eliah could feel the hair standing up on the back of his neck. What was happening? Hearing a terrified shriek from the dias where the king sat, he spun around. There above his throne was a disembodied hand writing on the wall.

If he hadn't felt totally frozen in his tracks Eliah would have broken into a smile.

I also smiled and approached closer. "This is what you asked for, my young charge," I whispered, wishing he could hear me.

Eliah's mouth dropped open. How appropriate it was for just a hand to appear. He had served at banquets after battles before where the generals had brought in basket after basket full of hands and dumped them on the floor before the king. It was the ancient Assyrian form of body count that the Babylonians had also adopted.

Now this disembodied hand writing on the wall was telling everyone that Belshazzar had a message from a defeated foe.

The holy vessel that he had been drinking wine out of now dropped out of the ruler's hand and clattered to the floor.

"What does it say? What does it say?" Belshazzar demanded.

The wise men who were present at the feast were as drunk as he was. Consisting of only four words, the message was difficult to interpret.

"Somebody tell me what it means," the ruler's voice rose from a demanding pitch to a scream. "Can't anybody tell me? One of you has got to know!"

Suddenly the whole room broke into chaos. Eliah slipped out of the hall and ran for his mother. She would know what to do.

Her chambers were at the other end of the hanging gardens. He knocked at the servants' entrance and asked for his mother, knowing that he could not enter into the women's quarters without permission. When she appeared he breathlessly told her what had happened.

"Go back," she said, "but stay near the kitchen area."

He wasn't sure what his mother would or could do, but only moments later she and the queen mother appeared in the doorway of the banquet hall.

Belshazzar looked up wild-eyed. "Mother," he said.

"My son." The older woman quickly glanced around the room, taking in the situation.

"I don't know what it says," he blurted out. "I've offered a gold chain and royal clothing and position as the third-level ruler in the land to anybody who can interpret it."

The queen mother nodded. "There is someone, you know."

"Really?" His face brightened and he sat up a little straighter in the throne on which he had slumped. "Who is it? Why have I not heard of him?"

"He's old and served Nebuchadnezzar under the name Belteshazzar as the chief of all the wise men of Babylon. His Hebrew name was Daniel."

Eliah and the coregent both looked up in astonishment. Belshazzar thought, *He has a name almost exactly the same as mine.*

"He is in retirement now," she said, "but you can send for him. He serves the God of Israel." She glanced at the Temple vessels on the floor. "But he will be able to interpret this."

"Send for him at once," Belshazzar ordered.

It seemed like forever before the older man arrived.

When he stood before the throne the drunk ruler almost babbled. "My mother claims you can tell us what this says and what it means and that you know the secrets of all the gods. I will give you anything you want. I will give you royal clothing and a gold collar and I will make you the third highest person in the kingdom. You know of course that my father has first place even though he's away in Tamar right now. And I have second place. So third is the highest I could give you. But I'll give you anything you want if you just . . ."

"I need no rewards," the old man replied, "but I will tell you what the God of heaven has written on the wall. The God of heaven gave a large kingdom to Nebuchadnezzar and blessed him.

Unfortunately, he developed a serious pride problem, so the God of heaven allowed him to lose his throne and take his glory away from him. He became like an animal for a while until he was willing to admit that the Most High God ruled in heaven and here on earth and that He could give kingdoms to whoever He wanted to. Nebuchadnezzar learned from this. You, Belshazzar, have not humbled your heart even though you knew all of this. Not only are you filled with pride, but you have desecrated the vessels from His Temple. And you and your lords have drunk wine out of them and praised your gods and dishonored the God of heaven and defied Him here in this banquet hall."

By now Belshazzar was shaking. "S-so what does the message say?" he stammered.

"The words are this: 'Mene, Mene, Tekel, Upharsin.' Mene means 'God has numbered your kingdom and your number is up.' Tekel means 'You were weighed in the balances and found wanting.' And Peres means that your kingdom has been divided. It's going to be given to the Medes and the Persians."

"Well," the ruler said, "at least you did what I asked. Here have this royal robe. Give him the chain. Go on. And make him the third highest ruler in the kingdom."

"I don't want your riches," the Hebrew prophet protested, "and I don't want a position in the kingdom. Your kingdom is over."

Belshazzar insisted and Daniel stood silently as servants put the robe and chain on him. Then he turned and walked toward the door, his eyes briefly making contact with those of the queen mother. She nodded her head in thanks and slipped out another door. The elderly statesman stood at the end of the banquet hall.

Eliah set down his wine jug. Something told him it was time to make a choice, and he headed toward the old man. "My name is Eliah," he said.

Daniel smiled. "I will need a young servant. Stand with me."

With a nod Eliah joined him.

The door at the far end of the chamber suddenly burst open. Shrieks and screams swept through the banquet hall like a wave of terror. Although everyone scrambled and clawed for some way to escape, the two Hebrews patiently stood, an island of calm in a sea of chaos.

"It is Cyrus," Daniel whispered to the boy. "We live under the rule of Medo-Persia now."

Eliah wasn't sure what to think, but remained with the old man.

The soldiers swept through the room. Blood splashed on the walls where the hand of God had written only a short time before.

One soldier, apparently higher ranking than the others, approached them. "You look important, yet we have killed the king. Who might you be?"

"My name is Daniel."

The officer nodded. "Come with me."

The prophet motioned to Eliah and they followed the man out of the gory banquet hall to meet the ruler of the newest empire.

As they stood out in the chilly night air, awaiting their audience with Cyrus, Daniel explained, "This is the kingdom that will send our people home. It's almost time."

Daniel was right. Cyrus would make his uncle Darius, the Persian, king of Babylon as he continued on conquering territories for his new empire. The Hebrew prophet would join King Darius' government.

Eliah closed his eyes. "You really heard me, God of Israel," he whispered. "You were listening. I promise to serve You the rest of my life in whatever way You want me to. For now I will loyally serve Your wise man Daniel until You let me know that it's time to go home—home to Jerusalem."

AIESHA

s Aiesha heard the summoning bell she and her friend, Saroja, scrambled to their feet and hurried to answer. They bowed low before Hegai, the chamberlain in charge of the court of women.

"As you know," he began, "a new batch of virgins will arrive this afternoon and you will begin instructing the new slave girls who will be their servants. I hope that you have divided the slaves up so that at least one experienced slave is in charge of each group. In time they will learn what they need to know, but some instructors are better than others. You are my best."

The servant girls smiled. Words of praise were few and far between for slaves, even though Hegai was a kinder chamberlain than many.

"I'm giving you each three new slaves to start with. And those of you who end up with a girl that looks like she has potential to be a royal wife will receive additional servants. After you receive your assigned servants, I'd like you to take them to the chambers and prepare the rooms for their new occupants. The first of the new virgins should be here this afternoon. That will be all."

Aiesha nudged Saroja. "Hear that? We're the best."

Saroja laughed. "We are slaves at the very bottom of the pecking order in this palace. But at least we're the best of the bottom, huh?"

"We won't be at the bottom anymore," Aiesha laughed. "There'll be at least three people beneath us. Did you ever think that would happen?"

Even though their backgrounds were very different, they had much in common. And once they had learned enough new language to communicate with each other, they had become close friends. Both of them had been brought to the palace of Shushan as spoils of war. Saroja had come from the campaigns to the east in India. Aiesha had been captured in the west. And while both girls were terribly homesick and adjusting to life as a slave was difficult, they had formed a close friendship and found many things in common.

Aiesha had received her three slave girls and had prepared the chamber. Incense burned in the corner to make the room smell good, and beautiful gauze hangings covered the window. She wondered what her new mistress would be like.

"Now remember," she said to the three newer slave girls, "we must make each wife as happy and as beautiful as possible. All of the girls coming in this afternoon will probably be just as frightened as we were when we arrived here. Their whole future depends on one night with the king, and if he's having a bad day, they may spend the rest of their lives in the harem never seeing their families again, but not being able to have one here either. It's in our best interest to make sure her night pleases the king. And to do that we need to make her happy. Do you understand?"

The slave girls nodded.

"If he does like her and he summons her again, our lives will be better, too. And should he actually choose her for his queen, we'll be some of the better-off slaves in all of Persia."

The girls smiled bashfully.

"Can you do that?"

They nodded eagerly.

"Then we may as well relax until Hegai summons us."

It seemed they had just sat down when they heard the bell. They hurried in to his chambers and lined up, eyes on the floor until he addressed them. Several other girls stood with him, all of them looking uncomfortable. Some appeared anxious and afraid. Others had tightly clenched jaws.

"Aiesha," Hegai said, "this one is yours." He turned to the young woman. "Tell her your name."

"Uh, Esther," she stumbled nervously.

Hegai laughed. "Don't get too forgetful. One has to at least remember one's name around here. If you want the king to remember it, you must remember it yourself."

Esther's face remained blank as the other girls laughed. *Great,* Aiesha thought, *I'm getting one without a sense of humor.*

She looked at her new mistress a little more closely and noticed the red puffy eyes. The girl was obviously beautiful, but she had been crying. Aiesha shrugged. She couldn't blame her for that.

"Esther," Hegai continued, "this is Aiesha. She will be your main servant. And these three slaves will assist her. If you have any wants or needs, tell Aiesha and one of the girls will take care of it for you. I will be by later to make sure everything is alright."

"Come with me, my lady," Aiesha said, bowing to her. "We have a chamber prepared for you." As Aiesha led her down the hall, the other three slave girls trailed behind.

When they entered the chamber Esther drew a sharp breath. "It's so tiny," she whispered.

Aiesha nodded. "Yes, the rooms in the harem are small. But at least you will have some privacy, something few of us had in our original homes. Even those of us who were taken from wealthier families."

Her eyes met Esther's. Suddenly a flash of understanding took place between them.

"You were brought here, too?" Esther asked.

"Most of us were war captives, gifts to the king," Aiesha said, nodding toward the other three. She hoped the admission would make the new wife feel more comfortable.

The king had sent out a call for beautiful virgins to be brought to the palace after he had exiled Queen Vashti for her disobedience. All of them had been very young and most of them seemed frightened when they arrived. Although some tried to appear proud and hopeful, Aiesha guessed that their families were much more proud and hopeful than any of the girls themselves.

"Your parents must be very proud that you are here in the palace and might someday be queen," she said politely.

"I have no parents," Esther replied slowly, "just a cousin. More like an uncle really. He has taken care of me as long as I can remember."

Aiesha did not know what to say.

"He works here at the palace as an official at the gate," Esther continued.

Suddenly it all made sense to Aiesha. This way the cousin would no longer have to support a daughter that wasn't even his and, should she receive favor from the king, he could stand to receive great benefit.

"Has anyone told you what to expect yet?"

Esther shook her head.

"Sit down." She motioned for the other slave girls to do the same. "Here's what we have planned for you during the next year. All of the virgins who come into the palace spend 12 months in purification before they ever see the king."

The new wife lowered her eyes. "Couldn't I just come back in a year when it was my turn to see the king?"

Aiesha laughed. "That would be nice, wouldn't it? But you'll be receiving a special diet from the king's kitchens. They want you to be strong and healthy, but if there's anything you would really like to eat that they don't offer you, let me know and I'll try and get it for you. For the first six months your beauty treatments will consist of special skin oils because the air is so dry here. You'll be receiving two oil massages everyday, plus the usual bathing and soaking. By the time we're done with you, your skin will be as soft and beautiful as a baby's.

"The second six months we'll be doing lots of perfuming. Also we burn spices on that incense over here so that they will soak into your hair and your skin and your body until you always smell fragrant."

Esther said nothing.

"This chamber is yours. We also have common areas where all of the women can go. There are no men in the house, except for the eunuchs, so you're never in any danger of being seen by men. The harem has its own private gardens and bathing areas. Do you have any questions?"

Slowly Esther shook her head.

Aiesha took both of Esther's hands in hers. "Don't be so sad. It really will be OK once you get used to it."

Esther raised her red-rimmed eyes and looked into Aiesha's.

Smiling gently back, Aiesha said, "Everyone here understands."

Although she nodded faintly, Esther still said nothing.

Turning to the other three servants, Aiesha directed them to prepare Esther a bath. "Then we will get her in to some more appropriate clothing and help her settle in. After your bath we will look at some fabrics and decide which colors are the most becoming for your skin tones." Aiesha drew a deep breath. "Let's get going."

The others hurried out of the room.

I smiled as once again I realized that the Almighty had handpicked the perfect companion for Esther. My charge would be a great comfort to her as she adjusted to harem life.

"My lady . . . Esther," Aiesha repeated.

The young woman jumped. "Oh, yes. I'm—I'm sorry I didn't hear you."

"It's a new name for you, isn't it?" the servant girl said quietly.

The young woman's eyes grew round. "Please don't tell anybody."

"My lips are sealed. And my loyalty is yours, my lady. I would never reveal any of your secrets. Besides, Aiesha is not the name I was born with either, but sometimes it's best to fit in where we find ourselves."

Esther smiled shyly.

"My friend Saroja, though," Aiesha continued, "she's the head maid for another of the harem virgins. She kept her name. Saroja. It's a different name, but it has a nice ring to it. And no one would ever forget it or confuse her for someone else."

"That could be either a good thing or a bad thing."

Aiesha laughed. "Yes, especially around here."

"Where is Saroja from?" Esther asked.

"She comes from a land far to the east, one of the king's most distant provinces. It's where we import many of the spices and silks from. I believe that her family was quite wealthy and that she had a good life before becoming a slave."

"Do you think she would tell me about her country?"

"Of course. She would probably love to have someone willing to listen to her talk about her country and her family, what life was like for her as a little girl, the things she saw. And her gods. It's all quite different. Perhaps if you were to invite her mistress to your quarters for an afternoon, we could all visit together."

"That would be wonderful. I'm always interested in other peoples and the way they do things and see things and worship."

"Well, you have come to the perfect place," Aiesha sighed, "because there are women here from everywhere in the world and most of them are lonesome for home and would enjoy talking about it. And I for one would be delighted to listen to something besides the usual palace gossip. Sometimes I think the fact that we don't have enough to do makes such malicious gossip more attractive to us. I would much rather hear about other countries and other people, too."

"Good. Let's do that. For now, tell me about your home."

"Ah, I've had several. I'm from Egypt, at least that's where my family lived when I was very little. But because my father was a merchant we traveled to other places. I did not come here until I was 12 years old."

"Tell me some of the stories that you heard when you were a little girl."

"Ah," Aiesha said , "my father was quite a storyteller."

"Good. I will wallow in as many of these beauty baths as you want if you will tell me stories."

"It's a deal. My dad told me this story once . . ."

* * * *

"Aiesha, how is your mistress doing? Is she adjusting well?" Hegai asked.

"Yes," the servant girl said. "She seemed very quiet and sad at first, but she's doing better, and I am finding out what her interests are. And that helps."

"She appears to be one of our virgins with great potential. I could see her greatly pleasing the king. Because of that, I would like to give her more servants and move her to larger quarters. I think it will be worth everything we invest in her."

He was thoughtful for a moment. "So what are her interests?" he continued. "Is it something we can help her with, give her more of? Does she have a favorite fragrance or fabric?"

Aiesha laughed. "She always dresses attractively, but she doesn't have much interest in those things. Instead, she's intrigued by different peoples and cultures, and she's always asking to hear stories about the other women's homelands."

"Does she have a particular country she's most interested in?"

"I don't believe so. I think she's just fascinated by people."

Hegai appeared to consider this.

"I have a suggestion," Aiesha continued. "If you wish to give her more slaves, selecting them from a variety of faraway places would probably delight her more than anything else you could do, especially if you found some who enjoy storytelling."

"Well, that could be done," he decided. "That is probably the easiest request I've had all week. Does she ever speak of her family?"

"Never. But she's fascinated by the families of everyone else."

"Hmm, that's very interesting. It's unusual for a Persian to care that much about conquered peoples." Hegai seemed to come to a decision. "Well, I will be sending you some more slave girls this afternoon. You may interview them and select the ones you think would be most interesting to your mistress. And let me know if there's anything else I can do for her."

"I will," Aiesha said. "I have to watch and see what it is that she wants since she asks for so little."

Hegai rolled his eyes and laughed. "And that is *really* unusual in here."

Aiesha selected three new slaves for her mistress, one from the cooler lands of the north, one with dark Cushite skin from the south, and a Judahite from the conquered lands to the west. She chose them not only for their distant countries, but also their willingness to talk.

The new servants delighted Esther. She seemed bored with many of the beauty routines, but enjoyed hours of stories, whether they involved the girls' families or histories, cultural practices, or the gods they worshiped.

It was good for the girls, too, to be able to speak of their homelands to someone who actually wanted to listen.

One day Branna had been describing her family and their life in the north lands. Most of the storytelling had been happy occasions, but today Branna was homesick and burst into tears mid-story.

Rizpah, the young Judahite, put her arms around her. "I know just how you feel," she said, tearing up, too.

"How can you?" Aneksi snapped.

"What do you mean?" Rizpah asked.

"I know why I'm here, and I know why Branna's here. Most of us belong to conquered peoples. What I don't understand is why Rizpah is here. Didn't the previous king give a decree that all of your people should go back to your country and rebuild your Temple? If you're far away from home, it's your own fault."

Rizpah caught her breath sharply as her eyes filled with tears.

At the same moment Esther jumped to her feet and stood with her back to the slaves, gazing out the window for a long time.

The girls fell silent.

"Leave me," Esther said.

They filed out of her room.

"Have we offended her?" Aneksi asked when they were outside. "We didn't say anything about her or her people, just about Rizpah."

Aiesha looked at them sharply. "She wants to hear your stories, but she doesn't want to listen to you girls fight." Still Aiesha shook her head. Although she greatly admired her mistress, there were times when the new wife seemed such a mystery. She really didn't understand her.

On impulse Aiesha followed Rizpah out to one of the ornamental pools in the gardens. "Are you OK?" she asked the Judahite girl.

"The reason it hurt my feelings," Rizpah said in a shaky voice, "was probably because it's true. My people did receive permission to go back and rebuild the Temple. But my family was doing well where they were in Babylon, so they chose not to go. Then there were problems and fighting broke out and—well, I ended up here. Maybe the God of Judah can't bless me when my family didn't go back to Jerusalem as He had arranged for us. And I'm almost sure He can't bless me here in a Persian harem."

Aiesha's eyes softened. "Oh, Rizpah, your parents may not have made the choices your God wanted them to, but none of this has been your fault or your choice. The things you have told us other times sounded as if your God treats each person as an individual. Would He punish you for the decisions of your parents?"

"I don't know. Sometimes I'm not sure of anything anymore. I used to be. Now I think maybe He has forgotten those of us who didn't go back and He's just going to bless the ones who are there."

"I don't know your God," Aiesha said, "but I hope it's not that way. Please try not to be sad and try not to do anything that will upset our mistress. Her 12 months of preparation has ended, and she should be going to the king any day now. We don't want anything to upset her. What happens when she spends the night with him will affect the whole rest of her life—and ours."

Rizpah wiped at her eyes. "I know that it will, and I wish I could ask my God for help."

"Well, please do. We all should pray to our gods."

"Do you think my God would listen to me here in exile when we Jews aren't supposed to be in exile anymore?"

"Please ask Him," Aiesha suggested. "If He helps us with this, perhaps I'll even worship Him."

The Judahite girl smiled. "I will," she promised.

* * * *

It was Esther's turn. The maids and Hegai fussed around her, rearranging her hair and adjusting her clothes.

"Esther," the head chamberlain announced, "I have had the women bring all of your things. Once you have spent your night with the king, you will not be in my palace of virgins anymore but the palace of concubines. Your new chamberlain will be Sha-ashgaz. Don't worry, you will have everything there that you have had here. I have added some jewelry that I think you will like and several robes and changes of clothing. Is there anything else you would like? Anything at all? You've been one of my favorites. I'm going to miss you."

The girl smiled nervously. "You've been very kind to me, Hegai. There is one thing that would make this easier."

"Anything, anything at all."

"Because I have grown fond of them, I would like to take my women with me. I've never had a family. As a child I always thought that one day I would marry and have a husband and children. Now it appears that I probably won't. These seven are the closest thing I have to family. I would like to keep them with me."

Hegai beamed and spread his arms to include all the servant girls. "You may take all of them and any more that you wish. I could not deny you anything you wanted."

"Oh, thank you, Hegai. Having them go with me will mean more to me than anything else you could give me."

"I have never met a woman quite like you, Esther. But if giving you a bunch of slave women makes you happy, it's certainly easy to do. May the gods favor you tonight so that the king loves you as much as I do."

"Thank you, Hegai," she said and turned and walked with her head held high down the hall toward the palace.

The next morning guards took Esther to the harem of the king's wives. Her servants, who had her quarters all fixed up with her things from the previous harem, now glanced at her shyly, waiting for her to initiate the conversation. She didn't.

One of the other concubines dropped by her room and boldly demanded to hear about her night with the king.

Her face coloring, Esther glanced up at her.

Aiesha stepped to the doorway, wanting to intervene, but understanding that it was not her place. She ranked below any of the concubines.

"The king is a very interesting man," Esther said finally. "And I enjoyed his company."

The other concubine whooped with laughter. "An interesting man. That's a good one. I don't think anyone here has ever called him that."

Esther blushed more.

"Word among the servants is that he found you pretty interesting. They say they could hear him talking and laughing clear down the hall. And that you two spent most of the night talking instead of, well—."

"Well, I guess no one will know exactly what went on in there," Aiesha interrupted, "unless Esther or the king chooses to tell you."

Still Esther said nothing.

When the nosey woman had left Esther slumped in her chair. "It's true, Aiesha," she whispered. "I guess I'm not a very exciting concubine, but we did talk all night. I asked him how he had learned how to rule such a diverse group of nations when they were all so different and had such different cultures and how he knew when to be tolerant and when to make everyone obey the same laws. It was fascinating. He was telling me all about the place he spent the past two years and what the people were like there. The king is a very intelligent man. All kings have wise counselors, but this one has wisdom of his own, too. I really liked him. As for . . ." She shook her head and stared out the window.

Aiesha placed a comforting hand on her shoulder. "Maybe he enjoyed your conversations as much as you did."

Later, as Aiesha stepped out of Esther's apartments, she was almost bowled over by Aneksi running down the hall.

"It's her! It's her! He's chosen," the girl squeaked out in an excited voice.

"Who's chosen what? Calm yourself."

"My lady, the king, the queen, the . . ."

"Our lady?" Aiesha asked, her eyes widening as she realized what the Cushite girl was saying.

Behind Aneksi she saw Sha-ashgaz, the king's chamberlain for his concubine harem. He bowed to Aiesha and said, "Is your mistress available?"

"I—she—she was going to, no—yes, she's fine. Come in," Aiesha stammered. She slipped in ahead of him and announced his approach.

Sha-ashgaz bowed even lower before Esther and then said, "The king has chosen you as his new queen. We need to move you to different chambers here. You will have your own private accommodations at the end of the harem and your own gardens. There will be a large wedding feast that will require some months of preparation. The king will invite his dignitaries from every province. And he says that you may ask them all any questions you like."

Esther burst out laughing. Sha-ashgaz did not.

"May I inquire what he meant by that?" he asked.

All of Esther's servants began giggling with merriment. Knowing Esther, they decided that she would do just that.

"Meanwhile," Sha-ashgaz continued, "I know that you are tired and probably need some rest, but while you do, your servants need to transfer your things to more fitting quarters for the queen of the Persian empire."

"Thank you," Esther choked out.

With a nod he left the room.

"I can hardly believe this," Esther murmured.

Rizpah and Aiesha glanced at each other. "I guess if I'm going to worship your God," Aiesha whispered to her, "you better tell me a little more about Him."

The Judahite girl broke into a huge smile. "Well, for one," she said, "He has great mercy and He's the God of second chances and thirds and fourths."

"It's just as well," Esther, having overheard Rizpah, murmured to herself.

Aneksi raised an eyebrow and shrugged. Rizpah and Aiesha grinned at each other. And Esther, the new queen of the Persian empire, stood mysteriously silent.

King Ahasuerus invited his princes and servants from all the provinces to the wedding feast and gave huge gifts to everyone as was his custom. The palace at Shushan was the most enormous and lavishly decorated hall of celebration in the world and it was all in honor of Esther that night. The king was delighted with his new young wife and her interest and knowledge of the peoples he ruled. Soon, though, the feasting and celebration ended and life settled into a new pattern.

As the days passed Aiesha often observed her queen staring out the window at the gate official below. She could have sworn they somehow knew each other, but she was never quite sure.

Her mistress was now the most powerful and wealthy woman in all the Persian empire. Yet she still had that mysterious sad streak. Aiesha often wished she could know the thoughts of the young queen. But Esther remained a mystery.

The usual political gossip continued in the palace. Some of it filtered up to Esther's apartments. Most of it she ignored. However, she was extremely interested when a gate official foiled an assassination attempt on the king.

Other palace intrigues continued. Haman the Agagite was always scrambling for power, even though he wielded more of it than anyone but the king.

Aneksi shook her head. "Some people never seem to have enough power," she commented one day.

Esther shrugged. "As long as there are kings, there will be others who want as much power or more as they have. But a wise king is aware of that fact and will rule appropriately."

* * * *

Time passed quickly. Esther had been queen of Persia for several years. The occasions Esther spent with the king were good ones and they genuinely enjoyed each other's company. But sometimes she had no contact with him for long periods.

One day Aiesha watched as the young queen went to her usual spot to stare out the window each morning. Suddenly Esther let out a cry.

"What is it, my queen?" the servant asked. "What's the matter?"

"Look," her mistress said, pointing.

The old Judahite who served in the gate area was dressed in sackcloth and ashes and wailing as he paced back and forth in the street below.

"He looks upset," Aiesha observed. "Strange, though, that he would permit himself to be seen like that. No one is allowed in the palace dressed that way."

"That's right," the young queen said, nervously biting her lip. "Please call Hathach, my chamberlain, and have him go down immediately and take a robe to the old man. Make him change his clothes, then find out what is wrong."

She watched as Hathach rushed down into the street and conversed with the Judahite. Some minutes later he returned, still carrying the clothes.

Several onlookers had followed him into the queen's apartment.

"Leave us," Esther ordered. "Everyone but my seven closest servants and Hathach."

The room cleared.

She grabbed Hathach's hands. "You must tell me. What is it? What is happening?"

"The old man says that there is a death sentence on all Jews."

"All Jews? All of us?" Rizpah said numbly.

Hathach nodded. "The gate official is a Jew. He has continually refused to bow to Haman, a fact that has been a thorn in the official's flesh for a long time. Mordecai claims that Haman convinced the king that there was a people scattered throughout his kingdom who were masterminding an insidious plot to overthrow him. The king gave him permission to write a law and offer money to all those who would kill these enemies of the king. They cast lots for the best time to hold the executions. It will be coming up in less than a year. Then all the Jews in the entire Persian empire are to die. And, your highness, he said—he said such odd things."

"Tell me everything," Esther persisted.

"He said not to think that you would escape the execution. What could he mean? Is he speaking treason against you, because I could have him arrested."

The queen shook her head and sank into a chair. "I am a Judahite—a Jew," she said after a moment. "The man speaks no treason—he's my uncle. Please go tell him that I have not seen the king for months. That I'm not sure I could do anything to help."

Hathach disappeared from the room and came back a few moments later. "Your highness, your uncle says that perhaps you came to the kingdom for such a time as this."

For a long time Esther sat in silence. Finally she stood, pulled her shoulders back, and lifted her chin. "Perhaps I did," she said. "My God is a God of second chances. Tell my uncle I will go to the king."

Aiesha caught her breath. "But my queen, how dare you without an invitation? You know how the guards deal with anyone who approaches without permission because of the danger of assassination. You could be executed!"

"Yes, I could be," she sighed. "And if I don't go, I could be, too." She turned to Hathach. "Tell my uncle to call all the Judahites together and have them pray for me. I and my servants will pray and fast and then I will go to the king. And if I die, I die."

The eunuch left with his message.

The women flung their arms around their queen and burst into tears.

"He is a God of second chances," Rizpah murmured. "He still hears me, even though my people didn't go back to Jerusalem."

"Nor mine," Esther added.

"And He heard me when I asked Him to give you favor in the king's eyes."

"True," Esther smiled through her tears.

"And He will hear us now."

"So you worship this God, too?" Aiesha asked her queen.

"Yes. But my uncle told me to keep it a secret."

"I, too, have been praying to Him for unto three years now," Aiesha explained.

* * * *

The week of fasting and prayer Esther had requested the Jewish community to have had come to an end. Aiesha dressed her queen in her most magnificent robes. Then she and her fellow servants prayed one more time together. Finally they stood. Everything was done. It was time to go.

Aiesha couldn't imagine life without Esther. The queen was the kindest person she had ever known. Yet Persian law demanded the death of anyone who approached the king without an invitation. Would he make an exception for Esther?

They reached the outer court of his palace. Esther stood in the doorway where he could see her. The voices in the chamber dropped to silence. Everyone stared in shock. Aiesha could hardly breathe.

Suddenly the king broke into a huge smile and held out his scepter to her. She approached, touched the end of it, and bowed.

"What is it you want, my pretty queen? I'll give you anything your heart desires—up to half of my kingdom."

Everyone caught their breath. What did the queen want?

"I would like you and Haman to come to my apartments for a banquet tonight," she said.

The king roared with pleased laughter. "I will be there."

That evening the king asked, "This has been a wonderful banquet. So what is it that is on your mind, my queen? What do you desire?"

She knelt by him. "Would you come back again, you and Haman, tomorrow night? I have enjoyed this so much."

The king enthusiastically accepted her invitation. Haman seemed especially pleased.

The next day as Esther and her servants nervously planned the evening's activities, Hathach, the queen's chamberlain, interrupted them. He was laughing so hard that he could hardly give the queen his message. "Your highness," he said, "you must look out the window. It will cheer you greatly."

"I don't have time," Esther replied, checking over baskets of fruit and other supplies for the banquet. "Just tell me."

"Haman is leading your uncle through the streets on the king's horse. Mordecai is wearing the king's robe. As he goes along Haman has to shout, 'This shall be done to whom the king wishes to honor.' "

Esther paused in total shock, then began to laugh. "How did this happen?"

"Last night the king couldn't sleep so he had the scribe read him from the royal chronicles. The scribe ran across the incident in which Mordecai exposed the plot that Bigthana and Teresh had made against his majesty. The king asked how Mordecai had been rewarded and, when he heard that he had not been, he immediately decided to do something about it. Unfortunately for Haman, a little later he came in and the king asked him what he should do for someone he wanted to honor. I assume Haman thought the king was talking about him, so this is what he suggested."

"It must be making him furious," she said.

"I think so, and he'll be worn out by tonight when he comes to your banquet."

That night, as Esther expected, the king was in a jovial mood and Haman looked like a thundercloud. She received them graciously and provided an even more lavish banquet than the night before.

"So my queen," said the king, turning to her, "you've entertained us beautifully two nights in a row. What is it that's on your mind? I'll do anything in the world you desire."

Instead of breaking into a smile, Esther's eyes welled up with tears. "Then save me and my people. Don't let us be killed." She started to cry.

The king jumped to his feet. "Who is it that's plotting to kill you? And how dare they!"

Esther rose to her feet and pointed. "This man," she said, indicating Haman. "This wicked Haman."

"Haman!" shouted the king. "How dare he!" He exploded out through the double doors into the gardens, pacing back and forth.

"Your highness, your highness, save me, I beg you," Haman squeaked. He flung himself at her feet, trying to grab her legs.

Esther fell over onto the couch.

Just then the king burst back into the room to see them both toppling over. "Would you attack the queen in her own apartments and in my presence?" he shouted. "Guard!"

* * * *

The queen's palace was quiet. The servants had all knelt and prayed with Esther and offered their thanks to the God of Israel, who was the God of second, third, and fourth chances. The God who had protected them, removed their enemy Haman, and impressed the king to allow the Jews to compose whatever laws they wished to protect themselves, though he could not reverse the one Haman had written earlier.

The date for the mass slaughter of the Jews had come and gone. None of God's people in the Persian empire had been killed, but many of their enemies did die.

And now seven women from seven different backgrounds all clasped hands with their queen and gave honor to the Mighty One who was not just the God of Israel, but every country they had come from as well as ruler of the universe. And I bowed with them as my heart swelled with pride in my King and My Creator. God of the angels and, yes, even God of humans. God of second chances.